Margaret Gaan was born in Shanghai into a family that was part Chinese and part European. After leaving China she lived in Bangkok where she served as Deputy Regional Director, South East Asia, to the United Nations Children's Fund. She now lives in Sacramento, California. Her autobiography, *Last Moments of a World*, won her a Reader's Digest Non-Fiction award. Her first novel, *Little Sister*, was published in 1983; *Red Barbarian*, the first in her Opium War triology, in 1984; and *White Poppy*, the second in the trilogy, in 1985. *Red Barbarian* and *White Poppy* are both available from Futura.

MARGARET GAAN

Blue Mountain

Futura

A *Futura* Book

Copyright © 1987 by Margaret Gaan

First published in Great Britain in 1987
by John Murray (Publishers) Ltd by arrangement
with Dodd, Mead & Co, New York

First published in paperback by
Futura Publications 1988
This edition published by
Futura Publications 1994

ISBN 0 7088 3930 4

Printed in England by Clays Ltd, St Ives plc

Futura Publications
A Division of
Macdonald & Co (Publishers)
Brettenham House
Lancaster Place
London WC2E 7EN

THE BOOKS OF THIS TRILOGY

Red Barbarian
White Poppy
Blue Mountain

Are for My God-Daughters

Innes
Jacqueline
Megan

With My Enduring Love

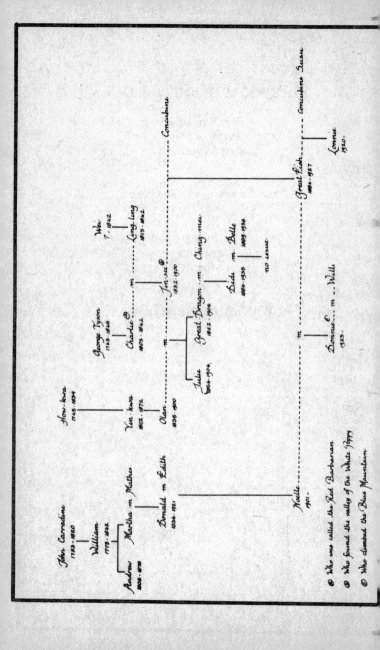

① who was called the Red Barbarian
② who found the valley of the White Poppy
③ who climbed the Blue Mountain

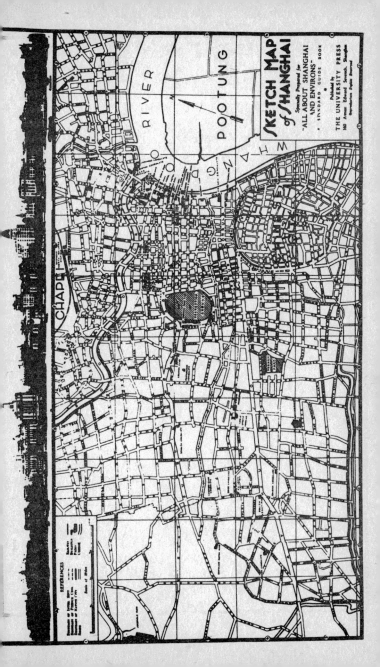

CHAPEI

RIVER

WHANGPOO

POOTUNG

N

SKETCH MAP
of SHANGHAI

Specially Prepared for
"ALL ABOUT SHANGHAI
AND ENVIRONS"
A STANDARD GUIDE BOOK

Published by
THE UNIVERSITY PRESS
160 Avenue Edward Seventh, Shanghai
Reproduction Rights Reserved

REFERENCES

Scale of Miles

Chapter I

1907

DIDI RECOGNIZED the street as soon as he stepped into it, though now he saw it from a different angle. Sixteen years ago his small boy's view had been obscured by the crowds that towered over him. Now, taller than most of the bustling pedestrians, he saw over their heads to the high walls that lined the street on both sides, hiding the secrets of the homes they guarded. A wave of nostalgia diluted the tightness of his heart. It was all so familiar! He began to make his way along the street, jostling and being jostled, peering at the house numbers. Halfway down he found the number he wanted, affixed to the same old sturdy gatepost.

But the gate was different. The old gate had been of worn, warm wood, with a little window through which the gateman could inspect whoever was seeking entrance. He remembered banging on the gate with four-year-old fists, heart bumping. Would the gateman hear? Would he open? The gateman opened his little window and looked around at his own eye level, way up there, muttering: "There's no one! It must have been a devil that knocked!"

"It's me! It's me!" the little boy shouted, tingling with suspense, and at last the gateman looked down, frowning severely. "It's you, is it? Well, I was right, wasn't I? You're the naughty little devil who ran out when I wasn't looking!'' But then he had beamed and chuckled and swung the old gate open on its well-oiled hinges.

This new gate was a cold, blank sheet of metal surmounted by strands of thickly barbed wire. Instead of a little window it had a peephole, a tiny, unblinking, sinister eye before which a knocker must stand helplessly while an unseen gateman inspected him. Didi shivered. Peking might be backward and overly ceremonious, but it wasn't heartless like this great, teeming, bustling city of Shanghai.

He took a big breath, stepped forward, knocked upon the gate as loudly as he could. At once he heard the click of the peephole being opened, as though the gateman had been waiting for his knock. He lifted his head to show his face to the eye in the peephole, trying for nonchalance, hoping the thudding of his heart didn't show in his expression.

From inside the gate, a harsh voice said, "What d'you want?"

Didi kept his voice steady.

"I want to see the occupants of this house, who are my aunt and uncle. My father, the mandarin Wei Ta-lung, is their elder brother—"

"Never heard of him."

"But you must have! He must be here. He came six weeks ago to see his sister and brother—"

"The owners of this house have no brother. You'd best leave quietly."

The peephole clicked shut.

Didi flung up his fists to hammer on the gate, then let them drop, the hot blood surging to his face. I must be bright red, he thought ashamedly. Why couldn't I be commanding, like my father? The gateman would never have dared speak thus to my father!

The gateman had denied speaking to his father at all.

Then where was his father?

Something was very, very wrong. Before leaving Peking he had put on a calm face to reassure his mother. "Father must have fallen ill or had an accident. He's probably in some Shanghai hospital with amnesia, like that time in Tientsin. Doesn't know who he is and has lost his papers, so the hospital people don't know who to get in touch with. Don't worry, Mother. I'll find out what's wrong as soon as I get to Shanghai."

But whatever was wrong was much more wrong than amnesia! For the hundredth time, his mind flashed to the story his father had told him the night before he left Peking. There must be some connection between that amazing story and his father's amazing disappearance. There must be . . .

He turned away from the gate and spoke to the first passerby, an old man with acid eyes, who answered him sarcastically.

"The *police station*? You want to *seek out* those bloodsuckers? Well, I suppose you're young enough to be foolish! Over there . . ."

He pointed over his shoulder and hurried on.

Two blocks away, Didi found the police station. Hesitantly, he entered the dirty courtyard and crossed to the tumbledown building, ignored by the gateman and the uniformed men who lounged about. In a dim, cluttered room, he found four men sitting at scuffed desks, sipping tea and talking. They paid him not the slightest attention. He coughed a time or two, unsuccessfully trying to attract notice, then remembered tales he had heard from Shanghai boys attending Peking University. He went back to the street and, standing in a doorway, tied one of his few silver dollars into a corner of his handkerchief. He slipped the handkerchief into the side pocket of his gown, leaving a bit of it showing, and went back to the police station, pausing in the gateway. He felt a tug as the handkerchief was slipped from his pocket. There was a slight pause. Then the gateman spoke, his tone grudging—a single dollar wasn't going to buy much.

"What d'you want?"

"I should like to speak to someone in authority, to report the disappearance of my father."

"This way."

The gateman led him across the courtyard, past the same loungers, into the same cluttered room in which the same four men still sipped tea and chatted. But this time one of them looked up and glanced at Didi. With a sense of shock, Didi stared back. Had there been a sudden intentness in those bold, hard eyes? But the gateman was saying deferentially, "Sergeant, this young man wants to report the disappearance of his father."

The sergeant looked back at Didi, his eyes blankly opaque.

"He's probably gone off with some woman. He'll be back when he's had enough."

"Oh no!" Didi cried. "You don't understand! My father is Wei Ta-lung, senior mandarin of the Ministry of Foreign Affairs in Peking . . ."

His voice trailed away. This time certainly the sergeant's eyes had flickered. Had the other men tensed? He glanced around, but they were indifferently shifting papers. The sergeant said lazily, "A Peking mandarin! Sounds like a long story, and it's nearly time for lunch . . ."

Didi faltered. "I'd be glad to invite you to lunch if you will listen to my story while we eat."

It was the right thing to say! The sergeant smiled genially. "I accept for all of us. We needn't go to a restaurant. I'll have a meal brought in."

He nodded to the gateman, who had lingered. The man hurried out, and the sergeant pointed Didi to a chair.

"You can start your story."

Didi sat down and drew a long breath.

"About six weeks ago my father left Peking to come to Shanghai to see his sister and brother, Wei Julie and Wei Ta-yu, who live in our family home two blocks from here. You must know the Wei compound? The very large one, with five houses in it?"

The sergeant nodded. The other men were still shifting papers, but very quietly. With heightened heartbeat, Didi went on.

"My father traveled to Shanghai by China Merchants steamer. China Merchants confirm that he was on the ship, and that it arrived here on time. After that, we have no trace of him. He would have written to my mother and me as soon as he arrived, so we expected a letter about three weeks after he left, but none came. We sent a telegram to his sister and brother. There was no answer. We sent two more telegrams, both unanswered. We tried to make inquiries through the Ministry, but the relations between the government in Peking and the Shanghai authorities are not too good . . ."

The men guffawed. Didi swallowed.

"Anyway, my mother and I finally decided that I must come to Shanghai to look for my father. I arrived this morning and

4

went at once to the family home. The gateman denied me entrance. He denied that my father was there. He denied knowing my father's name. He even denied that the occupants of the house have a brother!"

In spite of himself, his voice was rising and he was glad when the gateman entered with a waiter carrying two food baskets on a pole across his shoulders. While the waiter spread dishes out on the desks, the gateman presented the bill to Didi. It was not as exorbitant as he had expected, and he counted out the money with relief. The waiter dished rice into bowls and passed them around. The men began to eat, their chopsticks flashing. Didi watched them, feeling his gorge rise, pushing his bowl aside. After a moment the sergeant said, his mouth full, "Why did your father want to see his sister and brother?"

"On family business."

"Concerning money?"

"Well, yes . . . A mistake that my father had to straighten out."

"What mistake?"

Didi hesitated. This wasn't going as he had hoped.

"It's hard to explain, and it's not important. What I came for was to ask you to order the gateman . . ."

The sergeant stopped shoveling rice into his mouth and raised his hard eyes to Didi's.

"What mistake?"

Didi cleared his throat.

"A mistake about the remittances . . . The family business, the *hong*, is here in Shanghai, managed by my father's sister. Of course, my father's salary as a mandarin is not sufficient for our living, so his sister sends him a remittance every month. Suddenly, three months ago, the money stopped coming. My father came to find out what had happened."

The sergeant frowned.

"You said your father has a sister and a brother. Why is the sister managing the *hong* and not the brother? It's most unusual for a sister to be in charge of money when there's a brother around."

"That really has nothing to do with—"

"Why is the sister handling the money?"

"Because the brother is younger."

5

"How much younger?"

"Very much younger. In fact"—as the sergeant continued staring—"he's my age."

"*Your* age?" The sergeant snickered. "How does it happen that your father's brother is the same age as you?"

Didi felt himself flushing. Furious with himself, he said defiantly, "Actually, he's *exactly* the same age as myself. He's my father's *half* brother. My grandfather had a concubine who gave birth to him within the same hour as my mother gave birth to me."

He stared at the sergeant, trying to look icily challenging, as his father would have looked in the circumstances.

The sergeant said "Hmmm" quite mildly and turned back to his rice bowl. There was a silence, broken by the men's slurpings and belchings. Didi felt a little glow. Had he really impressed the sergeant with his imitation of his father's mandarin glare? He followed up what he hoped was an advantage.

"Of course, all that has nothing to do with my reason for coming here. I came to ask you to order the gateman at the Wei home to open the gate to me. I must talk to my aunt—"

"Hah!" one of the other men exclaimed suddenly. "I remember now! There *was* a woman living in that compound! I don't know about 'aunt,' but I think her name was Julie."

"*Was?*" Didi cried, heart thumping.

The man sucked up a morsel of chicken and spoke around it.

"Uh-huh . . . She died . . . Five, six weeks ago? They buried her in the compound—they have a kind of private graveyard. I happen to know because they came here to report it, and I told them they'd have to go to the Registry Office."

Something icy chilled Didi's heart. There *was* a kind of graveyard in the family compound—at least, there was a tomb in which a baby sister of his father's was buried. He could even vaguely remember the monument that marked it—a tiny pink marble house . . .

He turned to the sergeant.

"I *must* get into that compound! If it really was my aunt who died, why didn't my father send us a telegram? Something has happened to my father!"

The sergeant selected a piece of pork, popped it into his mouth, savored it, swallowed.

"We're policemen. We deal with crimes, not family squabbles."

"But a crime *has been* committed! My father has disappeared! He must have been harmed, perhaps he's dead! I'm asking you to find out!"

The sergeant yawned. "What you're asking me to do is force the gateman of that compound to let you in so that you can talk to people who you claim are your relatives . . ."

"They *are* my relatives! Here—look at this!"

He handed the sergeant the letter the Ministry had given him. The sergeant glanced through it indifferently.

"So? This says that the bearer is the son of Wei Ta-lung, senior mandarin of the Ministry of Foreign Affairs. You are the *present* 'bearer,' but are you the person to whom the Ministry gave the letter? Is Wei Ta-lung of that Ministry in Peking a son of the Wei family in Shanghai?"

"Of course he is!" Didi cried desperately. "He was born in Shanghai at the family house! So was I! I lived here until I was four years old, when I was sent to Peking to join my parents! We are indeed who I say we are!"

The sergeant shrugged. "I suppose I could find out if I spent a year checking, but why should I? As I said, it's a family matter. Not our business."

Didi licked his lips, his heart hammering. It was deliberate. They were playing with him. They were waiting for something to happen, and were dragging this act out while they waited. He'd arrived at a good time for them—the meal was a fine way to pass an hour, and they could even make him pay for it—but if he'd arrived at another time, they'd have found another way to make him wait . . .

The gateman came hurrying back into the room, looking important. He bent over the sergeant and murmured in his ear. The sergeant slurped up a last mouthful of rice, belched, and wiped his mouth on his sleeve.

"Well, sir"—he turned genially to Didi—"we must thank you. Very good meal. Sorry we can't help you, but I'll tell you what I'll do—I'll send the gateman to take you to the Registry Office. They may be able to do something for you."

He nodded to the gateman and turned away, belching again. Didi rose uncertainly. The other men were shoving aside the

7

dishes, going back to their papers. They had lost interest. Whatever it was that they had been waiting for had happened. It was hopeless appealing further to the sergeant. The next move was the gateman's. He was smiling, holding out an arm to shepherd Didi out. Didi turned on his heel and went with him.

On the street, the gateman walked ahead—it was too crowded to walk side by side—talking volubly over his shoulder, as friendly now as at first he had been hostile.

"From Peking, eh? How I'd like to go there! The real China, not like this bastard, half-foreign city! And home of the grand old Empress!"

Didi thought of the wizened, gaudily bedecked, willful, ruthless old woman who had successfully usurped the throne for fifty years.

The gateman nimbly dodged around a noisy crowd of children.

"Shanghai really is a bastard city! Here, where we're walking now, is the site of ancient Shanghai, that they now call the 'Chinese City.' When the foreigners came, they took over the surrounding sectors—to the north, the International Settlement—to the south, the French Concession that they call 'French Town.' Around the foreign sectors are more Chinese sectors—Chapei, Nantao, and Pootung across the river. So, you see, the city is governed by three different municipal bodies, Chinese, British, and French. We Chinese have nothing whatever to say in the foreign municipalities. Shame, isn't it? Foreigners owning sectors of China! All because of those damned Unequal Treaties that were signed after the Opium Wars!"

He shook his head piously, hawked up phlegm, and spat neatly onto an inch-square empty spot on the pavement.

"The place I'm taking you to now is the Registry Office for the Chinese City. Fortunately, I happen to know the chief personally so I can take you straight in to him. Otherwise you might have to wait for days . . ."

Didi stopped listening. There was no way a gateman could personally know so important a bureaucrat as the chief of a Registry. The gateman was merely the sergeant's messenger. While they were eating lunch, the gateman had hurried to the

Registry with a message from the sergeant to the chief—"The son of the mandarin Wei Ta-lung has turned up." And the chief had sent the gateman back to the sergeant with his answer—"Send the son right over, I'll deal with him." All prearranged. They had been expecting him. They must know what had happened to his father.

The gateman led him into another dilapidated building, much bigger than the police station but as cluttered. No one asked their business. There was no passing of silver dollars wrapped in handkerchiefs. The gateman ushered him through a maze of corridors straight to a room where a large fat man sat behind a desk that, in striking contrast to the rest of the place, was clean and bare. The man himself looked strangely clean and bare, his pudgy white face hairless and smooth as steamed dough. His eyes, sunk in the dough, were small and black and cold, a poor match for the warm smile that came to his soft lips as he looked up at them.

"Chief!" The gateman was ingratiating. "Have you had your lunch? We're not interrupting you?"

"No, no! What can I do for you?"

"A small favor . . . This young man says his father has disappeared. Since it's a family matter, our sergeant thought you might be able to help him."

"I'll do what I can!"

"I'll leave him with you, then . . ."

The gateman sidled quickly to the door. The chief turned his small, cold eyes and his warm, fat smile on Didi, waving him to a chair.

"Tell me what I can do to help you."

Cautiously, Didi began to repeat what he had told the sergeant. The chief listened attentively, then rang a bell and asked the secretary who entered, "We have a file on the Wei family of our district?"

"Certainly, sir."

"Bring it."

Didi sat back, prepared to wait: it would take a long time to find anything in all that clutter. But in a moment the secretary was back with a neat, thick file. The chief began to scrutinize it, turning the pages, nodding.

"Ah-hah . . . Ah-hah . . ." He looked up at Didi. "Well,

young man. I see that the Wei family properties were operated for many years through a *hong* managed by a daughter, Julie, under a power of attorney from her father, Jin-see. Her mother, Jin-see's legal wife, is dead. About a year ago, Julie transferred the power of attorney to Jin-see's concubine. In the case of the death of a legal wife, it is not uncommon for property to be transferred to a concubine, especially since in this case Jin-see is blind. But the concubine is illiterate. Therefore her son Ta-yu, Julie's half-brother, applied for and was granted control of the *hong* on his mother's behalf. About six weeks ago Julie died. Thus the half-brother is now in sole control of all the properties. Rather complicated, but all entirely legal."

He smiled benignly and continued smugly:

"So I don't see that you or your father have any rights at all in the properties—assuming, of course, that you do really belong to this particular Wei family."

Didi swallowed the constriction in his throat and tried to make his voice calm and cold, as his father's would be in the circumstances.

"Sir, if that is the Wei family file, you will find in it the record of my father's birth."

The chief smiled smoothly. "Ah yes . . ." He flicked over a few pages of the file. "Here is the record."

"Sir, you can see that my father is my grandfather's eldest son by his legal wife. Do you think my grandfather would disinherit him in favor of a younger son by a concubine?"

The chief's smile widened.

"I don't know, young man. You must ask your grandfather."

Didi's heart sank. Now they would get into the matter of his grandfather's death and why it had not been reported to this Registry! The chief's eyes were jolly. He knew about the unreported death. He knew he had Didi in a trap. Didi licked dry lips.

"I cannot ask my grandfather because he is dead. He was killed in 1900, in Tientsin, in a street battle during the Boxer Rebellion."

"Ohhhhhh?" The chief's twinkling eyes opened wide. "And why is there no record of his death in this file?"

"Because the bodies of those who died in the fight were not

recovered. My father and his sister decided not to report the death since there was no proof of it."

No proof—Didi clearly remembered his father's wry voice: "If we report his death without proof, our inheritance will evaporate. Everybody from the court gateman to the chief judge will be on to us for squeeze. The estate will never be settled until there's nothing left to settle." So the death had gone unreported, and Julie had continued to operate the *hong* under the power of attorney their father had given her when he began to go blind—that now, by some sleight of hand, was all in the half-brother's name.

The chief was beaming, hardly able to restrain himself from chuckling.

"You know, of course, that there's a law requiring all deaths to be reported. It's always best to obey the law, isn't it? See what happens when the proper reports aren't made? Now there's no proof of anything and we'll have to go by the power of attorney, which is clearly in favor of the half-brother."

Didi tried again to put some of his father's steel into his voice.

"May I remind you, sir, that I came here about *my father's disappearance*, not the settlement of my grandfather's estate. Clearly, nothing about the family properties can be settled until my father is found."

"Ah yes, of course!" The doughy forehead crumpled in a mock frown. "Now, let's see. What have you done so far to find your father? Knocked on a gate, been refused entry, and asked a policeman to force entry for you. Not much, you will admit. I suggest you try harder. A tour of the hospitals?"

Didi's heart pounded dully. Another put-off! If they sent him to the hospitals, he was sure *not* to find his father in any of them. Hopelessness began to creep into his spirit like slow paralysis. The chief rose and leaned across the desk to pat his shoulder kindly.

"That's the next step, I assure you! If you don't find him, we'll think of something else. Unfortunately, I have to leave now, but I'll send in an assistant who'll give you a list of hospitals and advise you how to go about visiting them."

He beamed at Didi as he bustled out of the room, an actor giving a fine performance of Benign Uncle. Didi stared after

11

him. An assistant with an already-prepared list of hospitals! Certainly, they'd been expecting him! He felt like a fly struggling in a web that grinning spiders spun around him ever tighter. Almost in tears, he slumped forward to rest his head in his hands . . .

Inches from his eyes was the file! Careless in his triumph, the chief had left it on the desk! Heart lifting, Didi quickly drew it toward him, flipped it open, riffled through it. It was nothing but a thick wad of discarded papers! Scribbled drafts that from a little distance looked as though they had meaning, but had none at all! Only the top page of the file was significant. Eyes jumping with excitement, Didi scanned it. A list of names, with dates and notations. At the top, his grandfather's name with the note: Died in Tientsin, Boxer troubles, 1900, not officially reported. The name of his aunt Julie, the date of her birth, another date six weeks ago, and the note: Buried in home courtyard. His father's name, and two dates: his birth . . . *and his death?*

A shadow fell across the paper. Startled out of his skin, Didi leaped up. A little old man was standing behind the chief's chair, his wrinkled face impassive. Didi said nervously, "I was just glancing . . ."

. The man gave a slight, dismissive shake of his head. Without a word he closed the file and put it away in a drawer of the desk. Then he sat down in the chief's chair, spread a sheaf of papers before Didi, and began to speak in a voice surprisingly loud for such an old man, and much too loud for a listener sitting hardly two feet away. Didi controlled an impulse to move his chair back. Was the old man making sure that people *outside* the room heard him?

The old man said, "Here is the list of all the hospitals in all parts of the city. One hundred and thirty-two altogether. I am told you intend to visit all of them to look for your father. Since that will take many days, I advise you to engage a hotel room, get a map of the city, locate the hospitals on it, then hire a rickshaw on a daily basis and let the coolie take you around, district by district. Do you understand?"

"I understand," Didi said, imitating the loudness of the old man's voice.

"Very well."

12

The man handed him the sheaf of papers, rose, marched to the door, glanced out into the corridor, stepped back into the room, and shut the door loudly, leaving himself still inside. Fascinated, Didi watched as he tiptoed soundlessly back to the desk, gestured for Didi to remain seated, and bent forward to whisper in his ear.

"I knew your aunt Julie. She came in here often to attend to your family's affairs and I used to serve her. She was a lovely lady, always kind and pleasant, even to an old fetcher-and-carrier like me. For her sake, I'm putting my neck on the edge of the ax. They"—he jerked his chin at the chief's chair, and his thumb in the direction of the police station—"are running you around. That hospital tour is rubbish. Go if you like, but instead I urge you to go and see this man."

He handed Didi a tiny scrap of paper on which a name and an address were written. Astonished, Didi saw that the name was English: Wilson.

"He's my son-in-law," the old man whispered. "He used to be on the English police force, but they dropped him when he married my youngest daughter. He knew they'd do that, but he married her just the same. A proper, legal marriage. He's a good man. Now he does private inquiries for a living. His Chinese isn't good, but you can talk to him in the foreign language—they say you're very good at it. Go and see him. He'll find out what's happened to your father."

Without another word, the old man tiptoed to the door and eased himself out soundlessly.

Wilson said, "I think I've got the answer."

Didi's heart thudded heavily.

Just yesterday he had found Wilson in a small, cheerful, spotless house on a back street in French Town, with his small, cheerful, spotless Chinese wife and two giggling children.

Wilson had said, "I'll see what I can do. I have a couple of old pals on the English force who're feeling damned guilty because, since I got married, they've never even asked me for a drink." He grinned cheerfully. "So when I ask them for help, they're only too damned glad to give it. Shouldn't take more than four or five days."

That had been yesterday, and here Wilson was in the cheap

hotel room Didi had taken, sitting on a rickety chair, saying, "I think I've got the answer."

Wilson rose and went to the window, leaned against the sill, shook his shoulders.

"I thought I'd start from the moment your father arrived in Shanghai, so I went first to the Yangtszepoo Police Station, which is in charge of the waterfront area where your father's ship docked. The superintendent of that station is one of the pals I told you about. First crack out of the bag, he came up with something that I think must be the answer."

He cleared his throat and frowned.

"I must warn you—it isn't good. The morning after your father's ship docked, the dock-master called in the police. The body of a Chinese man had been found behind some crates, naked, with a knife in his back. It seemed like murder in the course of a robbery. There're lots of thugs on the waterfront. But why was he naked? Thugs would hardly have wasted time stripping him. That made my pal curious, and he decided to take a look at the body himself. He came to the conclusion that the man hadn't died of the knife wound. There was almost no blood from that. On the other hand there was a heavy concentration of blood in the face, as though the body had lain face down for quite a while after death. My pal concluded that the man had died elsewhere of something else, probably poison, had been stripped and transported to the dock later and dumped behind the crates."

He paused, eyeing Didi watchfully. Didi said nothing— thought nothing, felt nothing. The world was nothing.

Wilson said, "There wasn't much the police could do. Nothing to go on. They circulated details of the case to other stations and waited for somebody to report a missing person. When nothing came in after a week, they had to bury the body—can't keep bodies longer than that. But before they buried him, they took some photographs."

Another pause. Didi thought that his father had never been photographed. When other mandarins in Peking had rushed to be photographed by the Italian, Beato, who'd made such a good thing of the Dowager Empress, his father had laughed. "So much money for an image of the same face that I look at every day in the mirror!"

Wilson said softly, "My pal lent me one of the photographs. D'you mind looking at it? It's the only way of knowing whether that was your father."

After a moment, Didi said, "All right."

Wilson proffered a small slip of stiff paper. Didi took it, glanced at it, handed it back.

This new technique of photography was much overrated. His father wasn't a crumpled-up, slack-jawed, staring-eyed bundle of discolored skin and disheveled hair. His father was aristocratic, handsome, immaculate.

Wilson said, "Is it your father?"

Didi said, "Yes."

Wilson muttered, "Sorry. And sorry I had to show you that photograph."

Didi said, "It doesn't matter. I know what my father really looked like."

He felt remote, untouched, untouchable. The photograph was offensive but unimportant. He'd known, of course, that his father was dead—known the moment the sergeant's eyes flickered when he said his father's name in the police station. Later—sometime much later when life began again—he would cry for his father. One night, later, he would lie in darkness and all the things about his father, the loving, beloved things, would come creeping out of his sleeplessness and he would remember them one by one, and cry for his father.

Wilson said carefully, "My father-in-law thinks that your aunt too didn't die naturally. He says that for a long time before she died she didn't go to the Registry. Her young half-brother went, and sometimes an associate of his, a one-eyed man who, my father-in-law says, anyone with sense should be afraid of. But once, about three months before she died, your aunt did go into the Registry. She was dazed and confused. She asked my father-in-law about the staff of her *hong*—did he know that all the old ones had been sent away? He said he didn't know— staff changes don't have to be registered. Tears rushed to her eyes, and she ran out. He never saw her again. He says she looked dreadful. Bone thin, hair all gray, skin transparent . . . He says she looked like a far-gone opium smoker."

Didi stared. "My aunt Julie? Never!"

Wilson leaned closer. "Think about it . . . She could have

been addicted without her knowledge. You said she lived in the family home with her half-brother. She'd trust him, wouldn't she? How easy to make her ill with a bit of something in her food. How easy to get a 'doctor' who'd treat her with opium. How easy, while she was dazed and bewildered, to get her to sign over the power of attorney."

Didi shivered. "That would be absolutely wicked!"

"Yes of course," Wilson said calmly.

"But—my grandfather left millions. If they had divided the estate, each would have had more than ample. He didn't have to kill my father and my aunt to get their share of the money."

"No. But he'd have to kill them, wouldn't he, if he wanted to use the *hong* to black-market opium?"

The words lay almost tangibly on the stale air of the little room. Didi watched a spider busily spinning a web between wall and ceiling, racing back and forth, constructing its intricate trap . . . Use the *hong* to black-market opium? It wasn't possible! It wasn't possible! But of course it was possible . . . there was that story his father had told him. He turned to Wilson.

"The night before my father left Peking, he told me an amazing piece of family history. We have an ancestor, an Englishman—they called him the Red Barbarian because of his red hair—who was an opium smuggler. When opium was legalized, his son, my grandfather, undertook for himself and his descendants the duty of dismantling the structure of legal opium trading in China. The 'life-duty' he called it. He and my father and my aunt Julie worked for that all their lives. Finally, last year, the Agreement with India was negotiated under which the British will taper off their opium shipments over the next ten years, and the Empress signed the Edict Against Opium, ordering that opium be abolished throughout China in ten years. On the night of the day she signed the Edict, my father told me all this. He hadn't told me before because he hoped that the life-duty would be accomplished in his own lifetime, that I need not inherit it . . ."

Didi's throat constricted. With what joy his father had said, "You are free, Didi! Your life will not be encumbered! The life-duty will be accomplished in my own lifetime!" And now, not two months later, he was dead. The life-duty had descended after all. From grandfather to father to son. To me, Didi thought. To me . . . His heart pounded.

Wilson had risen and was pacing the room.

"That is quite a story! Of course, the legal means of abolishing opium is now in place—the Agreement with India and the Edict Against Opium. But to make it all stick—that's another matter. I suppose your father thought that in ten years it would all come out right, but the immediate effect of the Edict is to shoot the price of opium sky-high. Black-marketing opium will become more profitable than trading it legally ever was. That must have been the half-brother's motive for killing your father and your aunt. He could never had got hold of the *hong* otherwise."

He came to a stop and stared at Didi somberly.

"And now there's you . . . Please believe me, Didi. If you go on prodding and poking into your father's death, you've an excellent chance of ending up a dead body yourself. It's crystal clear that the police sergeant and the chief of the Registry are part of a network of bribery supported by your relative that must include a whole gamut of people right up to judges. You'll never get the Chinese authorities to touch your father's case. And the British, of course, won't reopen it. They've got nothing to go on. Take my advice and go back to Peking. You haven't a chance, going up against your relative. In the first place, what would you use for money? You can't begin to fight this without gobs of money, and you haven't any, have you?"

Money. Didi had never before thought about money as much as he had in the last day or two. He rose abruptly.

"No. Being an honest mandarin isn't a lucrative profession. Apart from the family wealth, my father had nothing, and I have nothing. The Ministry loaned us money for my steamship ticket."

"Then you'll have to go back, won't you? Believe me, Didi, there may come a time when you'll find a way to fight this, but that time is not now. I'm even wondering why you've lived this long. You've been in Shanghai two days, haven't you, and he knew you were here two minutes after you knocked on that gate. Will you go back to Peking at once, and leave the fight to another day?"

"Yes. I'll have to. My mother's there. I'll have to look after her. Get myself a job."

"Good. Go on the next ship."

Wilson turned toward the door, then turned back.

"Do you mind if I ask a question? My father-in-law is curious about your family's names. Your father's name means Great Dragon, doesn't it? And his half-brother's name means Great Fish?"

Didi smiled wryly.

"My grandfather had the fancy that those names would protect the family from dangers from the land and from the sea."

"Ah!" Wilson raised an eyebrow. "He was wrong about the sea, unfortunately."

Didi said, "How much do I owe you?"

"Nothing. The inquiry took just a few hours that I'd like to donate to the service of your aunt."

"I'll gratefully accept on her behalf. I hardly remember her, but my father loved her very much."

At the door they shook hands. Wilson walked softly away and Didi turned back into the meager room which, in the few moments while he wasn't looking, had filled with loneliness and sorrow.

Two weeks later, in Peking, on a cold, snowy afternoon, Didi gazed at his mother in wonder and dismay. She was still weeping. He had returned yesterday, told her yesterday that his father was dead, and she was still weeping. It was the last thing he had expected. She was the daughter of his father's former teacher, a famous mandarin who had been torn between greed for the excellent salary his employer had paid him, and disdain of his pupil, the son of a merchant. Nurtured on her father's resentments, she too had disdained her husband. Didi had expected her to be annoyed by his death. Who had dared kill him? How had he dared to allow himself to be killed? But instead she appeared grief-stricken, shedding storms of tears. Tentatively, he put an arm around her. She clung to him, words pouring brokenly through her sobs.

"I loved him! In my heart, I loved him! I know I was often angry! I know I shouted at him! But that was because he was always withdrawing himself, withdrawing his spirit! If only . . . If only I had . . . If only my father had not . . . And now it's too late!"

He patted her back, thinking sadly that years and years ago it had already been too late.

Sobs choked her, and she began to gasp and shudder. He propelled her gently to her bedroom, made her lie down. She huddled into a ball, her body vibrating with the sobs that wouldn't stop. He began to feel worried. This really wasn't one of her dramatic tantrums. This was distressingly real.

He heard the doorbell ring and listened as one of the servants went to open it. There was a murmur of voices, then the servant mounted the stairs and pushed open the door of the bedroom.

"There's a messenger from the British Legation with a letter and a parcel. He says he must hand them to you personally."

"All right. I'll come down. Tell the cook to make some herb tea and bring it to my mother."

The servant left and he lingered a moment, watching his mother with concern. She lay tightly curled, shaking, abandoned to her sorrow. Her remorse? He drew a coverlet over her and went downstairs.

At the front door, the messenger handed him an envelope engraved with the handsome crest of the British Legation, and a small oblong parcel sturdily wrapped in brown paper and sealed with many official-looking red wax seals. He took them up to his bedroom, sat at his desk which was still littered with textbooks that he would probably never use again, and slit open the envelope. It contained a letter on British Legation stationery, and another envelope.

The letter was from the British Minister who had become his father's good friend while still First Secretary of the Legation. He offered condolences. "I feel your father's untimely death as a personal loss, as well as a great loss to the whole opium suppression effort. I have taken the liberty of suggesting to the Opium Suppression Bureau that you be appointed to a still-vacant position as Opium Suppression Officer to stop poppy cultivation in the province of Shansi."

He felt relief. The Bureau would of course take the suggestion of the British Minister. At least he needn't run about looking for a job!

He slit the second envelope and removed a few sheets of lined copybook paper covered with shaky handwriting. Curiously, he looked for a signature.

It was signed Donald Mathes.

He sat, staring at the straggling signature, his mind leaping back to that last night with his father. Donald's grandfather, his father had said, had been an opium smuggler too, the biggest, roughest, richest of them all. So Donald and his own grandfather Jin-see had become great and good friends, and Donald had shared the life-duty, had worked in London to persuade Parliament to abrogate the opium treaty . . .

Slowly, he unfolded the closely written sheets. The letter was dated the fourth of January 1907 and started abruptly, without salutation:

Though you do not know me, I knew your father Great Dragon and your aunt Julie. Your grandfather Jin-see was my dearest, lifelong friend. Please read carefully what I have to tell you. I was invited to Peking for the signing of the Agreement with India. I arrived in Shanghai on the twenty-fifth of November last year and of course went immediately to see your aunt Julie. The gateman refused me entrance. This was so astounding that I banged on the gate and shouted, which attracted a crowd. The gateman then let me into the courtyard, but would not let me go to the house. Thoroughly alarmed, I swore that I would not leave until I saw your aunt. After a long wait, she came out into the courtyard. I was absolutely shocked by her appearance. She looked dreadfully ill. I questioned her, but she would tell me nothing. Instead, she took me to the ancestors' house, where I was again shocked to see that your father Great Dragon was dead, for there were four soul tablets, the newest one being for him. She asked me to take the soul tablets to you in Peking. I agreed, of course, and put them in my pockets. Then she insisted I must leave immediately. "Before they come back and stop you," she said. She was so desperately urgent that, in spite of my trepidation, I did leave her, after seeing a servant take her back into the house.

As I left the compound, I saw two men approaching, one a one-eyed man, the other, I am certain, your grandfather's younger son, Great Fish. He looked much like your grandfather. I walked quickly away, but they saw me. Fifteen minutes later, as I made my way toward French Town, a laden handcart somehow got out of control and ran me down. Thinking of it now, I am sure that the accident was contrived. Those handcarts are too heavy to run amok of themselves. At any rate, I was seriously injured. By the time I regained consciousness, I found myself on the way back to England. I am now in a London hospital, having just recovered sufficiently to write you this letter. I am very sorry about your father's death, and I fear greatly to think what has happened to your aunt. The accompanying parcel contains the soul tablets of your ancestors.

Didi laid the letter down, his heartbeat pulsing slow and heavy in his ears. The house was utterly still. He took up the parcel, cut the strings and seals, removed the wrappings, uncovered a white box, opened it. On a bed of cotton wool lay the tablets. His heart swelled. He had been in their presence only twice before, once on the night of his birth when his grandfather had presented him, together with his birthmate Great Fish, to the ancestors. And once when he was four years old, before he was sent to Peking to join his parents.

Now, with reverence and awe he took the tablets from the box and set them upon his desk.

The first, of white marble, was carved in gold with the name WEI. His great-great-grandfather who, during the first Opium War, had spied against the British in a doomed attempt to recapture the city of Ningpo, had been caught and beheaded. His head had been exposed on a spear above the city gate as a warning to other foolish Chinese patriots.

The second tablet, a match of the first, was carved with the name CHARLIE in English. The Red Barbarian. The English great-grandfather who had married Wei's lovely daughter Ling-ling and started it all by smuggling opium.

The third tablet was of dark green jade, carved with the name JIN-SEE. His grandfather, son of Ling-ling and the Red Barbarian, the first to give his lifetime to the life-duty.

The fourth tablet . . . his father's tablet! His blood drummed. It was exactly the same as Jin-see's, dark green jade carved in gold. TA-LUNG. GREAT DRAGON.

He sat back on his heels. The room was almost dark and the four tablets on the desk seemed to draw into themselves all the light there was—and everything else as well, everything of joy and hope and love, of life itself. Suddenly, the room was full of emptiness. His father would never again push open the door, peep in with that faint smile, murmur, "Son? Can we talk for a while?" Never again.

He had thought that he would cry for his father on a dark and sleepless night, but he cried for him then, on a gray winter afternoon, cried with wild, fierce sorrow, as though his heart lay crushed beneath the little jade tablet, as though hot blood dripped from his heart as hot tears dripped from his eyes.

But gradually, through his desolation, he became conscious of a relaxing of tension. The house felt calm, as it always had when his mother was out. He and his father had always known when she was out, when they were alone together . . . He looked at his father's tablet. It seemed to pulse, to be apart from the others. He rose and took it in his hand. It seemed warm, with a life of its own. Holding it, he went to the room where his mother lay.

"Mother?"

She didn't answer.

He went to the bed and touched her shoulder.

She didn't move.

He lit the lamp on the table beside the bed.

She lay on her back, her face lifted to the ceiling, white and calm now, almost smiling.

On the table beside the lamp were the empty cup in which the servant had brought her tea, and the bottle of her sleeping pills, empty too.

When the doctor had gone, Didi closed his mother's eyes, folded her hands across her bosom, knelt wearily beside the bed, waiting for the pain of the long, long day to come cracking down.

But what came to him was a kind of peace. The anxiety was over. The weeping was over. The future was clear. His father's gift to him, the freedom of his first twenty years of life, was all used up. Tomorrow he would arrange his mother's funeral, put the house up for sale, accept the job of Opium Suppression Officer in Shansi.

Tomorrow was the first day of the life-duty that, after all, he had inherited.

Chapter II
1909

G REAT FISH looked discontentedly around the shabby private office of the family *hong* on the third floor of an old building in the Chinese city. Big-ears thought it would attract too much attention if he were to move to better quarters. Julie had occupied this room for more than twenty years, during which it had grown more and more threadbare, but it served its purpose and Julie had considered it a waste of money to move. Julie never wasted money. She'd been a wonderful businesswoman, quick and clever and tenacious. Pity she'd had to die! She'd have made a wonderful partner in the *hong*'s new line of business—but of course she'd never have agreed to it! All those years she'd run the old lines of business, just the way their father had, with the sole objective of seeing to it that every conceivable antiopium activity—as well, of course, as Elder Brother Great Dragon in Peking—were amply supplied with money. A couple more years of that and the family would no longer have been in the multimillionaire category. He'd seized control only just in time.

He'd been twelve years old when he realized that the Edict Against Opium for which his father worked so hard and spent so lavishly would drive the opium trade underground and raise prices sky-high—which would be the proper moment for easing the *hong* into opium. Listening with eager face and utmost boredom to his blind old father waffle on and on about the life-duty, he had decided that *his* life-duty would be to keep the family fortunes well within the multimillion bracket.

He'd had to wait awhile, but as soon as it became clear that the Edict Against Opium would be issued, he had moved against Julie and Great Dragon in perfectly planned maneuvers. He smiled to himself. He'd done well! Still, it really was a pity about Julie. She'd been *nice* as well as clever and efficient. Mandarin Great Dragon, on the other hand, was totally unmourned as far as he was concerned. He'd have brought the Opium Suppression Bureau down on Fish's head like a ton of bricks, brother or no brother. And he hadn't been nice like Julie—just stuffy in that officious mandarin style.

Now the family consisted only of Fish himself and his birthmate Didi, who was helpfully running around Shansi suppressing poppies. Fish laughed aloud.

One-eye, entering the room in his silent way, growled, "What's so funny?"

"I was thinking how upset my only relative would be if he realized how much he's helping us! The less opium there is, the higher prices will go."

One-eye's single eye flicked maliciously.

"Your only relative shouldn't be alive! He's got a perfectly legitimate claim on the estate you stole from him, and he might one day find someone to listen to him!"

Fish frowned. "But—"

"But . . ." One-eye cut in sarcastically. "But you've got to let him live in case he knows who Ah-fet is." His smile became vicious. "I'll bet that Julie knew. I'll bet anything that Julie fooled you."

Fish's good humor vanished in a hot surge of fury. For the millionth time his mind flashed to the brief note in his father's straggling, half-blind writing that he'd found one day while prying through his father's papers.

Since 1885 I have been accumulating about four hundred pounds a year of top quality opium, as good as Patna. Ah-fet is my agent. He knows why I am doing this, where the poppies are grown, where the opium is stored.

He'd known at once that his father meant the note for Julie to find in case of his sudden death, and he'd left it where it was until his father did die suddenly. Then he'd removed it quickly before Julie found it. After the Edict was signed, he'd asked Julie who Ah-fet was, never doubting that she knew. She'd been their father's eyes ever since he went blind. She knew all about his affairs. It had been a thumping shock when she said, "I don't know. You should have asked Elder Brother before you killed him." Furious as that had made him, he'd believed her. Why not? By then the "doctor's" treatment had addicted her heavily to opium. Even as he asked her the question she had been showing signs of craving—yawning, languor, sweat. She couldn't have retained the wit to fool him! She couldn't have!

"She fooled you all right!" One-eye said coldly. "We should have kept her alive a few more days and got it out of her. But you flew into one of your rages and couldn't wait to be rid of her. That temper of yours is going to do you in one day."

Biting back a curse, Fish strode to the window, stood looking down at the narrow, crowded street. That devil-cursed One-eye, always needling, always flicking! At first he'd been so great! On Fish's thirteenth birthday, when he had rushed away, bursting with frustration, from the solemn ceremony at which his doddering old father had conferred upon him his version of the life-duty, One-eye had been standing outside the main gate of the compound. He'd had his eye on Fish for some time, Fish learned later, somehow scenting that Fish would make a good disciple for himself. In the months that followed he had dazzled Fish with the glamour of his gangland connections, his wide acquaintance among sing-song girls, his entrée into palatial brothels.

But the day had come when he'd had to introduce Fish to the king of that exotic underworld, Big-ears Doo. Ever since, he had burned with jealousy of Big-ears' interest in Fish, for Fish represented qualities Big-ears didn't yet have in his ever-growing arsenal: education, good-family breeding. One-eye had entrée into brothels. Fish had entrée into society.

Staring at his own reflection in the windowpane, Fish suddenly smiled. He could pay One-eye back immediately for that crack about Julie. All week, at Big-ears' behest, he had been attending the meetings of the International Commission on Opium, a job that only he could do because of his near-perfect knowledge of English, and all week One-eye had been fulminating about it. Today was the closing meeting. Fish turned back into the room, saying jauntily, "Well, time I left for the meeting!"

One-eye glowered as he gathered up his papers—all in English—and put them into his handsome calf leather briefcase. As he went to inspect himself in the mirror that hung behind the door, One-eye brushed passed him roughly and snatched the door open, banging it behind him. Fish's image in the mirror bounced and shivered. He grinned at it as it settled down again. So much for One-eye!

He preened a little. He was handsome. He had inherited nothing from his peasant mother and much from his father's English father. The foreign-looking features enhanced his youthful attractiveness. One-eye really had no chance against him. He raised pleased eyebrows at himself and left the room.

That evening, in Fish's family room, One-eye, who was well known for his bad digestion, looked on stonily as Big-ears wolfed food and slurped wine. Big-ears had no objection to eating and drinking at others' expense, and the food and drink at Fish's were lavish.

When he had finally had enough, he belched, patted his stomach, and began to prowl around the room. He had no appreciation of the elegance of Fish's huge estate—the marble courtyards, the graceful houses, the exquisite furnishings and ornaments. His interest was only in their value—particularly, at the moment, in the value of the curios Fish's father had collected. He was keenly aware of the huge sums that changed hands over pieces of porcelain, and he had recently started a factory that made curios. "They don't have to *be* a thousand years old. They only have to *look* it." Now he picked up a Sung dynasty *m'ei p'ing* plum blossom vase that Fish knew to be virtually priceless and turned it around carelessly in his rough hands.

"My factory can turn out things like this."

"Oh?" Fish held his breath until Big-ears put the vase down safely.

"And those ancestor tablets of yours." Big-ears jerked a thumb in the direction of the exquisite little ancestors' house that stood in Fish's courtyard, with its golden moon door and its floor and walls of precious woods. "My factory can turn out things like that too. Are they valuable?"

"Er—quite," Fish said, trying to sound judicious. They were, at least, expensive. He had ordered them from a famous stone carver to replace the real soul tablets that Julie must have spirited away. They had disappeared the day that nosy Englishman came to see her.

Big-ears wandered back to Fish's brocade-upholstered couch and threw himself down, yawning and belching. His nickname came from his grotesquely battered and misshapen ears. In addition he had scarred lips, eyelids that drooped over misleadingly dull eyes, and a voice that grated through a larynx that had at some time been badly damaged. Now he rasped, "I ate too much . . . Well, those meetings you attended sound like a waste of time, but go over the whole thing again. Maybe we can find something useful in all that mouth shit."

Fish collected his thoughts. This was his first real chance to get ahead of One-eye in the race for Big-ears' favor, a race that Fish was surer he would win the more One-eye feared he would lose. He began to speak with youthful earnestness, portraying gratitude for the confidence Big-ears had placed in him. He knew that this particular approach was charming: Julie had always been enchanted by it.

Thirteen nations, he said, had been represented at the Commission, which had been arranged by the American President Roosevelt. There had been a large number of formal speeches which could all be summarized in a very few words: all the delegates except the British thoroughly deplored the trade in opium. Many resolutions had been taken, all condemning opium, consequently the British attitude toward opium. There was to be another meeting at The Hague in 1912, at which the delegates would be plenipotentiaries, empowered to commit their governments to action against opium-producing and -trading nations.

Big-ears snorted with amusement. "More mouth shit! That's the way *not* to have action!"

Fish, grinning attractively, agreed. The informal talk in the lobbies had been much more straightforward than the fancy speeches. The British delegates had frankly cursed the Americans as busybodies and hypocrites, arranging international meetings as though they too didn't deal in opium. The Americans had pointed out contemptuously that Americans who traded opium broke their own country's law and laid themselves open to prosecution by their own government, whereas the British government protected British opium traders.

Fish laughed his charming, boyish laugh. The talk in the lobbies had become daily more acrimonious. Whenever the British mentioned the Agreement with India, somebody asked, why take ten years to tail off your shipments of opium to China? Why not just stop immediately? The British had had a rough time of it, not only from all the other delegates, but also from one of their own.

Fish turned to One-eye with a charming smile. "You remember that nosy Englishman, that old friend of my father's, who came one day to see Julie? You thought Julie might have told him something, so you arranged that 'accident'?" His smile widened. One-eye hated to be reminded of that hastily conceived, ill-executed accident. "Well, that Englishman is here, attending the meetings. He must be over seventy and he doesn't seem too healthy, but he's lobbying hard against his own delegation for an immediate halt to all production of opium except for strictly medical purposes."

"Very interesting," One-eye said coldly. Then, countering, "Did you get any clues as to who Ah-fet is?"

Big-ears grunted, lifting his droopy eyelids, "Did you?"

"No . . ." Fish deflected the thrust with a shrug of his shoulders. "I didn't look for Ah-fet at an international meeting! But I did get a clue that might be useful to us in future . . ."

He turned to Big-ears, intensifying his open, youthful, earnest expression, and began to speak softly, looking directly at him.

"All the delegates praised the Chinese government for unswerving sincerity in trying for the past hundred years to get rid of opium. They recommended that all nations should follow China's example. The British promptly said that every nation has the sovereign right to decide what it will do within its own jurisdiction. That means that, even if the British must stop

28

shipping opium to China, they intend to continue selling it in their own colonies—India, Burma, Malaya, Singapore. The French will do the same in Indochina and the Dutch in the East Indies. They say they'll control sales by establishing government monopolies, but that only means higher prices . . ."

He was speaking quickly and smoothly, using classical language in spectacular contrast to the coarse vernacular sprinkled with obscenities that was Big-ears' and One-eye's medium of expression. His education and his fine-family polish were showing; Big-ears was absorbing it all and One-eye was helplessly fuming . . .

"The French and Dutch don't produce opium, so they'll buy from the British. But *we* can produce opium much cheaper than the British. Not so good, but *much* cheaper . . . In the southwest there's a territory, very rough and mountainous, inhabited by tribal peoples, where our Yunnan province has contiguous borders with Burma and Laos. In a few years' time, when we've got the opium trade reorganized properly, we might consider growing opium in Yunnan and exporting it directly through that territory. We'd be in a fine position to compete with the British for the French and Dutch markets, and any other markets, of course, that might be interested."

In the pause that followed, One-eye petulantly changed his position. Big-ears mumbled, "Mmmmm." It was extraordinary how dull and stupid he could look and sound. But now, in addition to the mumble, a gleam showed from under his hooded eyelids. Well satisfied, Fish rose to pour more *mao tai*.

Chapter III

1911

THAT YEAR the rains came early in Shansi province. In June, trickles started in culverts of the craggy mountains and swiftly swelled into gushing streams that tumbled down the slopes and roared through the terraced fields, the foothill villages, the bamboo forests, before plunging into the swollen Yellow River. As always, year after year, farmers toiled from daybreak to nightfall, hauling rocks to shore up the terraces their forefathers had carved out of the grudging mountainsides. As always, precious loess washed away into the river, but as always some of it clung to the fields in a rich yellow-brown crust that rejoiced the hearts of the farmers.

In Taiyuan-fu, the provincial capital, the rains churned up bogs of yellow mud, which sucked sluggishly at the granite blocks that paved the center of the roads. Wheelbarrows and Peking carts crowded the narrow stone strips, forcing foot traffic into the ankle-deep ooze, where pedestrians slithered, porters cursed, and screeching children darted under everyone's feet.

Didi urged his pony through the bedlam, making sure that his long silk gown was safely tucked away from the splashing mud. The days when long silk gowns had been ordinary dress were dim and distant. Most of the time these days he was dressed like the mountain men in padded cotton jacket and calf-high boots of quilted cloth, riding his tireless mountain pony from village to far-flung village among the peaks and valleys that covered the landscape of Shansi like paper crumpled by a giant's hand.

But today he was going to see the governor. He had great news. He and his staff of nine officers had just returned from a month-long field trip. They had divided the province between them and ridden up and down every detectable trail, and none of them had seen a single poppy!

Well . . . with a wry grin, Didi made a superstitious sign. They hadn't *seen* a single poppy, but there were all those hard-to-find dips and dales in the mountains where a poppy field might so easily be hidden! Yet perhaps indeed they had missed nothing. Perhaps indeed this season no Shansi farmer had planted poppies. At first it had seemed an impossible task to dissuade them. Two hundred thousand acres planted to poppies in the season, producing more than three million pounds of opium, the most lucrative of crops! But he and his officers had doggedly gone about persuading, cajoling, haranguing, threatening, calling on morality, patriotism, omens, everything they could think of. And gradually, wheat and millet and persimmon orchards had begun to replace poppies in the fields. The gentry had agreed to go easy on the farmers' rents in the hard years while they were changing to crops less lucrative than opium. The governor had mitigated local taxes. And this season, barely five years into the ten years of the Edict, no single poppy had been seen!

The pony's hooves ceased squelching and began instead to clip-clop—they had reached the well-paved precincts of the Yamen, the massive building that housed the provincial offices. At the front steps, a servant took the pony's reins and another led Didi directly to the governor's office. Surprised at not being kept waiting, he entered. The governor, sitting squarely in his carved armchair, his long-nailed hands spread out on the table, eyed him with an arrogant stare.

"You took your time! I sent for you three days ago!"

Undisturbed, Didi bowed. Arrogance was part of the mandarin stock-in-trade. His own father had had the same stare, that he had tried hard and unsuccessfully to copy. The governor was, in fact, a kind and dedicated man whom Didi had learned to respect and like.

"I am sorry, Excellency. The message didn't reach me because I've just returned from a month-long field trip. I have good news, Excellency." Again he made the superstitious sign under the table. "It seems that the whole province is clean. Neither I nor my officers saw a single poppy!"

"Then somebody kept his eyes tight shut," the governor snapped. "I sent for you precisely because an army officer on maneuvers in the Chungtiao Mountains has reported finding a valley in which a big crop of poppies is flourishing."

Didi bowed his head and sighed philosophically. So much for superstitious signs!

"I'm not *blaming* you," the governor went on brusquely. "I know those mountains are rugged, and the rains came early. But I want you to act fast now to clean up that field of poppies. We're going to have a visitor . . ."

He relented enough to wave Didi to a seat.

"Under the Agreement with India, the British are to reduce their shipments of opium by ten percent a year, *provided* we reduce domestic production at the same rate. Actually, we are doing better. In Shansi alone we are one hundred percent clean—or almost—in only five years. But, Peking informs me, the British don't believe our figures. They're sending inspectors to see for themselves. One of them is coming to Shansi, and of course I want that field of poppies cleaned up before he gets here."

"Of course, Excellency! I'll go at once!"

He would have to hurry: in the high mountains the time for harvesting opium was due—he must reach that field before the poppy capsules were milked.

The governor's lips turned down in his version of a smile.

"Kindly delay your departure a moment . . . I've arranged for the lieutenant who found the field to accompany you. He will have a squad of twenty soldiers to dig up the crop and burn it. Later, when the English inspector comes, you are to take him around the province. Prepare a map, and let him choose the itinerary. You speak English, I know, and that will help establish good relations."

He paused and coughed, then looked up again, frowning severely.

"You have done a fine job, young man. Your fame has spread. I've had requests from other governors to pass you on to them when your job here is over, but I fully intend to keep you here. There's a very great deal yet to be done—the whole opium trading organization to dismantle. Wholesalers, retailers, middlemen, divans. To say nothing of the smokers: I suppose there's nothing to be done about them but wait for them to die off. Anyway, there's still a big job to be done, which I will entrust to you with every confidence."

"Thank you, Excellency!"

Didi left the room in a little glow of gratification. He was doing the life-duty in a different way from his father and grandfather, but he was doing it! If he had his ancestors' tablets on an altar, he'd go now and kowtow to them and report what the governor had said. But of course he had no altar. The tablets, still in the box in which Donald Mathes had sent them, were in the governor's safe.

After three days of southward travel, Didi and the lieutenant and his squad of twenty soldiers reached a village that lay eerily silent in the gray drizzle. The lieutenant said sharply, "This is the village that owns that poppy field! When I was here two weeks ago, it was full of people and dogs and chickens. They must have realized that I'd found their field and would report it. They've gone up to protect their crop. They're going to fight for it!"

Didi said reasonably, "Maybe they've gone up to harvest it."

"*All* of them? The babies too, and the grandmothers? I tell you, they're going to fight for it!"

He glared around at the little mud-walled village houses as though they hid an enemy. Disturbed by his intensity, Didi said soothingly, "Maybe they're just hiding up there, hoping we'll search a bit, and then go away, not finding the valley."

"Don't you worry, I'll find it!"

The lieutenant began to rattle off orders to his little squad of twenty men. They would bivouac in the village and start out at first light to climb to the valley. They should reach the valley by midafternoon—sooner, if the devil-cursed rain would stop. They would eat a good meal now, and a light one in the morning. They would not stop to eat on the way up.

The men moved to obey the lieutenant's orders. Still uneasy,

Didi murmured, "If it's such a hard climb, shouldn't we travel as lightly as possible? Perhaps the men could leave their weapons here, and carry only the spades and hoes."

The lieutenant glared. "Are you proposing that *soldiers* leave their *weapons* behind?"

Didi turned away silently—the lieutenant was very young and very proud of his command.

Even in the rain, the view from the village was beautiful, perhaps more beautiful because of the rain, which gave it a muted kind of mystery. Rolling fields of wheat and millet rose to a feathery wall of bamboo that marked the beginning of the foothills. The persimmons were ripening: thousands of red spots hung from angular branches. All around, water dripped and whispered. Above everything, dwarfing everything, the great peaks towered.

The lieutenant came and stood beside Didi. With the men working hard to obey his orders, he had relaxed a little.

"Pretty, isn't it? But what's really pretty is that valley where the poppies are. It's in a ring of mountains like a giant rice bowl, the field at the bottom. There's only one entrance, a kind of cleft in the mountainside. When you enter the cleft, you can't see the field because there's a broad shelf of rock with a farmhouse on it. You have to go to the edge of the shelf—then you look straight down on the field. When I was there two weeks ago, the poppies were in flower, like a white carpet covering the floor of the valley. Beautiful!"

He coughed and grunted, as though ashamed of having noticed beauty.

"But what I really like about that valley is how hidden away it is. I found it by the sheerest accident. It's a near-perfect military stronghold."

In the morning, the rain had stopped. In watery sunlight, the climb to the valley was made with speed but a great deal of noise. The path was so twisting and narrow that the soldiers were forced into the underbrush. Their guns and equipment clanked against stones and branches that rattled away loudly to be lost in the leafy depths. In places, the clinging forest was so thick that the light turned green. In places, open fields rose skyward in terraces like mighty stairways. As they climbed higher, vegetation became sparser. Bare patches of rock and clay began to show among the greenery. The ground, stripped of its loess, became harsh and dry, drained already of yesterday's rain. Didi's ears hummed and popped: they were very high up. The valley of the poppies must be very deep among these peaks. To be fertile enough for poppies, it must contain centuries of loess washed down and trapped within its bowl.

Shortly after noon, they came to a bend in the path where the lieutenant halted his men. Giving them an order to be silent, he took Didi's arm and almost tiptoed him forward.

Around the bend was a rocky plateau, comparatively flat. Beyond it, steep cliffs rose to a lofty rim, unbroken except for a deep V that cleft almost down to the plateau. It was a bare and eerie place, no leaves to rustle in the mountaintop breeze, no birds to whir their wings. The jagged rocks were sadly gray in contrast to the pale sky that showed through the cleft. The cleft seemed to beckon—unbreached, soundless, enticing.

The lieutenant whispered, "They know we're here—they must have had sentinels out who heard our noise. So I'll make my move at once. I'll send a scout in first. If everything looks all right to him, he'll signal and we'll rush the cleft."

They retreated quietly. Behind the bend, the men were sitting cross-legged on the ground eating cold rice and drinking cold water. The sergeant jumped to his feet and grinned at the lieutenant.

"Didn't think we had time for a fire."

The sergeant was a middle-aged man who, beyond token respect, treated the lieutenant like a son. The lieutenant was brusque with him, but accepting, as though he found a secret security in the fondness of the older man. Now he said, "Sergeant, take the men very quietly around the bend, where they're to wait at the ready. You yourself are to go through the cleft into the valley. You'll find yourself on a rocky shelf with a farmhouse on it. The villagers will probably all be there, eating their noon meal. They must have heard us arrive, but they'll expect us to eat too before we attack. So I want to attack at once. If you think it's feasible, signal, and we'll rush the pass."

The sergeant saluted and turned to give quick orders to the men. They crowded around the bend, Didi and the lieutenant following. At the foot of the plateau they halted. The sergeant went forward alone, quick and noiseless in his straw sandals. At the entrance to the cleft he stopped and looked back, raising a hand in a gesture of—comradeship? Anticipation? Farewell? His body was a thick, black splotch against the glow of the sky, his hand a small black spider. Then he turned and climbed through the cleft.

They waited, all eyes fixed on the spot where he had disappeared. Didi felt a pain under his ribs and realized that he was holding his breath. So were the others: their postures were tense and strained, their eyes staring. The silence deepened, seemed to take on a pulsing rhythm.

And then was monstrously shattered. A shock wave of sound burst through the cleft—the ragged roar of many shouting voices, the thud of many rushing feet, the clash and clang of metal. Didi's heart leaped as though it would leave his breast. The men stood frozen, open-mouthed. For long moments the hullabaloo went on, the watchers silent and unmoving as though hypnotized by it. Then words began to be distinguishable in the torrent of sound:

"Got him!"

"Got the pig!"

"His skull's cracked!"

"He's dead . . ."

". . . dead!"

". . . dead!"

Beside Didi the lieutenant began to whisper monotonously, "They killed my sergeant . . . *my sergeant* . . ."

The corporal came padding up to him, gray-faced. For a moment the lieutenant stared at him unseeingly. Then his body snapped erect, his eyes took fire, his lips began to pour out a stream of orders.

"You . . . you . . . you . . ." He selected ten men, pointing at random. "Up the cliffs on each side of the cleft! We'll fire on them from the top! We'll trap those stinking murderers! You others—be ready to rush the cleft as soon as I signal!"

"Wait!" Didi shouted, grabbing at the lieutenant's arm. "You can't do that! We're here to dig up poppies, not to kill farmers!"

The lieutenant flung off his hand.

"I'm in charge here! They killed *my sergeant!"*

"But—"

36

It was no use. The men had already leaped to the cliff face, were hauling themselves up, climbing, crawling, zigzagging on the slenderest of toe- and finger-holds. Their straw sandals on the slippery surfaces were like the hooves of mountain goats. As they went higher their gray-green uniforms became invisible against the gray of the jagged rocks and they seemed to disappear, but soon they reappeared, their heads and shoulders popping up over the cliff top to be outlined blackly against the sky. They maneuvered into position, sprawled on their stomachs, legs braced. They unhitched their rifles from their backs, pointed them into the valley, turned to stare down at the lieutenant, waiting his signal to fire. Their white faces, far away, high up, seemed to shine like the sky behind them. It was a moment that would be etched forever in Didi's memory. The men clinging to the cliff top, the men clustered on the plateau, the farmers' voices still tumbling out of the cleft, joined by the shriller voices of women and children, quarreling now over the sergeant's belongings.

"The gun's mine! I hit him first!"

"No, I did . . . I did . . . I did . . ."

"The coat's mine . . ."

"Mine . . . mine . . . mine . . ."

The lieutenant stepped forward, a white cloth held at full stretch between his raised hands. He flexed his arm sharply, and the cloth fluttered in a long arc. From the cliff top the guns spoke, volley after volley, echoing from peak to peak in demonic repetition. From within the valley there was dead silence, then a great, swelling wail of fear, then a whirlwind of rushing feet as the villagers ran for shelter. The lieutenant dashed forward, the men followed. In moments, they were through the cleft and into the valley.

Didi followed slowly, heart pumping, blood prickling, muttering idiotically, "We came to dig up poppies . . ." As though bullets could be shot back into the muzzles of rifles, blood sucked back into wounds, the dead called back to life.

He stepped through the cleft.

On the slope that led down to the rock shelf, the dead lay in careless abandon. A pile of three or four together, arms and legs entangled. A woman tumbling downhill, head lolling lower than her heels. A child caught in midflight, arms outflung. The sergeant . . . his skull chopped open, blood and brains spilled out in the dirt. He was naked, his body white and bony, his clothes clutched in the arms of the men sprawled about him.

Thirteen dead, Didi counted. The latest of the millions who had died because of opium. A century of deaths. Smokers. Smugglers. Soldiers. The terrified and innocent bystanders of the Opium Wars. And now, these latest . . .

He raised his eyes to the rim of the mountains. It was indeed a beautiful valley, hidden away like a playground for the gods and spirits of the heights, who now had punished its desecration. Thirteen dead men and women, and a child.

He heard a cry and walked quickly down the path, peered around a rock. Not thirteen—fourteen, the fourteenth a woman, half sitting on the other side of the rock, still clutching in her dead arms a living, squalling baby.

He took the baby and started walking down to the farmhouse. With the movement, the baby quieted and cuddled against him, sucking its thumb. He approached the crowd of surviving villagers, who were herded into the narrow space between the farmhouse and the mountainside, some wounded and moaning, all white-faced, in shock. He held out the baby.

"Whose child is this?"

At first they gazed at him, blank-eyed. Then a woman came forward timidly, bent to peer at the baby, and became suddenly animated.

"It's Li-po!" She beamed up at Didi. "It's the great-grandson of our headman! He's alive! He's alive!"

A murmur fled backward through the crowd and soon there was a ripple as an old man came forward, the people patting him, murmuring, smiling in spite of their fear and sorrow. Didi went to meet him.

"Sir, your great-grandson."

With a little cry the old man took the child, clutched him to his bony chest, covered his face with kisses.

"I thank you! I thank you for saving the life of this child!"

"I didn't save him," Didi said gently. "The gods saved him. I am ashamed that he was ever in danger."

But the old man had not listened. He was murmuring to the child, cuddling him, trembling with emotion. Didi put an arm around his shoulders to help him to the farmhouse. A soldier came forward in a halfhearted attempt to stop them, but a glare from Didi sent him scurrying back. Inside the farmhouse, Didi struck a match and lit a lamp. They were in a sleeping room. Along one wall was a wooden platform on which twenty or thirty men could sleep side by side, warmed by the quilts piled on the platform and the small clay stoves underneath. Didi helped the old man onto the platform, laid the baby across his lap. The old man fell instantly asleep. The baby clutched one of his fingers and gurgled.

For a time, Didi watched them, the pounding of his heart beginning to slow. At least the child was alive—the precious great-grandson, the inheritor of the rituals he would one day perform for the old man who nodded and drooled over him, and for those other ancestors who had gone before. . . .

When the child too fell asleep, Didi wandered outside, found himself at the top of a stairway that must have been cut into the mountainside a very long time ago, the steps were so smooth and slippery. Carefully, he descended to the poppy field, where the soldiers were busy pulling up the plants. Indeed, they had been ready for harvest—straggly, almost leafless, the capsules heavily pendant at the end of long, thin stalks . . .

The capsules were enormous! The biggest and plumpest he had ever seen! He picked one and incised it with a thumbnail. At once the white opium latex began to ooze, thick and strong-smelling. It was top-quality opium! As good as Patna—and Patna was the best in the world. No wonder the villagers had been determined to protect their crop! Where had they got seeds for poppies like these? The old village headman must know!

Quickly, Didi climbed back to the farmhouse. In the sleeping room, the old man stirred and gave him a toothless smile.

"I thank you again for this child's life!"

Didi perched on the platform beside him.

"Sir, I say again that the gods saved him, not I. But if you are grateful, you can do something for me. You can tell me where you got the seeds for your poppies."

"Oh—that!"

The old man—his nap had considerably refreshed him—cocked his head and looked crafty. Then he shrugged.

"I promised never to tell, but I don't suppose it matters

anymore. That devil-cursed government will make us plant wheat and millet in this beautiful valley where our ancestors planted poppies for a hundred years!"

He sighed and coughed and dilly-dallied, and finally raised filmy eyes to Didi.

"It seems like a fairy tale . . . It was many years ago, nearly thirty. I was still young enough to enjoy my wife." He chuckled rheumatically. "She was a one! Flesh on her that a man could get hold of! Now I'm so old it's too much trouble even to look! Well, about the poppies . . . we were growing ordinary opium in this valley, about two hundred pounds a year, and selling it to the Opium Merchants Guild, which handled all the opium in China, everybody had to sell to it. We thought we were doing fine, but a man came from Shanghai, a very rich man, who offered to buy our valley, for a great price. Not only that. He said that if we would sell to him, we could go on growing poppies, same as always, but he would give us seeds of the Indian poppy that would produce much better opium, and twice as much—four hundred pounds a year. Also, he would buy our opium at ten percent more than the Guild's price. Now—wasn't that like a fairy tale? We couldn't believe it at first. I asked him why. He couldn't sell the opium without the Guild knowing, so why did he want it? He said he had his reasons. We thought him mad! But how could we refuse an offer like that?"

"Did he say how he got the seeds of the Indian poppy?"

"He said he had bribed an Indian farmer to let him have twenty poppy heads. We grew poppies from that seed the first year, and the seed has held true ever since."

"And he bought your opium every year, as he promised?"

"Yes, every year, regular. He didn't come himself. He sent an agent—an Englishman, if you'll believe that! An Englishman with a Chinese wife, whom we already knew because he had come up many times before to inspect our poppies—he used to buy our opium through the Guild."

"Did you expect him this year?"

"Yes! That's why we were so anxious to save our crop! We hoped to sell one last crop before we had to obey the Edict."

He sighed and shook his head and rubbed away an old man's tear with a gnarled and dirty fist.

Didi contemplated him. It sounded fantastic. But that capsule he had picked was fantastic too.

"What is the Englishman's name?"

"Ah-fet."

"*Ah-fet?* That's not an English name. It's not even a Chinese name!"

"It's a nickname. That's what we call him. I don't know any other name."

"What did he do with the opium?"

"I don't know. We never asked. Every year he came up here and paid us, and we delivered the opium by pony-back to a landing place on the Yellow River, and he took it from there."

Nearly thirty years at about four hundred pounds a year—between ten and eleven thousand pounds of top-quality opium. Not an awful lot, but enough to have made a great big splash if it had ever been put on the market. It must be hidden somewhere, in storage . . . But *why?* Why go to such enormous trouble and expense to produce Patna-quality opium domestically, then hide it away for thirty years?

The old man was nodding again, eyes closing. Didi touched his shoulder.

"Who was the man who bought the valley?"

"Mmmm?" The old eyes stared vacantly.

"The man who bought the valley—what was his name?"

"Ah . . ." A cracked smile, a little nod. "He got something else from us too, besides our valley. A girl. We threw her in with the deal, free of charge." He shook with silent laughter. "She was a widow from our village who was eager for city things, and one night while he was here she got under his quilt. When he said he'd send for her to Shanghai, we were glad because she used to ogle us men and our wives didn't like it. She got pregnant by him. Until he sent for her, we watched her very carefully. We didn't want him to say the child wasn't his."

"What was his name?" Didi asked patiently.

"Didn't I tell you? Wei Jin-see. His name was Wei Jin-see."

If a great fist had shot out of the heavens and clobbered Didi, he could not have been more stunned, his heart could not have leaped higher, his mind could not have jangled more bewilderingly. Wei Jin-see, his own grandfather, whose green jade

41

soul tablet rested in the governor's safe, waiting for its place on his ancestral altar! The sun stood still, the moon and stars hesitated in their courses, as he sat staring at the nodding old man.

At last, when it grew dark and he could no longer see the old man's face, nor the child in the crook of the old man's arm, he rose and left the room. Stars were shining overhead, so low that it seemed impossible he could not touch them if he reached up. Other stars were shining below him—the lanterns of the soldiers. A tongue of flame leaped up: they were burning the poppies.

He climbed to the cleft, the thin, chill air whistling in and out of his lungs. In the cleft, he turned to look back at the valley, lying in the dusk, shadowed, peaceful, and mysterious. The beautiful valley where, thirty years ago, for some unimaginable reason, his grandfather had arranged for the best opium in China to be grown and then had caused it to disappear through the hands of an Englishman nicknamed Ah-fet. And where, in the womb of a peasant, his grandfather had given life to his younger son, the fratricide Great Fish.

He turned and stumbled out of the valley, the secrets of the past pressing heavily on his spirit, the stars twinkling merrily overhead, unconcerned with mortal pain.

Chapter IV

1911

THE RAILWAY CARRIAGE was painted orange-red. Gold paint (gold leaf?) trimmed its windows. A large placard on an easel stood beside its steps: HIS EXCELLENCY INSPECTOR OF POPPIES.

The Chief of Protocol bowed. "For only you, Sir Hosie. Please have comfortable journey."

Sir Alexander Hosie gravely bowed back and entered the carriage. A conductor in livery led him to an armchair by a window. When he was seated, the conductor signaled to someone on the platform and, a moment later, the train jerked and started. The conductor bowed and withdrew.

Alex looked admiringly around the palatial parlor-on-wheels in which he was to journey to Shansi in lonely splendor. Rich woods, marbles, brocades . . . The carriage had belonged, he had been told, to the Old Empress. Though she could hardly have used it! Alex reviewed what he had read about the Empress, preparatory to this trip to China. She had died in 1908, and before that her last trip out of Peking had been in 1900, when she fled in an oxcart in the midst of the Boxer Rebellion, after the Boxers had failed to prove their claim that they were bullet-proof. She had returned to Peking two years later, after the Boxer Protocol with all its punitive provisions had been signed.

She had never left Peking again. She had set herself stoically to woo the invincible foreigners, even allowing herself to be photographed with the much-taller wives of foreign ambassadors towering around her. That must have been galling to the occupant of the Peacock Throne, whose subjects had routinely prostrated themselves at her feet and banged their foreheads on the floor to acknowledge that she was above humankind and endowed with celestial sanctions! Not that she had had any real right to the throne she had adroitly usurped. Still, the old mandarins, now defrocked by the Republic, referred to her as the Old Buddha and, like millions of her other subjects, believed she had had more right to govern than the jumped-up warlord Yuan Shi-kai, who was now first President of the Republic of China. Certainly, she had had more finesse in the art of governing! It was an unholy mess in Peking now!

Grimacing, Alex opened his briefcase and spread out on the table the reports he had been given by the Minister of Foreign Affairs. A sheaf of thin rice-paper sheets, covered with names and figures: every district in the province of Shansi was listed, with the acreage planted to poppies and the quantity of opium produced in every year since the promulgation of the Edict Against Opium. He turned to the neat summary on the last page, which set forth the English equivalents of the Chinese dates, weight, and measures.

	Acres Under Poppy	Pounds of Opium Produced
Thirty-second year of Kuang Hsu (1906)	198,000	3,300,000
Thirty-fourth year of Kuang Hsu (1908)	58,000	1,068,000
Second year of Hsuang Tung (1910)	10,000	172,000
First year of the Republic (1911)	—	—

Alex had looked skeptically at the last entry, but the Minister had assured him that it was correct. Although three calendar months of 1911 remained, the growing season for poppies was over. It could therefore be said with truth that no opium had been produced in Shansi this year.

But poppies had been planted! There was that report that had reached Parliament before he left London about a riot over poppies somewhere in the Shansi mountains that had given rise to a number of killings. The Opposition had raised questions in the House of Commons about the "massacre," claiming that the Chinese couldn't enforce the prohibition on poppies, that the situation was out of hand, that therefore the British opium traders should not be forced to curtail shipments of Indian opium to China. It was worrying. There were many, especially in the India Office, still violently opposed to the closure of the opium trade in China.

Alex had consulted old Donald Mathes who knew the ins and outs of the China opium trade better than anyone else in England. Donald had proposed ensuring that the Chinese punish whoever was responsible for the massacre. They might try to let him off if he were highly connected. But if Alex could show that he had been punished (imprisonment? dismissal?), that would be proof that the Chinese were taking action to control the situation, and that would scuttle the Opposition.

Accordingly, Alex had discussed the matter with the Minister of Foreign Affairs. He felt exhausted now, just thinking of that discussion! The Chinese knew how to do things on the grandest of scales, but they also knew how to evade questions, especially when the questioning had to be done through interpreters!

At last, Alex had got the Minister to admit that, yes, there had been a little disturbance in Shansi last June. Something about farmers who had illegally planted poppies and then refused to give up their crop to the proper officials. Yes, perhaps a farmer or two had been killed in the resulting struggle to destroy the poppies before they could be milked of their opium. The action against the farmers had been initiated by an army lieutenant. No, of course the Minister of Foreign Affairs could not punish an army lieutenant! But . . . The Minister, suddenly perceiving the way out of this difficulty, had become affable . . . If it would reassure the British Parliament that the government of the Republic of China was firmly in control of the poppy situation, the Shansi Opium Suppression Officer, a civilian, who had been present during the incident, would at once be dismissed. The necessary steps would be put in process immediately.

Alex turned to the window, sighing. He hoped the Opium Suppression Officer was one of the fawning, favor-currying types liberally sprinkled around Peking . . .

The scenery was changing. Dusty plains were giving way to

hills—in the distance, mountains. Those improbable-looking mountains on Chinese scroll paintings actually existed! Misty, gray-green precipices tumbling almost vertically into leafy depths, trees clinging here and there, a temple perched where no building could possibly have been constructed . . . Alex settled down to forget the Opium Suppression Officer and enjoy the trip.

Thirty-six hours later, the train huffed into the station at Kwanglin on the northern border of Shansi province. Alex watched amusedly as person after person on the platform stopped in mid-movement to stare at his ornate carriage. When he himself descended to the platform, the starers had become a phalanx, all dropping their jaws at the same moment. A foreigner! A "Redface"! Donald Mathes had said, "They'll call you Redface. It used to be Red Barbarian. Now it's Redface."

A young man came pushing his way through the crowd, stopped before Alex, bowed politely, and said in excellent English, "Sir Alexander, I'm to be your guide for the next ten days. I'm the Opium Suppression Officer of Shansi."

Alex felt his heart begin to sink. This was no fawner. This was an alert, handsome, efficient-looking young man. To hide his consternation, he harrumphed loudly.

"Young man, where did you acquire your English?"

The young man smiled pleasantly. "From my father. My father was senior mandarin of the Ministry of Foreign Affairs. Until he died five years ago, he handled all the correspondence with your Foreign Office, especially about opium."

Alex barely prevented himself from goggling.

"Was your father's name Great Dragon?"

The young man laughed delightedly. "Yes!"

Alex somehow managed to keep his expression neutral. Oh God, what had he done! This young man must be the Didi of whom Donald had spoken, son of the mandarin Great Dragon, grandson of Donald's dearest friend Jin-see, with whom he had worked all his life to end the opium trade! God in Heaven, could that dismissal be recalled?

Didi was looking a little anxious. "Sir, are you feeling quite well?"

"Yes, yes . . . Perfectly . . ." Alex shoved aside the tumble of his thoughts. "When do we start on this tour?"

Didi looked relieved. "As soon as you like. The governor sends his compliments and says you're to pick the itinerary. We'll have to travel by pony-back—hope you don't mind, but there's no other way of getting up and down the mountains. The governor would like us to end the tour at Taiyuan-fu—he'd like to meet and talk with you. You can get the train back to Peking from Taiyuan-fu—even that carriage . . ."

He grinned, and Alex found himself grinning back . . . A perfectly charming, straightforward, competent young man! Hell and damnation!

For ten days they rode the mountains and the plateaus, up and down and roundabout, stopping at farms of all sizes, digressing sometimes at Alex's whim along trails that led nowhere or ended suddenly in tiny lost villages. They did not see a single poppy. Several times, Alex himself took up a rake and rummaged through rubbish piled up for burning outside villages: not a single dried-out poppy head, not a single dead plant with the fusiform root that characterized the poppy. Day by day Alex's spirits rose: by God, Shansi was indeed clear of poppies!

And, day by day, his spirits fell as he saw more and more clearly the impossibility of recalling that dismissal, and yet could not bring himself to say anything about it to Didi. He was funking it, he knew. For the first time in his life he was funking a distasteful job. But what good would it do to tell Didi now? It would only spoil a delightful companionship. Each evening, at the end of the long day in the saddle, they sat together in village inns, drinking piping hot, harsh-tasting green tea, eating prodigiously of whatever the innkeeper provided. Alex forgot all the London strictures about being careful what he put in his mouth and enjoyed the food thoroughly. Each night, the ponies huffing gently nearby, they lay under the frosty stars, wrapped in bedrolls, preferring the chill air to the flea-ridden fustiness of the inns' sleeping rooms. And each night, for a moment or two before tumbling into sleep, Alex regretted bitterly that conversation with the Minister. But it was too late now. He could only hope that the dismissal order wouldn't arrive until after he had left. Cowardly. But there was nothing he could do.

47

On the eleventh day, in Taiyuan-fu, the meeting with the governor took place. Alex was glad he had brought his dress uniform, for the governor wore a splendid brocade robe and a hat cockaded with his badge of office. In a glow of mutual goodwill they sat down opposite each other at the large round table, their interpreters beside them. The remaining seats at the table were occupied by the members of the Provincial Assembly. Didi sat to one side, with the governor's secretary. Smiling, the governor opened the meeting, speaking through his interpreter:

"His Excellency Sir Hosie has seen for himself, not only through reports, that we in Shansi have suppressed poppy cultivation in only five years of the ten prescribed by the Edict Against Opium."

Alex bowed. "Indeed, I have seen for myself. I congratulate His Excellency the Governor, the Provincial Assembly, the people of Shansi, and especially the Opium Suppression Officer, for a most remarkable achievement. I should like to add that it makes me personally happy, for I hate opium."

"Ah!"

The President of the Provincial Assembly bounced to his feet, beaming, and began to speak animatedly, gesticulating with his fine, long-fingered hands. When the interpreter began to translate, Alex sighed inwardly. This wasn't going to be as pleasant as he had hoped!

". . . since we in Shansi," the interpreter said, "have worked so hard and so successfully to get rid of poppies, would it not be right for a great and honorable nation like the English to reciprocate by terminating your opium shipments *now*, instead of in another five years? It is not good for one nation to be obliged to accept from another what it does not want!"

Alex turned gravely to his own interpreter, cursing the fact that in London the Opposition would demand that the minutes of this meeting be read into the Record, therefore he must now speak sternly.

"Let me remind the Honorable President of the Provincial Assembly that the right of the British to ship opium to China is guaranteed in the Treaty of Tientsin of 1860. In consenting to terminate shipments, the British have made a great concession to China, sacrificing a revenue to the British Indian Govern-

48

ment of more than four million pounds Sterling per annum . . ."

Startled glances flashed around the table, and again Alex cursed inwardly. Why had he mentioned figures! Clearly, they hadn't known the extent of the opium revenues . . . He finished as quickly as he could.

"Moreover, other provinces of China have not been as prompt as Shansi in suppressing poppies. For these reasons, I regret that my government cannot consider the suggestion of the Honorable President."

There was a little silence. The President looked crestfallen. Alex tried to look both stern and sympathetic.

The door opened and a messenger came hurrying in with a scroll that he handed to the governor's secretary. The secretary glanced at it, and looked up in amazement, his eyes flashing to Alex, then to Didi. Alex's heart lurched. Oh God! Everything was going wrong! That must be the dismissal order!

The secretary hurried to the governor and handed him the scroll. The governor read it, his face changing, goodwill giving way to icy anger. He spoke sharply to his interpreter, who looked startled then began to translate woodenly.

"His Excellency the Governor was given to understand that His Excellency Sir Hosie's mission in Shansi was simply to verify whether poppies were still being grown."

Alex bowed silently. There was nothing to be said. He must simply endure until he could flee to the refuge of that damned red and gold carriage.

The Governor spoke again, and the interpreter translated.

"Nevertheless, His Excellency the Governor has no objection to informing His Excellency Sir Hosie that the questions asked in the British Parliament referred to some farmers who thought they could hide a poppy field high in the mountains and then tried, with violence, to defend it. In spite of their resistance, the poppies were destroyed before they could be milked. Unfortunately, some deaths occurred by order of the lieutenant commanding a squad of soldiers who had been sent to destroy the poppies. The Opium Suppression Officer was present but conducted himself throughout with the high honor that distinguishes his character."

Alex bowed again, trying to look imperturbable, feeling as

miserable as he had ever felt in his life. The governor let a few very long moments pass, during which the growing anger of the members of the Assembly communicated itself to Alex, as they began to realize that somehow he had hoodwinked them. But worst of all was the shock and pain on Didi's face. Alex took one look at it and averted his eyes.

When the silence became unbearable, the governor rang a little silver bell. The doors were opened, and the ceremonial tea was carried in.

While the tea was being drunk, Didi slipped from the meeting room and walked out to the portico. It was raining. Ten days of lovely sunshine to ride through the mountains with Redface, and now it was all over—the good feeling as well as the good weather. He felt cold and empty. Whatever was written in that scroll, it was clear that Redface had taken him in. It hurt more sharply than he would have thought possible. He had liked Redface very much. He had even thought that Redface was more like his father than any man he had met since his father's death. How had he been so easily duped? What signs had he missed that should have tipped him off? He was a fool! Fine with unsophisticated farmers and rural gentry, but put him up there with the Redfaces where the politics were and he was a simpleton. He had inherited absolutely nothing of his father's acumen. He would never, never be like his father, no matter how hard he tried. Perhaps if his father hadn't gone so suddenly . . . He felt the sob rising in his throat and strode briskly out into the rain. His gown was instantly soaked and his skin began to shiver, but he walked up and down, heart aching, until a servant came to recall him to the governor's office.

The governor was alone, the scroll spread out on the desk before him. He spoke with contempt.

"A real traitor, that Englishman! Sat at our table, complimented us, made us all think he was a nice man—and he had already stuck the dagger into your back."

He pushed the scroll toward Didi.

Over its big square official chop, the Government Council had written:

> Because of questions raised in the British Parliament about the massacre last June, the British Inspector of Poppies has de-

manded that punitive action be taken. Therefore, the Opium Suppression Officer of Shansi is to be dismissed instantly upon receipt of this directive.

Didi laid the scroll down and went to the window, his wet gown clinging about him. The rain was still falling thick and fast in big, fat, gray drops. It would be raining for a long time now, if not out there in nature, then inside, within his spirit . . . He felt the governor's hand on his shoulder—astonishingly, the proud old mandarin had risen from his chair and walked clear across the room. He spoke gruffly.

"I am more sorry than I can say. I have never before had such an efficient officer, and I have rarely trusted anyone as I have you. Well, at least you won't have to worry about a job. As long as your name is removed from the Shansi rolls, those idiots in Peking won't notice if it reappears on another roll. I'll pass you along to one of the governors who've been begging for your services. The two best choices are Chekiang and Kiangsu. Which d'you want?"

A bubble suddenly swelled in Didi's throat. Kiangsu meant Shanghai, and Shanghai meant Fish—and Ah-fet . . . He swallowed.

"Kiangsu, Excellency."

"You'll probably be assigned to Shanghai, which must be *the* most difficult place for opium control. Are you sure?"

"I'm sure," Didi said softly, feeling the high beat of his heart.

Chapter V

1912

ONALD MATHES carefully shifted position on the hotel couch. He had never really recovered from that "accident" and now, at seventy-five, he became painfully stiff if he didn't move frequently. Apart from which, the couch was hard. The hotel facilities of The Hague were strained to capacity by the delegates of the twenty-seven nations attending the Second International Opium Conference. He hadn't decided to attend until all the good hotels had already been booked. Noelle had finally persuaded him to attend because of her eagerness to meet real Chinese people and test her Chinese on them. But now he wished he had resisted her. The Conference had been bitterly disappointing.

He called "Come in" to the knock on the door, and Alex Hosie entered, frowning.

"You're not looking well, Donald."

"I'm all right. A bit tired. And disappointed."

"Don't be, Donald. At least the Chinese are in the clear. They're virtually rid of poppies, and we'll have to stop shipping them opium within the year. As to the rest—what did you expect? Those resolutions of the 1909 Conference were too grand not to be watered down. Did you really think our India Office would piously give up *all* opium revenues? It really would play havoc with the India Office budget. So they'll continue producing opium for monopolies in our own colonies, and the French and Dutch will buy from us for monopolies in Indochina and the East Indies . . ."

Donald laughed, creakily furious.

"And do you really think opium smoking will die out because smokers can't buy opium except at high prices from government monopolies? Of course not! The high prices will simply create black markets and smuggling will start all over again! The whole thing is poppycock!"

"Well, at least now we're talking of monopolies and not free trade for any Tom, Dick, or Harry who wants to buy and sell opium. I only wish . . ."

He fell silent, looking gloomy, and Donald said, "Alex, stop blaming yourself for what happened to Didi. You had no possible way of knowing that he was the Opium Suppression Officer in Shansi, and it was *my* suggestion in the first place that somebody should be punished. Besides, in a topsy-turvy kind of way, he was serving the 'life-duty' by being dismissed."

Alex shrugged. "That may be, but what I really hate is that he took it as a personal betrayal. He didn't give me a chance to explain before I left, and the letter I wrote him later came back to me 'unable to deliver.' He must have left Shansi. Well"—he rose and buttoned his jacket—"the closing meeting starts in a few minutes. Coming?"

Donald shook his head. "It'll be nothing more than a pompous requiem."

"Can I get you something, then? You really do look tired."

"No, thanks. Nannie's taken Noelle for a walk and they'll be back soon. You go along."

When Alex had left, Donald gingerly stretched himself. It was only five o'clock, but winter dusk was already invading the dreary hotel room.

Jin-see hated the dusk. "I hate the dusk. The day dying, and the night not yet born." Donald could almost see him, standing at their office window, looking out over the Whangpoo River. They had been feeling distressed, both of them, having just decided that Donald must return to England to fight the antiopium battle in Parliament. But even that separation had not disrupted their friendship. The friendship that had started in 1861, at three o'clock one morning, with a joyful handshake in Jin-see's splendid marble courtyard. And ended in 1900 when Jin-see and Olan died in that Boxer riot in Tientsin. Nothing in Donald's life had ever quite measured up to that comradeship with Jin-see—not marriage, not even the marvelously unexpected gift of a daughter. For Jin-see it had been different. He had had Olan, whom he had loved with all his being from the time they were children in her father's fabulous Canton courtyards . . .

The light came on. Donald sat up too suddenly, back aching, mind groping for the time and place . . . Of course, here were Noelle and Nannie back from their walk.

"Sir?" Nannie's voice was light and pleasant. "Did I startle you? I'm sorry! I thought you'd be at the meeting with Noelle."

"I decided not to . . ." His heart thumped. "What d'you mean, with Noelle?"

"She said you were going to take her."

"I thought she was with you!"

They stared at each other, alarm flaring. Nannie went quickly across to the bedroom she shared with Noelle, glanced in, came back.

"Not there. I'll go down and look in the public rooms. You phone down, sir, and ask the desk if they've seen her, and if not, ask them to ask the doorman."

"Yes."

But the desk had not seen her, nor had the doorman. He set the phone down and rested his head in his hands. Oh God, the child was so willful! He'd made such a botch of bringing her up! She'd been such a miracle. He sixty-five and Edith forty-five. At first they'd thought that Edith was menopausing—then the wonder, the slow believing, the careful waiting, and at last, on Christmas Day 1901, the beautiful child. Edith had been better than he at handling her. After Edith's death he'd felt helpless. They'd had nothing to talk about, apart from the Chinese language lessons. The stories about China, about the fight against opium, about the events that had been the mainspring of his life, bored her. She treated him with a kind of indulgence, as though she were the adult and he the child. "You told me that yesterday, Father . . ."

54

The door was flung open by a stern Nannie, and the child came in, her golden hair a little mussed, her blue, blue Carradine eyes flashing stubbornly. Nannie gave her a little push.

"Go on! Go and tell your father you're sorry!"

She came and stood before him, startling eyes cast down.

"I'm sorry . . . But you *knew* I wanted to meet some real Chinese people, and we're leaving tomorrow."

He put an arm around her. Over her head, he saw Nannie frown—the child should at least be scolded!—but he said gently, "Is that where you went? To find some real Chinese?"

She flashed into life.

"Yes! The Chinese delegation was in the dining room. They were *amazed* how well I speak Chinese! They invited me to China! Oh, Father, may I go to China?"

He laughed. "You're much too young to go to China alone!"

"Not alone! With you of course!"

He felt the tired grayness in his heart.

"And I'm much too old!"

She set her lips determinedly.

"Well, *one day* I'm going to China!"

Chapter VI

1916

THE WATER WAS an uneasy flow of black ink, the sampan's wake a thin, silver ruffle. The tall figure of the boatman loomed on the tiny aft deck, a shadow darker than the night, wielding his single oar. Fish and One-eye sat facing each other on the thwarts, knees almost touching. Fish had ushered One-eye into the boat before him, hoping that he would seat himself on the forward thwart facing forward, but One-eye had taken the rear thwart and Fish had been obliged to squeeze past to the forward thwart, where he had turned to face One-eye, no more willing to have his back to One-eye than One-eye had been to have his back to him.

The boatman rhythmically swished his oar, grunting with each backward swing. A few lights bobbed about them: other small craft, homing. Fish thought, Not yet. Go slow. Talk a little. Put him off guard.

He said conversationally, "What's this hulk we're going to?"

One-eye answered promptly, "It's an abandoned opium clipper, one of the old sailing ships. Pock-marks likes to use it for the Red Gang's secret meetings. The initiations are held in the hold, which still stinks of opium. Sometimes you can hardly breathe down there."

A very long speech for One-eye . . . Was he nervous? Did he

suspect something? Fish grinned in the darkness. When One-eye had turned up at the wharf alone, when there'd been but this one sampan waiting instead of the usual dozen, he'd been sure that tonight was the night Big-ears meant him to kill One-eye. For weeks Big-ears had hinted at it. "Hard to keep two fighting cocks in one coop!" and "Well—that's life. The day comes when the younger cock jumps higher than the older, and that's that." And, "Of course, Pock-marks expects you to perform a test for your initiation—a kind of blood test." And, last night, the message, "One-eye will fetch you to your initiation."

Fish swallowed, pulse thudding, blood thundering through his veins. When Great Dragon crashed over the dining table after drinking the poisoned soup, it had seemed like an independent action, nothing to do with himself. And Julie . . . it had been One-eye who had handed Julie the final dose of poison. But this, tonight, had to be done by himself, and there was no way of doing it but with a knife.

The sampan was moving fast downriver. The lights of the other boats had disappeared. It was so dark that Fish could see no more than the outline of One-eye's head against the sky. That was good: One-eye could see no more than that of himself. His hands, hidden in the long sleeves of his black gown, would be invisible as he reached for the knife strapped to his ankle. He shifted on the narrow thwart and let his right hand drop. Bilge water swishing about the bottom of the boat had wet the hem of his gown, which was clinging to his ankle. Gently, he peeled back the silk to free the hilt of the knife, grasped it, began to draw it from its sheath.

At that instant, One-eye lunged at him. He caught the glint of One-eye's blade flashing at his gut and flung himself backward, falling off the thwart. His feet thrashed in the air and he felt a hard blow on his left foot as One-eye's knife glanced off the leather sole of his shoe. Then One-eye was on him, pinning him over the thwart, the knife raised high. Frantically he twisted his head and felt the knife whistle past his cheek, heard it thud against the bottom of the boat. One-eye wrenched at it, grunting: it was stuck in the wet wood! With a heady rush of triumph Fish bunched his young muscles, heaved the older man off his body, put the heel of his right hand against his chin, and shoved with all his strength. There was a loud splash and the boat swung wildly: One-eye was overboard. Fish scrambled to his knees, eyes devouring the darkness. He heard One-eye surface, heard his heavy panting as he struggled toward the boat. His hand appeared, a pale blotch reaching for the gunwale. Fish lunged to chop at the hand—and was suddenly shoved aside. The boatman had stepped down from his tiny deck, holding his oar like a weapon. He cracked the oar down on the reaching hand. There was a loud, bubbling cry of pain. He raised the oar again and began to thwack it down on the water where the cry had sounded, at first raising only splashes, then a series of dull, squelching thuds. He paused a moment, listening, then swept the oar from side to side just above the water. It encountered nothing. There was no sound but the creak of the rocking boat and the tiny slap-slap of the water. He grunted and stepped back onto his tiny deck. A moment later, the boat resumed its forward motion.

Heart pumping like a piston, Fish crawled back onto a thwart. If not for the boatman, One-eye might still be swimming around out there, maybe getting to the bank, climbing out, *alive* . . . Big-ears would be livid! And the mysterious Pock-marks, whose very name Fish had only recently been allowed to hear—what would *he* think? It would have been the end! Fish would never have made the Red Gang! If not for the boatman . . .

Why had the boatman helped him?

His breath caught in his throat. Icy fingers ran up and down his spine. He found himself staring at the boatman's bare feet, just visible six inches from his eyes, the toes splayed . . .

The boatman said softly, "Which are you, the one-eyed one or the other?"

Fear gushed through Fish's veins like another kind of blood. *The boatman didn't know who he had helped!* He towered up there on his little deck, pretending to row, waiting to raise that lethal oar again and thwack it down on *the other head* . . .

Fish wrapped an arm around the boatman's ankles and jerked his feet from under him. With a hoarse cry, the man toppled backward. Fish dragged him forward over the thwart, down into the bilge, and crawled over him, pinning his arms. He slipped the knife from its sheath and pricked the point into the man's throat. The man cowered away, stretching his head back as far as it would go, rolling his eyes. His voice came in a strangled whisper.

"Don't kill me! I have children and a woman. I just did what they paid me for . . ."

"What did they pay you for?"

"To kill the one of you that was losing."

"Who paid you?"

"I don't know. Truly I don't. A man came an hour before you and gave me a hundred dollars . . ."

The icy fear in Fish's veins turned to red-hot fury. A hundred dollars! A hundred miserable dollars for his life, or One-eye's! And a miserable boatman as executioner!

He buried the knife to its hilt in the boatman's throat. Blood welled, gushing warmly over his hands, flowing neatly in a dark little waterfall to mingle with the bilge in the bottom of the boat. The man gurgled and was still.

Frantic now, disgusted, the pit of his stomach quivering, Fish scrambled off the body and began to heave and tug at it until, an arm first, then a shoulder, then a leg, he got it overboard. But it didn't sink. It floated, bumping against the boat. He wrenched the oar from the rowlock and poked at the body, pushing it downward and outward, and at last, the clothes sodden, it began to submerge and disappeared into the darkness.

Replacing the oar in its rowlock, Fish's hand struck a bucket. With it, he scooped water from the river, poured it over the gunwale, the thwarts, the deck, scooped it back out of the bilge and flung it back into the river. Scooped more water and poured it over his head, let it run down to wet his gown thoroughly. The gown was sticky with blood, but it was black, the blood wouldn't show.

When he had done what he could to clean up, he sat down on the little deck, hugging his knees to keep his feet out of the still-bloody bilge, his mind humming, his blood bubbling. Devils take Big-ears! It must have been he who arranged this! Devils damn him to the seventeenth story of hell! But *why*? And what now? Go back upriver to the city? Or to the river bank—scramble ashore and try to escape? No use! If Big-ears meant him to die, he would be hunted down without mercy. Better go on to the hulk. The boatman had been bribed to kill one of them—the other would be expected at the hulk. Find it, then.

Present himself. Tell some story. Big-ears wouldn't believe it, but it would buy time.

Shivering in his soggy clothes, Fish climbed onto the little deck and awkwardly began to work the oar, his mind racing, searching for a story that would account for the absence of the boatman and also hide the fact that the boatman had told why he had been paid . . . Lights glimmered ahead and voices bounced over the water. Fish stopped rowing, straining to hear.

A big, jolly-sounding voice saying something unintelligible. Then Big-ears' voice, strangely ingratiating: "Right! Right!" Then Big-ears, shouting, "That sampan out there! Who's the mother-sticker in it?"

Fish didn't need to make his voice sound breathless and shaky. "It's Fish! Great Fish!"

"Get him in!" Big-ears roared.

People came paddling in a dinghy bringing the end of a rope with which to pull the sampan to the hulk. Fish perched tensely on a thwart. In the light of flaring lanterns, he saw that the hulk had once been a great wooden sailing ship, three decks deep. Now it was rotting, stripped of every movable thing, but its name in faded paint was still visible on the transom. *Falcon*. A bird of prey. A small, compact bird, very swift and sure. It was an omen.

Hands reached down to help him climb onto what had been the top deck. Shadowy figures gathered around him in the flickery light. Big-ears' voice rasped, "You're alone? What happened?"

To hesitate would mean disaster . . . Fish took a great breath and plunged into his half-formed story.

"We had a collision! A big launch sideswiped us! It was traveling so fast that we almost capsized . . ." The words were magically forming themselves, pouring out with just the right mixture of excitement and lingering fright. "I thought we were finished! But the sampan came right side up again, bouncing like crazy, half full of water. By the time I managed to cough the water out of my lungs, I saw I was alone! One-eye and the boatman must have been swept overboard!"

The big, jolly-sounding voice guffawed loudly. For an instant, its owner's face showed in the flare of a lantern. A big, flat, wide-nosed face, heavily pockmarked. Big-ears laughed too in that same ingratiating way, but his hand gripped Fish's arm roughly, moved to his shoulder and down his body, feeling the wet silk of his gown—and the stickiness of the blood. But he made no comment, merely turned and walked off. The others followed him, melting away, taking the lanterns with them. Suddenly, it was very dark and very silent, and Fish was alone, heart pounding. Had he got away with it? What now? His breath seemed to whistle in the emptiness.

A hand touched his arm, sending his skin a-crawling. A voice behind him whispered, "I am Straw-sandal, the messenger. Are you ready for your initiation?"

Fish gulped. "I am ready."

"Come."

Shakily, Fish followed the shadow-figure of Straw-sandal across the deck and down a creaking ladder. On the second deck it was even darker. Another whisper came rustling, "I am Incense-master, the initiator. Come."

They crossed the second deck and descended another ladder to the lowest deck. Here it was not dark. Light came out of a big, square opening that gave access to the ship's hold. With the light smells rose—ancient, musty smells of dirt, mildew, rot, and opium. Fish felt his stomach heave. Straw-sandal whispered, "Wait here." He and Incense-master moved forward and disappeared down a ladder into the hold. Fish stood alone, tension building on tension, the moments passing, excruciatingly slow. Deliberately, he set himself to relax . . . It was nothing! It was childish playacting . . .

From behind, a hand closed around his throat. His sphincters spasmed and he stood deathly still, afraid to move, slithering his eyes from side to side to try and see who was holding his throat in that delicate, threatening grip. The hand—a right hand—tightened, the fingers like steel. Then it gently left his throat and was raised up before his eyes, the palm toward him, the thumb extended, the fingers close together. With shock, he saw that the first two fingers were of equal length . . .

A Silent Killer!

He stood totally still, barely breathing, fearfully remembering schoolboy stories he had scoffed at. Silent Killers were trained from childhood to stab those first two fingers into a bag of rice. Gradually, over years, more rice was added to the bag until it was hard as stone, and the two fingers were of equal length and hard as steel. Fully trained Silent Killers could knock a single brick out of a solid brick wall with those stabbing fingers . . .

The hand was withdrawn. A voice whispered with a friendly chuckle, "I am Red-pole, the enforcer. Go on down."

Shaking, Fish went down the ladder, Red-pole behind him. The hold was large. Around its shadowed edges, Fish sensed an audience, but only the center of the space was lit. Many flickering candles stood on a long, narrow table, an altar, draped with red paper scrolls on which were written bold, black characters: Secrecy. A closed mouth. Trust. Betrayal. Swords. Between the candles were strewn a number of small red flags. In front of the flags stood a heavily patinaed bronze urn and a bowl filled with raw rice in which were stuck many unlit incense sticks.

On the left of the altar stood Straw-sandal, masked, but identified by a traveling cloak and straw sandals. On the right stood Incense-master, decked out in an embroidered robe and a tall conical hat, a black mask hiding his face. Red-pole still lingered behind, unseen.

Straw-sandal beckoned. Fish stepped forward. Incense-master signaled to him to kneel. Incense-master took an incense stick from the bowl and lit it from one of the candles. When it was glowing, the musky smoke swirling, he passed it to Fish, intoning words, nodding at Fish to repeat them.

"Humbly, I knock on the door of the Red Gang."

Incense-master took the smoking stick from Fish, replaced it in the bowl, lit another.

"If the door of the Red Gang is opened to me, I will enter on my knees."

Another stick.

"I shall obey the Masters without question."

Another stick.

And another.

And another.

Fish felt nervous laughter rising in his throat. The oaths went from trivial to nonsensical. If they couldn't think up sensible oaths, why didn't they cut down on the number of incense sticks? But on and on it went until at last there was only one stick left—the twenty-seventh, by Fish's count. Incense-master solemnly lit it.

"I swear on the heads of my sons that I shall never reveal any secret of the Red Gang."

Fish mumbled the melodramatic words, inwardly sighing with relief. Thank the gods that was over! He didn't even have sons—though perhaps soon. Susu was pregnant again. Perhaps this time it would be a son.

Straw-sandal and Incense-master retired behind the altar. There was a slight pause. Then another man moved into sight, an ordinary man, not tall nor short nor thin nor fat, dressed in ordinary clothes and unmasked. A man one might see a hundred times and forget a hundred times—except for the fingers of his right hand, which he was holding up before him.

Red-pole.

Again, Fish felt tension. But Red-pole casually took the bronze urn from the altar, placed it on the floor in front of Fish, and took Fish's right hand. With a dagger as tiny as a large needle that he took from his sleeve, he lightly pricked each finger of Fish's hand and squeezed a drop of blood from it into the urn, intoning almost in parody of Incense-master's gravity, "Your blood lies here with that of ten thousand brothers. If you betray them, those who are alive will hunt you and those who are dead will rise to haunt you."

Fish felt sudden anger. The whole thing was ludicrous! Was it for this that Pock-marks had required a "blood test," that Big-ears had engineered the murderous sequence in the sampan? He looked around with a flashing desire to vent his anger somehow, but the hold was emptying. He heard the rustle of the audience rising and the creak of the ladder as they went up on deck. Red-pole had disappeared. Straw-sandal came back from behind the altar and said in a friendly tone, "That's all. Go up on deck. You'll find a launch tied up in front. Big-ears is waiting for you."

The anger mounted, hot and explosive, but Fish clamped down on it. This was going to be the real initiation: facing Big-ears and coming to terms with him. To let him see anger might well mean a death sentence. Devils curse Big-ears! That tricky, traitorous piece of garbage, holding all the cards, moving all the pawns on both sides of the board!

He climbed slowly up to the deck, saw the big launch chuffing alongside, the engine revving up a little as though beckoning. As soon as he stepped aboard, the craft surged smoothly forward. From a bench across the stern, Big-ears waved. Heart bumping, Fish went to join him.

"Well!" Big-ears was shouting to make himself heard over the roar of the engine, but his voice blew back in the rush of wind that the launch's speed created, and no one but Fish, sitting beside him, could hear him. "Well!" Big-ears shouted again, very hearty. "That was a fine story you told! You heard Pock-marks laugh? A real smart-shit story! A compromise!"

Fish said nothing. Big-ears put a confidential arm around him.

"That was One-eye's trouble. He never learned to compromise. Bang 'em over the head and if they won't bang down, kill 'em. That was his style. Dangerous and useless." He paused a moment. Then, "That's why I paid the boatman to help you finish him off, just to be sure."

Fish slitted his eyes against the tear of the wind. So that was the line! Believe, or pretend to believe, the big damned lie I've just told you, and we can go on from there. Otherwise, you're not going anywhere . . . Fish swallowed the hard lump that was clogging his throat.

"Thank you . . ."

Big-ears slapped his back.

"Good! It's only smart to compromise! Look at Pock-marks. He's getting old. His style's antique. Those boring initiations! Who cares for those silly oaths? But he's still on top because he's a champion compromiser. He's chief of detectives in the French Town police force. He keeps the street gangs quiet, and in exchange the French Town police give him a lot of leeway. When it comes to an argument between me and Pock-marks, I can tell you that *I* always compromise! He could use police power in a war against me that I couldn't win. In exchange, he's grateful to me for not forcing a war on him—he doesn't want the bother of a war, he's got a new young concubine and he wants to take life a little easy now. So we compromise, and we get along fine."

Big-ears cackled and dug an elbow into Fish's ribs.

"I'll compromise with you too—I won't ask what happened

to the boatman . . . You're smart, Fish. You're a fast learner. That's good, because some big changes are coming up. I'm going to put Tall-short in One-eye's place . . ."

Fish's anger flared again. Had he been maneuvered into getting rid of One-eye for Tall-short's benefit? That limping ruffian, risen from the gutter . . .

"He's better at running the everyday stuff than you'll ever be." Big-ears was going on smoothly. "He was born street smart. For you I have other plans, Little Fish."

Fish smiled sardonically. A nickname, to confirm his entry into the higher echelons of the Red Gang, and to soften him up for some appointment that he wasn't going to like.

"D'you know Soong Chiao-shun?" Big-ears' sudden change of tone brought Fish up short. Big-ears was through with conciliation. He was back to menace.

Fish nodded sullenly. Everybody knew "Charlie" Soong, educated in America by the Methodists, a missionary himself for a while, now making a fortune printing bibles.

"You mean the man who owns the Commercial Press?"

Big-ears nodded. "Jesus books aren't the only thing he turns out. He also does all the printing for the Red Gang. Now, listen . . . Soong's second daughter, Ching-ling, has run away from home to join Sun Yat-sen. Her father is spitting fury. He has been Sun Yat-sen's best friend, and one of his best financiers. The girl met Sun at home, in her father's house, and has been carrying on with him under her father's nose . . . her father's friend, more than twice her age! But she's a revolutionist, and she's in love with what Sun Yat-sen stands for—China's great revolution. She and Sun are in Japan now, and I hear that he's putting away his old wife to go through a marriage ceremony with her. That might make her father's headache a little better, but I don't think it's going to open up his purse again, at least not as wide as before."

Big-ears glanced sharply at Fish. "That's one side of the picture. The other side is this: Ching-ling's older sister, Ai-ling, is married to the banker Kung. He's not too bright, but she is . . . she helps me put schemes together that her husband's position as a banker is very useful for carrying out."

Big-ears and the missionary's daughter defrauding the public through the Kung bank! But Fish kept his face straight.

Big-ears went on. "Through Ai-ling, we can get close to Ching-ling—and Sun Yat-sen, who's very short of funds now that his old friend Soong—his father-in-law!—is furious with him." Suddenly, Big-ears let out one of his rasping cackles, putting menace aside for malice. But a moment later he was intent again. "D'you get it, Little Fish? Sun Yat-sen's Kuomintang party is growing strong. Sun Yat-sen is a very good bet for the presidency, once Yuan Shi-kai falls on his face, as he's bound to one of these fine days. But Sun is hurting for money. If he becomes the next president of China, *and we helped him*, there's no limit to the possibilities."

Fish licked suddenly-dry lips. Big-ears leaned closer.

"The Kungs live in French Town—very rich, very grand. When Sun Yat-sen and his new wife come back to Shanghai, they're going to be living with the Kungs—what's more natural, the two wives are sisters. Pock-marks' boss, the chief of the French Town police, is a good friend of the Kungs. High society. Big manners, grand clothes, parties. Everybody talks English—the Soong sisters were educated in America." He became expansive again, digging Fish in the ribs. "Those people can't deal with an old crook like Big-ears. Big-ears is going to have to appoint a representative who can fit into their society . . ." He grinned his shark grin, showing all his brown and broken teeth. "So, Little Fish. What d'you say? We'll compromise, won't we?"

His heart hammering in his throat, Fish nodded silently. Big-ears laughed raspily, his hooded eyes gleaming with triumph. Devils curse you, Fish thought. *Devils curse you* . . . But his heart kept on hammering. The prospects were dazzling.

The noise of the engine was suddenly silenced, and the boat began to drift toward the wharf. Big-ears dropped his voice to a whisper.

"All right . . . You'll have to wait for that. It'll take a year or two to develop. In the meantime"—he raised a hand to stop his bodyguards who were coming smartly along the deck—"*find Ah-fet.* I want that opium of your father's that he's got in his possession. Before somebody else gets it—*find him.*"

Fish said sullenly, "I've been trying, but it's practically impossible. That's just a nickname."

Big-ears flashed his frightening grin. "Try harder . . ."

66

He rose, beckoned to his bodyguards. As they surrounded him, he turned back to Fish.

"By the way, I've got a new workman in my curio factory who's a genius. His vases look exactly like the one you have. I can start selling now. I want you to set it up. The best curio dealer is an old Englishman who lives on Bubbling Well Road. You can easily find out his name. He's been dealing with the foreigners for years—they all trust him. His usual commission is ten percent. Offer him fifty . . ."

His voice trailed off into the darkness. Fish stared after him resentfully. Do this, do that . . .

But a moment later, excitement overlaid his anger. The future looked wonderful! He saw himself in white tie and tails, bowing, smiling, foreigners exclaiming, "How marvelously you speak English!" He alone, Great Fish, Little Fish, unique in the Red Gang, able to play such a role. Attending parties. Giving parties too. He'd have to marry. Not Susu, of course, though he'd never let her go. Some well-educated, high-society girl, whom he'd marry legally. A big wedding. Foreign style, maybe. Reception at the Palace Hotel. Hundreds of wedding guests. Perhaps even, by that time, Sun Yat-sen himself . . .

He sighed, suddenly exhausted, the night's events tumbling before his mind's eyes as in a kaleidoscope. A chill wind ruffled his hair and wafted the dank smell of the river to his nostrils. One-eye was down on the muddy bottom, his body washing gently to and fro. The boatman too. The knife had slid in so easily. The sharp little knife. He had honed it for hours, sitting in the pink marble courtyard where his father's mad wife Olan had been locked up for thirty years. There was only one gate to that courtyard. When it was locked, he could be sure of being alone. It was a fine place to be alone in. The reflecting pool peaceful and hypnotic. Beyond the pool, the doll-size pink marble house that marked the grave of the crippled baby daughter Olan had killed. When Julie died, he had had the whim of having her buried under the tiny house, in the same grave as her long-dead baby sister.

Had Julie known who Ah-fet was? Had she fooled him, as One-eye had always maintained? She couldn't have! Yet she might have . . . Julie had been very, very clever . . .

He sighed again. How was he going to find Ah-fet? Beyond

pure luck, there was only one chance—that Didi knew who he was. Didi was alive now only because of that one chance. And at last, Didi was actually in Shanghai. After being fired from his Shansi job for killing farmers—Fish laughed shortly. That was funny! The upright Didi—he had been assigned to the Yangtsze River ports. A month ago, he'd been transferred to Shanghai. Fish had employed a man called Zung who worked at the Opium Suppression Bureau to watch him . . . it was just possible that he would lay a trail to Ah-fet.

Chapter VII

1916

"AH-FET . . ."

Alfred Pratt turned to the door, smiling. "Come in, Mei-mei."

He watched his wife cross the room with her energetic stride and plump herself into the chair beside his desk. She was short and stocky, with bluntly bobbed black hair and a broad face saved from homeliness by bright black eyes and a sparkling smile. He thought her beautiful and loved her with all his heart.

She put his four o'clock tea on the desk. "Ah-fet . . ."

He interrupted her teasingly, "Try and say my name properly. *Alfred* . . ."

He spoke in the Shanghai dialect, which was the only language she knew, and said the English name distinctly, giving it its English pronunciation: *Ahlfred*.

"That's what I said!" she exclaimed. "*Ah-fet!*"

He laughed. He was "Ah-fet" to all his Chinese friends. The only one who had not heard "Alfred" as "Ah-fet" was Jin-see, but then Jin-see had spoken perfect English in an English accent far classier than Pratt's own.

Mei-mei had taken up one of the photographs on his desk. "That's beautiful!"

"That's a Sung dynasty *m'ei p'ing* plum blossom vase, about a thousand years old."

69

"It must be very valuable!"

"It is. There're not many like it. One is in the National Museum in Peking. I gave one to my friend Jin-see many years ago. This one belongs to an old schoolteacher who has no idea of its value in today's curio market. I'm selling it for him to the American ambassador. He'll get more money than he's ever seen before, and I'll get ten percent, which will also be a lot of money."

She turned to leave the room, laughing. "And you won't spend a cent of it! You'll put it all away for me and Belle!"

Naturally! He picked up his photographs again . . . He was considerably older than Mei-mei, and she had no resources. She was illiterate. And Belle, though highly educated and brilliant, was very frail.

When it was growing dark, Belle came in.

"Here are the London papers, Father."

His heart moved, as it always did when he saw her. How fortunate he and Mei-mei were to have Belle! There had been an older brother, stillborn, and old Dr. Macpherson had been gruffly discouraging about the possibility of another child. "Your wife's history . . . poor chances . . ." But a few years later Belle had come along.

She bent to kiss his cheek. "Father, is your mind in the present, past, or future?"

"The present!" He smiled at her. "What's in the papers?"

"The Japanese have declared war on Germany! Ostensibly, because they're selling munitions to the Allies and want to wave the flag on the Allies' side. But I believe it's an excuse to land troops in China to attack the German Concession in Shantung province. You'll see. When the war is over, that territory won't be returned to China. The Japs will claim it on the strength of having declared war on Germany. The Japs have big designs on China, Father. They're bursting the seams of their islands, and China is nearest, and China is huge."

He didn't answer. Her grasp of the intricacies of politics always amazed him. She turned to him with the sweet smile that gave her plain face an esoteric kind of beauty.

"Father, I've joined something called the Socialist Youth Corps. The members are mostly university students and some of the younger professors. There're chapters of the Corps in all the big cities. Our aim is to 'explore socialist theory.' That's rather less vague than it sounds when you take into account that socialism looks very democratic in comparison to warlord politics! But we do have one very concrete objective, which is the real reason I joined: we're promoting newspapers written in the vernacular."

"You don't know anything about running a newspaper!"

"No, but I do know how to write. And I do believe it's high time for ordinary people to have some means of informing themselves. For centuries all newspapers, proclamations, edicts, everything, have been written in the classical language which ninety-five percent of the people can't read. They simply don't know what's going on, and there's simply no way of informing them, which is why the wildest rumors gain currency. Now that we're a republic, it's more important than ever for people to be properly informed. When Yuan shi-kai is dethroned, we should *vote* for a new president, but the presidency is going to be grabbed off by whoever's nearest or strongest because most Chinese have never even heard of voting!"

She rose to pace the room, frowning.

"No wonder we have warlords! What else would a country like ours have but warlords? And who's to stop the warlords? That bungler Sun Yat-sen? His new wife Soong Ching-ling is more of a real revolutionist than he! It's most certainly high time for ordinary people in our country to have newspapers they can read!"

Her passion seemed to set the air swirling. He regarded her, worried but admiring. She got it from her mother, he thought— that decisiveness, that buoyancy, that preparedness to *do* something . . .

"Dinner's ready!" Mei-mei called.

Pratt rose and led the way toward the dining room. The lamps were not yet lit and the corridor was dim. He shivered. Belle took his arm.

"Are you cold, Father?"

"No. I was taking a look at the future."

"And what did you see?"

"Things that frighten me."

"They frighten me too," she said.

* * *

After dinner, when Pratt returned to his study to read the London papers, he heard the tinkle of the bell over the front gate. A minute later, a servant came to say that a young Chinese was asking to see him. About curios.

"Show him in," Pratt said.

Hospitably, he rose to set a chair for the visitor. With his back to the door, he did not see him enter. It was not until a voice said "Good evening" in excellent English that he turned around, smiling a welcome—and was shocked into immobility.

There, by the door, stood a young Jin-see . . .

"My name," the young man said, "is Wei Ta-yu."

With effort, Pratt broke out of his paralysis—Great Fish, Jin-see's younger son! Heart banging, he stepped forward.

"Please sit down. What can I do for you?"

"Thank you." Fish sat in the chair Pratt had set and laid on the carpet beside him the parcel he was carrying. "I have come to see you, Mr. Pratt, because you are the foremost authority on Chinese curios."

He smiled attractively—Jin-see's smile! Almost, Pratt cried out, "You are so like your father!" But caution held him back. He had waited for years to find out whether this young man was trustworthy. He could wait a few minutes more. He said deprecatingly, "You are too kind. I know something about Chinese antiquities, but there are others who know as much as I do, and many know a great deal more."

"Perhaps. But you have the great advantage of being believed without question. Foreigners who buy curios all buy from you."

A cold little finger touched Pratt's heart.

He pointed at the parcel.

"You've brought me something?"

"Yes. Something I'd like you to sell for me. I've been told it's very valuable."

He unwrapped the parcel, and placed on Pratt's desk a Sung dynasty *m'ei p'ing* plum blossom vase.

Pratt began to tremble. The vase he had given Jin-see! He could hear Jin-see's voice: "I can't accept this, Pratt! It's far too valuable!" And Julie's soft voice: "Mr. Pratt *wants* to give it to you, Father. Don't you see?" Perceptive Julie, so bright, so loving. How she had loved her father, and he her!

Tears came to Pratt's eyes. To hide them, he picked up the

vase and carried it over to a lamp, turned it in his hands as though inspecting it . . . It was a fake!

Heart thudding, he kept on turning the vase in the light of the lamp until he felt he could face Fish calmly. Then he came back to his desk, put the vase down carefully.

"I'm sorry. I can't accept this commission."

Fish's eyes became sharp and angry.

"Why not? You're a dealer, aren't you?"

"I'm more or less retired."

"That's not what I heard. I heard you're in the process of selling a vase exactly like this to the American ambassador."

"Not *exactly* like this . . ."

Fish hesitated. Then: "Well, the sale of *this* vase will give you a commission of fifty percent instead of your usual ten. And I can supply more vases—as many as you can sell."

Pratt smiled grimly. "That wouldn't be a good idea. Fifty percent on many more of *these* vases would amount to about a dollar."

Fish flushed. "If not this vase, other things. I can provide copies that would fool anyone but you, of any item you suggest."

Pratt stared down at his desk. Poor Jin-see! Had he found out before he died that his younger son whose birth had so overjoyed him was a criminal? Wearily, he raised his eyes.

"Let me make myself plain. I'll have nothing to do with you and your fakes."

Fish leaned over the desk. His face was pale with anger, but his voice was soft: "You'd do well to reconsider, Mr. Pratt . . . I'll give you a few days to think it over. I'll be back next week."

He rose abruptly, thrust the vase back into its wrappings, and left the room. He was quiet, yet it seemed that a storm had blown through. Pratt felt confused and empty, as though something had drained out of him. He looked up blankly as Mei-mei entered.

"Ah-fet, what happened?"

"Nothing," he said automatically.

"Don't lie to me, Ah-fet!" She was pale, her eyes wide. "That young man passed me in the hallway. He was so angry that he was burning inside . . . Ah-fet, if something happens to you . . ."

He tried to laugh. "Why should something happen to me just because a man comes to see me and gets angry?"

73

"I don't know," she said slowly, "but I feel it. That was not a good man."

Her fear was calming him. He rose and put an arm around her, led her to the window. It was dark outside, but light from the street lamps glittered on the thick shards of glass cemented into the top of the high garden wall. He pointed.

"See that glass? See how high our wall is? And the gate is covered with a solid sheet of metal and is always locked and barred. Nothing's going to happen to me. And even if it should—I suppose I could be run over on the street!—you'll survive. There's a tough little heart beating away in there"—he patted her bosom—"and it'll keep right on beating."

After a moment she said soberly, "It's true that I have lived through a lot of things."

He hugged her. "That you have! You lived to become the apple of my eye."

"What?"

The English phrase made no sense translated into Chinese, and he laughed.

"It means that I love you very much."

"And I love you. I can't say that I love you more than my life because you *are* my life. Without you, I would have no life."

She kissed him quickly and left the room.

He turned back soberly to the nighttime garden . . .

Jin-see had said, "Don't tell anyone about the opium from the valley. Can you imagine what the Guild merchants would do to get hold of opium of that quality? No one is to know about it—not where it's grown, not where it's stored, not that it exists."

"Dead secret," he had promised solemnly.

And he had kept the secret. Was still keeping it. The opium was all there in the warehouse in Chengchow, 10,768 pounds of it, in heavy wooden chests lined with leaded paper. After Great Dragon and Julie disappeared as though snatched from the face of the earth, he had not been able to make up his mind what to do with it. Jin-see's younger son, Great Fish, had suddenly seemed to be in sole possession of all the family properties. Why was the grandson, Didi, not sharing in his grandfather's wealth? He had made inquiries and learned that Didi was working as a provincial opium suppression officer.

74

Was it likely that Jin-see's only two living descendants had no connection with each other? Was it possible that the two were in collusion, the opium suppression officer in ideal position to buy opium and channel it to his relative, the relative in ideal position to pass it through the family *hong* into the black market?

Pratt, who had few illusions, had waited and watched for a sign as to which, if either, could be trusted with the secret of the Chengchow opium. Today, one sign had come: certainly it was not Great Fish who could be trusted! Now he would have to make up his mind about the other. He had kept track of him through the Opium Suppression Bureau. A month ago, he had been transferred to Shanghai. Tomorrow, Pratt would go to the Bureau, see him, try to make a judgment.

Pratt sighed, some of the tension leaving his body. Perhaps at last he could settle what to do with the opium. If not—let it stay where it was! No opium smell would leak through the heavy lead-paper lining of the cases. They would stay in the warehouse perhaps for generations until one fine day somebody would say, "What the hell is in these cases? They've been here forever!" But by then he would long be dead, like Jin-see, whom he had loved.

Chapter VIII

1916

WILSON POURED BRANDY while his wife urged the children into the kitchen to help with the dishes. Didi pushed back his chair, feeling replete, satisfied, and sad. Rarely these days did he dine as well as he had tonight, but it was a farewell dinner. Wilson had said, "We're leaving! I'm not able to make a decent living as a private detective in this city. I could take a desk job—bank clerk!—but that's not my style. Besides," he grinned ruefully, "the English dropped me because I married a Chinese lady, and the Chinese regard my wife with suspicion because she married a foreigner! It's no use! We'll take our chances in England."

"I hope it'll be good for you," Didi said, meaning it. "But it's bad for me. You're my only friend in this city."

"You've hardly been here long enough to make friends. How about the chaps at the Bureau?"

"There's one I like who's very nice to me, a chap called Zung. The others—well, they just ignore me. I'm not sharp enough or smart enough or quick enough . . ."

"Or crooked enough!"

Didi laughed wryly. "There's that too!"

Wilson leaned forward. "Listen, I asked you here tonight, not just for a farewell dinner, but to pass on things I know that might be useful to you. Also, something I heard recently that I think concerns you personally."

Didi felt a twist of apprehension: somehow he didn't think that that was going to be a good thing. But Wilson was leaning forward intently.

"What d'you know about the Red Gang?"

"The biggest gang in the city. The most dangerous. But I don't know any details."

Wilson nodded grimly. "Details about the Red Gang aren't easy to come by, so listen carefully to what I'm going to tell you. The Red Gang is going to have a lot to do with how your life goes from now on."

He pulled his chair closer.

"The Red Gang has a complete monopoly on crime in this city. All the other gangs are under its control. Anyone silly enough to break its rules gets taken dead—no warning, no mercy, no second chances. On the other hand, those who keep faith get a fair share of the profit-making activities—not the juicy ones like opium, brothels, and gambling, those the Red Gang keeps for itself, but the petty stuff—pickpocketing, robbery, begging, waterfront, and so forth. They also get excellent protection."

Didi was startled out of his fascinated concentration by the entry of Mrs. Wilson, who had come to say good night. He rose to offer his good wishes for the move to England. She asked if he remembered her father at the Registry Office, who ten years ago had sent him to Wilson. Her father was dead now—his death had made it possible for them to plan the move. "Of course, we couldn't go while he was alive. He always remembered you. He loved your aunt Julie."

Didi settled back into his chair feeling unreal. Life was flowing by on two dissimilar levels. On one hand, the sweet solidity of family life that he missed so sorely. On the other, the dark realities . . .

". . . *excellent* protection," Wilson was saying. "Not just from gang members. From the police themselves. The chief of the Red Gang is a fat, jolly, pockmarked joker who laughs a lot, who is simultaneously chief of detectives of the French Town police force . . . That's the big secret. He controls the minor gangs, and in exchange the French Town police accommodate him. It's a good, reasonable compromise. Neither side goes too far, and it has worked well for a long time now. A number of subagreements have evolved, like the take on opium. The Red Gang lets the French police collect 'tax' from the opium outlets in French Town that the Red Gang owns and/or supplies. The amount of the 'tax' is agreed beforehand. It's all cut and dried, and it works very smoothly."

Didi sat back. That explained a lot! It explained the difference between entering No. 386 Loh Ka Pang to look for opium—that was in Nantao—and No. 388 next door, which was in French Town. Leave the French Town premises alone, he'd been warned by colleagues at the Bureau. If the French feel like making a fuss, you could create an international incident. Not surprising, if the French police were collecting from the Red Gang's opium outlets in French Town!

"Listen," Wilson said. "Pock-marks Huang is the chap with the connections, but the chap who actually runs the Red Gang, who has more or less taken control of it from under Pock-marks' nose, is a chap called Big-ears Doo. He is the most dangerous man in Shanghai. He treats Pock-marks like a kind of Elder, is extremely polite to him, and I'm sure would get rid of him but for the connections Pock-marks has. Big-ears is a very rare creature: a pure criminal. Son of a Pootung prostitute. When his mother died, her brother took him in, starved him, beat him so unmercifully that he's permanently marked—his nickname comes from his disfigured ears—and inculcated in him the unalterable conviction that man survives only by the ruthless use of tooth and claw."

Wilson rose to pour more brandy.

"Now, as I said, Big-ears runs the Red Gang, but he has special interests of his own. The latest, I'm told"—Wilson laughed shortly—"is a factory that manufactures fake curios. He's into anything that offers a profit, and the curio market is remarkably profitable—when you come to think of it, it depends mainly on availability, and what could be more available than antiques from your own factory! But opium is his mainstay—opium is his big bonanza—"

To Didi, that explained a lot more. "You mentioned corruption," he broke in. "I've been wondering! 'Gifts' come in to the Bureau—great baskets of fruit, with hundred-dollar notes cushioning each orange and apple. Cases of brandy, each bottle standing on a stack of notes. Those are the visible sources, and they must be trifling because the chaps have allowed me to see them. They're quite casual about those. But the invisible sources—what must those be like! For the kind of salary we make at the Bureau, my colleagues couldn't last four days at the rate they spend!"

Wilson laughed. "You're learning fast . . . Now, I'm going to tell you something that I got from an old friend on the French Police force who hangs around a lot at the Blue Villa, not because of those poor, damned lily-footed whores, but because it's Big-ears' headquarters where he holds court every night. My friend tells me that there used to be a one-eyed chap always at Big-ears' table who seems to have disappeared in the last few weeks. His place has been taken by a young man who, from his description, must look a lot like you . . . My friend says he must have foreign blood somewhere in his ancestry. He's handsome, obviously well educated, obviously of good family. My friend says he's out of place running around in Big-ears' entourage with ruffians like the man they call Tall-short, and that drunken maniac Chiang Kai-shek. His name, my friend says—his nickname—is Little Fish."

Didi lay on his hard bed in the narrow little room, listening to the usual nighttime sounds. The rooming house had common walls with its neighbors, and they with theirs, so all up and down the alley neighbors willy-nilly listened to the sounds of each other's lives. Anger, arguments, fights, beatings, lovemakings, sometimes even laughter.

Didi stared at the murky ceiling and thought how futile it was to keep on wishing that his father's acumen had descended to him. In Shansi he had been successful because he'd dealt with rural folk. For the last four years, in the Yangtsze River port cities, he'd more or less held his own: they were essentially small-town. But here in this huge, diamond-hard city he was a bewildered country bumpkin.

Well, take stock.

Fish was beyond him. Even before, there had never been a handle to take hold of. Now, under Big-ears' protection . . . He clamped down on the useless anger that churned in him until his insides felt like a cement grinder at work.

The life-duty. Not accomplished. Opium went on and on.

Enormous stocks hoarded from the happy old days of legal opium were hidden away in this city, in tumbledown houses, ruined temples, half-submerged hulks abandoned in backwaters, a thousand unguessable places. The search for hidden opium was infinitely difficult, and further complicated by the need to tiptoe through the forest of sensitive antennae of the three different municipalities of Shanghai.

And the search for Ah-fet. How to find an Englishman nicknamed Ah-fet? He laughed aloud, heard the bitterness in his laughter, and turned over wearily.

When the first street vendor dragged his iron-wheeled cart into the alley below, Didi gave up trying to sleep. The nightlife of the rooming house hadn't yet ended, but the day-life of the alleys was already beginning. He went down to the backyard, fetched a jug of cold water from the pump, climbed back to his own room, gave himself a towel bath, and dressed in one of the old gowns from Peking days. It was too short and too tight, but of too good quality to throw away. Anything he could afford to buy now would be cheap stuff. He left his room, locking the rickety door behind him, and went down to the alley. Several vendors were out now, with their carts and kitchens. From one of them he bought breakfast—a twist of fried dough wrapped in a circle of unleavened bread. He ate it standing at the corner waiting for a tram. It seemed to occupy about half his stomach: the other half was a vacuum pleading to be filled. The sleepless night hadn't helped. Did Fish have sleepless nights? Certainly Fish's stomach never went half empty!

The tram was jam-packed. He found a fingerhold on a strap to which several others were already clinging. When the conductor struggled through to him, he offered the usual four coppers. The man angrily demanded six. He was on the wrong tram! He inched another two coppers from his pocket, barely able to move his arm in the crush of people. It didn't matter. He was scheduled to inspect a shop that had formerly sold opium to make sure that the owners had turned their remaining stock over to the Bureau for destruction. He could go straight there, instead of stopping first at the Bureau.

The shop was one of the small, scruffy, open-fronted "money shops," so-called because they made change for silver dollars. For a while, Didi stood in the alley outside, watching the stream of customers (that was one way of judging whether the shop was still selling opium), and reflecting on the complexities of Chinese life . . . A hundred cents in coins didn't add up to a dollar. The quality and quantity of silver in the several kinds of dollars and ten- and twenty-cent coins varied considerably, and the price of silver fluctuated daily. Thus, change for a silver dollar consisted of a hundred cents in ten- and twenty-cent coins, plus a varying number of coppers. The money shops kept some of the coppers as their commission. They also sold a vast array of small merchandise, including one-smoke packets of opium.

But that was no longer legal. All remaining stocks of opium were supposed to be turned in to the Bureau. In this shop the opium had been kept in a cupboard under the steps in the back room behind the long counter that ran across the rear of the shop. Today Didi would have to verify that there was no more opium in that cupboard, and try to satisfy himself that it wasn't hidden elsewhere on the premises.

The shop was owned by a small, timid man with bad teeth, and his large, bossy wife. There were several children who helped in the shop from the time they could toddle. Two of the children were now serving customers, and the woman was sitting behind the counter taking the money, her sharp eyes darting about, watching the customers. Didi saw her spot him standing outside the shop. Her eyes jumped away, and she nudged the child who happened to be beside her, jerking her head toward the back room. The child seemed puzzled for a moment, then, after a second, emphatic jerk of his mother's head, caught on and went scurrying toward the back. When the child disappeared, the woman waved a genial hand at Didi.

"What are you doing out there, Mr. Bureau Agent? I thought we'd finished with the Bureau! We've turned in our opium, according to the law. Funny it's always us poor people that the law applies to!"

She laughed loudly, her eyes darting from one to another of the customers, marshaling them on her side.

Didi entered the shop and went to the counter.

"I'm sorry to bother you, but I have to check your shop to verify for the Bureau's records that . . ."

From the inner room came a thud, a man's curse, a child's

cry . . . They were moving the opium . . . The man or the child had dropped the container . . .

The woman said loudly, merrily, trying to hold his gaze, trying to convince him that he hadn't heard what he'd heard:

"You government people with your fat salaries writing records all day while we poor people work our backsides to the bone!"

She stared at him, her eyes hard and shiny, tense with anxiety. When he made no response, she became suddenly furious, but still she tried to avoid confrontation. She leaned over the counter, hissing, low-toned, *"We already paid the other one!"*

"What?" he said, startled. "What other one?"

She lost control.

"The other mother-sticker of a Bureau agent!" she howled. "The one who came yesterday! And we paid the protection man! And we paid the French police! And now *you* come with your shit-stink records! How many more of you bloodsuckers? Or isn't our blood enough for you? D'you want our guts too? If I chopped my baby up and fried the pieces for you, would that fill your rotten stomach?"

Saliva dropped from the corners of her mouth. Her eyes danced with frenzy. He stared at her, aghast. She wasn't just angry. She was desperate!

Suddenly, he was jostled. . . . The inevitable crowd had materialized, drawn like magic by the woman's screaming. They filled the shop and spilled into the alley outside. They were staring, open-mouthed, avid.

Didi stepped up onto a ladder that was used to reach the upper shelves of the shop. Head and shoulders above the crowd, he held out a hand to them.

"I *did not* come for a bribe!"

A jeering roar answered him. A man struggled through the crowd to the foot of the ladder, a tall man, dirty and unkempt, but with a kind of presence. He held up his arms and slowly shot his sleeves, and the crowd quieted, accepting him as their spokesman.

"Well . . ." the man drawled derisively, "if you didn't come for a bribe, Mr. Bureau Agent, what did you come for?"

Didi looked down at him earnestly. "I came in the course of my regular duties to check that the owners of this shop have

82

turned in their opium to the Bureau for destruction. As you know, it's now against the law to hold opium. But the opium's still here, I think. Ask the woman . . ."

The woman glared at him malevolently, but said nothing, satisfied to delegate her fight to the spokesman. One of her daughters, as mettlesome as she, had come from the inner room and stood beside her, glaring like her mother, arms akimbo.

The spokesman grinned. His appearance was deceptive. He was an educated man. He spoke banteringly. "What law are you speaking of, Mr. Bureau Agent? The law of the warlords, who're fighting each other on battlefields thick with the bodies of peasants? Or the law of the puppets in Peking whose bones are rattling with fear? Or the law of the city streets? These streets here"—he gestured broadly—"where, if we ask a policeman for help, he's likely to throw us into jail for the crime of not being able to afford his protection money?"

He paused dramatically, turning to the crowd like an actor, lifting his chin as though to ask, "How am I doing?" The crowd roared approval, and he turned back to Didi, eyes gleaming. "Or d'you mean the law about destroying opium? But of course that isn't a *real* law! It's just a stick that you use to beat us with. Destroy opium! That valuable commodity that you Bureau pigs can confiscate and sell back to the owners, over and over? It would be mad to destroy it!"

He hawked up a glob of phlegm and spat it onto the patch of dusty floor between him and Didi, where it lay, glimmering slimily. He glanced around again, and turned back to Didi.

"Let me explain to you what *we* believe to be the law. . . . Like you, like anybody, we must live as long as we can and we must make our children live: any way we can do that is the law to us . . . Take these poor people who own this shop. They're honest. They bought their opium back from the Bureau pig who confiscated it. They paid the regular protection man, and they also paid a French policeman who came by. You can't be much more honest than that, can you? And now they want to sell the opium that they bought the right to sell. What's wrong with that? Go to any of the divans and brothels around here—there're a dozen you could walk to in fifteen minutes. They're all well supplied with opium. So why did you pick these people to bother? And what about *us*? We can't afford Blue Villa prices, but once in a while, we people who live in this alley, once in a while we can afford to buy some opium from this shop. Why shouldn't we have our source, like the Blue Villa patrons? Isn't that democracy? Isn't that what Sun Yat-sen spouts about?"

The people, who had been silent in admiration, now broke out in a chorus of agreement and praise. A decibel below their noise, the spokesman said to Didi, his tone icy with contempt, "I saved your skin because if you were harmed here it would give our policemen a new excuse to gouge us. Now, *get out*."

Didi stared down at him . . . He couldn't leave like that! He must convince this man at least that he hadn't come for a bribe!

He said hoarsely, "*Truly*, I didn't come for money."

The man's bright black eyes taunted him.

"Who cares why you came? Just *go*—and leave us alone from now on."

Didi looked into the anthracite eyes a moment longer. Then he stepped off the ladder, slipped on the glob of phlegm, and fell to his knees. The man helped him up, calling out mockingly, "Mr. Bureau Agent repents his evil ways! Mr. Bureau Agent kowtows to ask our pardon!"

Amid roars of jeering laughter, Didi stumbled through the crowd.

Zung said, "I'm really giving up hope for you! What possessed you to go to that shop?"

His tone was bantering: he was trying to lighten the sting. But Didi was too tired, too discouraged, to respond in kind. He said dully, "I was scheduled to go there today. I got on the wrong tram, so I went straight there, instead of checking in here first."

Zung shook his head. "My poor simpleton, *always* check here first! If you had today, you would have seen that the schedule was changed. We settled with the owners of that shop yesterday, after some bargaining, for a sum that they can afford. A bit stiff, but they can make it with a little effort. They appreciated that we didn't force them any higher. No wonder they got excited when you went there today! They're poor people, trying to stay alive . . ." He laughed and banged Didi on the back. "I'm kidding! But seriously, from now on check in here before—"

He stopped suddenly, staring over Didi's shoulder.

"How long has *he* been there?" he muttered.

Didi turned.

At the counter stood a short, tubby, balding foreigner who, when he saw that he had attracted attention, said hesitantly, "Er . . . I'd like to see one of your staff members . . . the name is Wei."

An Englishman, Didi thought, as he rose and walked toward the counter. Curious . . . The man was staring at him fixedly with—recognition? Sympathy? *Love?* It almost seemed that the stranger loved him! A dreamlike feeling drifted out of nowhere to envelope him.

The stranger said, "You are the grandson of Wei Jin-see."

Unsurprised, Didi nodded.

The stranger said, "My name is Alfred Pratt. Your grandfather and I were friends. Can you come to my home at seven tonight? Number 507 Bubbling Well Road."

It seemed an entirely natural request. Again Didi nodded. Pratt's eyes deepened with pleasure. He smiled and left.

At Didi's elbow, Zung whistled.

"Bubbling Well Road! Going up in life! Is he going to give you dinner? Seven o'clock's dinner time for rich foreigners."

Didi gave him a friendly bang on the shoulder. His fatigue, the sting of the event in the money shop, were gone, absorbed into a feeling of tranquility. He thought of his father who had once said, "Success brings tranquility, not triumph." The thought floated calmly in his mind.

Didi arrived at seven at the sheet-metaled gate of Alfred Pratt's house. He was admitted to a sandy path that led to the front porch where a Chinese woman waited. In the dusk he had an impression of bright eyes and a sparkling smile. In the flat accents of the Shanghai dialect she said, "You are welcome! My husband is waiting for you."

She led him into a spacious hall, to a closed door that she opened.

"Ah-fet, your visitor is here."

Alfred. Ah-fet. Of course! How simple!

They dined at a small round table—Didi, Pratt, his wife, whom he called Mei-mei, and their daughter Belle, a plain,

85

frail-looking girl who smiled occasionally in a way that transformed her looks. At the table, conversation was mostly in the Shanghai dialect, which seemed to be the only language Mei-mei knew. But Belle's English was as good as Didi's, and she and her father both spoke Mandarin, he with a heavy accent.

"Your grandfather and I always spoke English," Pratt said to Didi. "He thought my Chinese accent atrocious, which I suppose it is, and his English was better than mine! So was your father's."

"You knew my father?"

"Yes. And your aunt Julie. Her English too was very fine."

"She was six years old and my father only two when they started learning English . . ."

"From a genteel English lady down on her luck called Miss Crachett." Pratt's smile was wide. "I know—your grandfather and I were friends from 1885 until his death."

Mei-mei rose.

"Are we finished? Then, Ah-fet, we will go into your study and you will tell all of us, Belle and me too, not only this young man, the secret you've been keeping from me all these years."

"Very well."

Pratt laughed and pinched her cheek and led the way to his study, which was plainly furnished except for a luxurious Peking carpet and three rosewood pedestals on which stood curios that seemed to Didi to be exceptional. When they were seated around the desk, Pratt was silent for a moment, his head turned toward the window. Didi watched him, the tranquility deep now in his spirit. Soon, in the next few minutes, he would know the secret of that lovely valley in Shansi.

A servant brought tea and Mei-mei poured it with quick, impatient movements. Didi watched her, smiling. She was almost childlike in her eagerness to get to the secret, but she was fully a woman. He sensed in her a solid strength, a kind of buoyancy. Belle watched her mother too, smiling her charming smile. Outside it had begun to rain. Drops pattered lightly against the windows, making a merry sound. In the mirrorlike black of the windowpanes, Didi glimpsed mysterious reflections—the polished brass of the desk's appointments, the silken glow of the peach-colored carpet where the lamp highlighted it.

Pratt said, "I met your grandfather in 1885, on a ship steam-

ing up the Yangtsze River to Hankow. During that trip I told
him about a man called Tong Shao-yi, who was my Chinese
teacher, whom your grandfather later financed as head of the
National Anti-Opium Movement that played a vital part in ending the legality of opium in China. I know all about the 'life-
duty,' which I suppose you have inherited?"

He looked inquiringly at Didi, who nodded. Pratt smiled.

"Good . . . Well, on that trip up the Yangtsze I also learned
from your grandfather that he was looking for a place with soil
good enough to grow opium of Patna quality. He had obtained
seeds of the Patna poppy, and he was looking for the right
place to have them planted. I thought at once of a valley that I
knew in Shansi province. I had been going there for years to
inspect the poppies, with a view to buying the opium. I knew
that the land was wonderful for poppies. And it was a very
secret place, hidden high up in the Chungtiao Mountains. A
beautiful valley . . ."

Didi said softly, "I have been there."

Pratt stared at him, astonished.

"The 'massacre' five years ago," Didi said. "You read about
it in the papers? It took place in that valley. I was there. I saw
those marvelous opium capsules. I talked to an old, old man,
the village headman. He told me how the valley had been sold
to a merchant from Shanghai, who I learned was my grandfather, and how an Englishman called 'Ah-fet' came every year to
buy the opium . . . I have wondered every day for the last five
years how I could find you, Ah-fet. There are many questions
I want to ask you, but the biggest one is *Why?* Why did my
grandfather want that opium?"

Pratt said simply, "In case the British couldn't be stopped
from shipping Patna opium to China. In that case he planned
to dump it on the market—Patna-quality opium, at the price of
cheap domestic. That would have gone a long way toward
ruining the British opium trade in China."

No one said a word. The answer was so simple that it needed
no comment. Didi drew a long, long breath.

Pratt went on, "Of course, he wanted it kept absolutely secret because it was a big risk. The Guild merchants would have
done anything to get their hands on domestic opium of that
quality. Every year, when I bought the opium, the farmers

delivered it to a landing place on the Yellow River. I had it moved across the river and packed in chests lined with heavy leaded paper. The chests are stored in a warehouse in Cheng-chow, not a hundred miles from the valley. I didn't want to risk moving the opium any further. There are 10,768 pounds in that warehouse. The storage receipts are in my safe deposit box at the Hong Kong & Shanghai Bank."

Again no one spoke. Mei-mei's bright eyes were fixed on her husband's face. Belle was frowning, gazing at the black windows. Didi felt his heart beating strong and steady and thought that his father was right. Success brought a wonderful tranquility.

Pratt said, "Because your grandfather wanted it kept absolutely secret, only he and I knew about it, apart from the farmers in the valley. I told him I didn't want the responsibility in case something should happen to him, so he wrote a letter to Julie telling her about the opium, and left it among his papers for her to find in the event of his sudden death. But when he did die suddenly, the letter had disappeared. Somehow, it had disappeared . . ."

He paused, and in that instant Didi knew—knew as surely as if it had been whispered in his ear—that Fish had taken the letter. Fish knew about the opium. Fish was seeking Ah-fet too.

His throat went dry.

Pratt continued, "Well, I told Julie and Great Dragon about the opium, and the three of us decided that I should go on buying it as your grandfather had arranged. Julie gave me the money every year, as your grandfather had. But suddenly, in the year the Edict was signed, both she and Great Dragon simply disappeared. I didn't know what to do. I continued buying the opium, using my own money, because the farmers were continuing to produce it—until the year of the 'massacre'."

He shook his head wryly at Didi.

"If I had only known you. But I didn't. And I didn't know Great Fish. Since your grandfather wanted the opium kept absolutely secret, I never went to his house and I never met him. I got very suspicious when Fish seemed to be in sole charge of the properties, and you didn't claim your share. I thought you two might be in collusion, you buying opium, he selling it through the *hong*. So I decided to sit tight on the storage receipts until something happened to make up my mind. And yesterday, at last, something happened."

He turned to Mei-mei.

"That young man who came to see me last night, who got so angry—that was Great Fish. He wanted me to sell fake curios for him, and I refused. So of course I knew he wasn't to be trusted. So today"—he smiled at Didi "—I went to see you, to try and judge if I could trust you. I think I can."

A great wave of gratitude washed over Didi.

Fish had found Ah-fet first, and hadn't known it!

Fish had come to Ah-fet first, for the wrong reason!

But—his heart pinched.

"Mr. Pratt, last night, when Fish came—did he happen to hear your wife call you Ah-fet?"

It was Belle who answered, very sharply. "No! I was with my mother in the kitchen. We saw him pass in the corridor, but he didn't hear her speak at all . . . Why? Do you think he stole the letter your grandfather left for Julie?"

How bright she was! He nodded slowly. "He may have."

Pratt said, "That would explain the disappearance of the letter. But we don't need to worry, because he came to me about curios, and he has no idea I have anything to do with the opium."

He turned to smile reassurance at his wife, and at Belle, but they did not smile in response. He smiled more insistently.

"Of course he doesn't! I wouldn't be alive if he stole that letter, and if he knew who I am!"

"Don't talk like that!" Mei-mei shouted angrily, but Belle said, "I suppose you're right. He doesn't know."

Didi thought with relief that Fish couldn't know. If he knew, Pratt would have died long before now.

"He killed my father and Julie," he said aloud. "I can't prove it, but I know he did, so that he could use the *hong* for blackmarketing opium. You were right about that, Mr. Pratt, but he's not getting the opium from me. He doesn't need to. He's a member of the Red Gang."

Pratt nodded slowly. "So that's it. That's why you're not claiming your inheritance. You couldn't get a lawyer to touch your case with a ten-foot pole . . . Well, what are we going to do? We have to act quickly. That opium must be destroyed."

Didi said promptly, "We can't let it fall into the Bureau's hands."

"No, of course not. But how do we get it destroyed?"

They stared at each other. Didi thought of the miserable few pounds of opium in the money shop that had attracted three sets of extortioners. The slightest hint that ten thousand pounds of Patna-quality opium was available would bring criminals from far and wide, buzzing like bees to honey. That opium was a lethal bomb waiting to explode.

Belle said suddenly, "Give it to the British. *They*'ll see that it gets destroyed!"

Simultaneously, Pratt and Didi laughed aloud. Didi said, "That's brilliant!" and Pratt turned to his wife:

"Didn't I always tell you our daughter is a genius?"

She smiled her sweet smile. "Yes—but how are you going to get it to the British?"

"That's easy!" Didi said. "We don't have to get the whole lot to them physically. We'll just give them the storage receipts, and they'll be happy to take it from there. One of my father's best friends is now the British Minister in Peking. He'll remember my name. I could sail for Peking as soon as possible—there're sailings every day—and take the receipts to him."

They all laughed again, looking gaily at each other. Pratt said, "What will you tell the Bureau?"

"Nothing! I'll just disappear. I'll get another job later."

"I'll give you a job! Know anything about curios?"

"Not a thing! But I'll take your job!"

They were all laughing, lighthearted with pleasure. Then Mei-mei suddenly sobered, looking at her husband.

"But what if Fish *does* know you're Ah-fet?"

"He doesn't! He *can't* know!"

They were silent. After a moment Belle rose and went to stand behind her father, put her arms around him, kissed the top of his head.

"All the same, Father, will you be careful? Fish didn't suddenly become a crook yesterday . . . I'm going to bed. Goodnight."

She gave Didi a quick smile and left the room. Mei-mei rose to follow.

"Ah-fet, you heard our genius daughter. Be careful."

Pratt smiled fondly as the door closed behind her.

"What do they think! Of course I'll be careful. We'll both be!"

They arranged that on the morrow Didi would buy a steamship ticket for the night sailing. Pratt would go to the bank and fetch the storage receipts. After office, Didi would come directly to Pratt's house to pick up the receipts, then go straight to the ship and stay aboard in his cabin until it sailed.

Pratt looked at his watch. "The ship will sail with the tide, about nine tomorrow night. In less than twenty-four hours, those receipts will at last be on their way to destruction!"

He walked Didi to the gate.

"Tomorrow evening, then. About six?"

Didi nodded, smiling. "About six."

And left Pratt, feeling lighthearted, feeling glad.

Chapter IX

1916

Ιτ was ten to six as Didi walked along Bubbling Well Road toward Pratt's house, his heels tapping steadily on the pavement, his heart tapping in time. Everything was ready, the steamship ticket in his pocket, his belongings in the bag he carried. He smiled, rejoicing in the unaccustomed lightness of his heart. Zung had come to his desk that morning while he was hurrying to finish the last report he would ever write for the Bureau.

"Nobody should work as hard as you do for pay as miserable as ours. Why d'you do it? To shame the rest of us?"

He had laughed, and Zung pretended vast astonishment.

"That's the first time I ever heard you really laugh! What happened last night? Let me guess . . . The girl gave in! The rich one, who lives at 507 Bubbling Well—there *is* a girl there?"

Didi laughed again. "Yes!"

"And she gave in last night! You're a fox! Great worker by day, great lover by night!"

"Nice, if true!"

"For you it makes sense, chasing a rich girl. You'll never get rich, chasing opium the way you do it!"

What a nice chap Zung was!

Pratt's tall blank gate loomed in front of him. He pulled the chain that activated a spring-suspended bell on the inside of the gate. Footsteps came hurrying down the path and Mei-mei herself flung the gate open. Her smile dimmed a little when she saw him, but she was welcoming.

"Come in! Ah-fet isn't back yet. He left at two o'clock to go to the bank. I thought he'd be back by four, but sometimes he goes into curio shops and forgets the time."

In the nicely furnished parlor, she asked him to sit down.

"Excuse me. I'm cooking dinner. I usually cook myself because Ah-fet likes my food. I'll ask Belle to keep you company."

She bustled out, and a moment later Belle entered. Didi stood politely, but she waved him back into his chair and sat down opposite him.

"Let's talk English," she said abruptly. "I don't want my mother to understand. Father does like to rummage around in curio shops, but I'm sure he wouldn't do so today. Yet he's very late. I'm uneasy."

Something icy stirred in Didi's gut.

But it couldn't be anything serious! The vault door got stuck. Or the bank mislaid the matching keys to the safe deposit boxes. Or—an accident? Here they were in the Settlement. The British police were in charge. There'd be no game-playing. He could simply go and inquire . . . *What was he thinking?*

The gate bell rang.

Mei-mei called from the kitchen, her voice light, relieved, "Here he is!"

They heard her run out of the house. Belle went to the window and Didi joined her. They watched Mei-mei hurry to the gate, draw the bolt, fling it open.

Nobody was there.

A large piece of white paper that had been thrust into the crack of the gate fluttered to the ground.

There was a blank, motionless moment. Then Mei-mei picked up the paper and came running back to the house, carrying it at arm's length like a precious but terrifying burden. Belle said, "She can't read!" and rushed out to meet her. Didi followed. They stood in a tight group at the top of the porch steps. Mei-mei handed the paper to Belle, her hand trembling. Belle glanced through it and turned white. Licking dry lips, she read it aloud.

> Tomorrow evening at nine o'clock there will be a basket outside
> your gate. Put two hundred thousand dollars wrapped in brown
> paper into the basket. Open the gate just enough to slide the
> parcel out. Do not look out. Do not tell the police. Your husband
> will be returned before midnight.

Again, a moment of motionless silence. An icy wave rose in
Didi's stomach. Mei-mei and Belle stared at each other, women
made of ivory. Then Mei-mei spoke briskly, "We have that
much money, Belle?"

"Yes," Belle said steadily. "I'll get it from the bank tomorrow. Didi, will you stay with us tonight and come with me to
the bank tomorrow?"

He stared at her, his tongue paralyzed by dread. Pratt wasn't
locked up somewhere, still breathing, awaiting deliverance.
Pratt was already dead.

She said, "Didi?"

She was white as a ghost. He wrenched himself back to the
moment.

"Yes, of course, I'll stay tonight and go with you tomorrow.
But—"

"No police!" Mei-mei cried. "The letter says no police!"

Her voice had risen and she was beginning to shake. Belle
put an arm around her.

"Come indoors, Mother. There's nothing we can do tonight.
We should have something to eat."

"I can't eat!"

But she went indoors with her daughter, Didi following. In
the hallway she stopped again.

"I hate opium! *I hate opium!*"

Her voice was raw. Belle held her tightly.

"Hush, Mother! The secret of the opium started thirty years
ago! Whether or not Father told us about it, it would have
caught up with us sooner or later. It's no use to look into the
past. Now the only thing is to do what the letter says, and to
hope."

"You are right."

She became calm. Didi could almost see the strength of the
will with which she took hold of herself. She turned to him,
ashen, but in control, and quietly spoke the words that were in
all their minds, that he was dreading to hear.

"Fish did this. He stole Julie's letter. Somehow, I don't know how, he recognized Ah-fet. But it's not your fault, Didi. Don't feel bad. Ah-fet likes you very much. He told me last night 'that young man is truly his grandfather's grandson!' "

She kept her bright black eyes on his, compelling him to absolve himself. With a rush of gratitude, he cried, "I'll do everything I can to help!"

She turned to her daughter. "I'll go to bed now."

"I'll give you something to make you sleep."

They went upstairs together, walking steady and erect. Didi watched them, horror hovering in his spirit like a great bird of prey.

He smelled something burning and was glad to hurry to the kitchen where Mei-mei had left the pots on the stove. A frightened servant was already there, moving the blackened pots. The servant poured tea for him, then sidled out, casting covert looks over her shoulder.

He sat at the kitchen table, irony a bitter taste that seemed to pervade his body. He and Fish, searching for Ah-fet all these years, wondering who he was, wondering how to find him, then finding him together, and Fish somehow getting his blow in first. Fish again! Fish winning, Fish gloating. And, worst of all, the victim not himself but Mei-mei and Belle.

Belle came into the kitchen, poured tea for herself, sat opposite him at the table.

"She's asleep . . . We'll go to the bank tomorrow as soon as it opens. It'll take a long time to get the money. I'll have to arrange for a loan against Father's bonds and gold bars. There'll not be enough time to sell them."

The money would buy nothing . . .

"I know," she said. "If Fish did this, Father is already dead. Mother knows it too. But we have to pay the money. What if Fish didn't do it? There are kidnappings every day in Shanghai. It's possible that somebody other than Fish got Father, not for the storage receipts, simply for ransom. So we have to pay."

He nodded silently. She was right.

She sipped tea, her hand steady. "How did Fish guess that it was Father who had the opium? He wasn't here for more than ten minutes. The only person he spoke to, besides the servant who let him in, was Father. And Father was sure that when he left here he didn't suspect."

He glanced at her. Her eyes were sunk in pools of shadow. Her frail face seemed transparent, like gauze.

He could only say, "I don't know . . ."

After a while, Belle rose and fixed him a bed on the couch in the parlor. He thought he would not sleep, but he slept deeply, swathed in comfort for the first time since Peking days. But when he woke in the morning the lump of ice was still in his stomach and the dread bird of prey still hovered.

They went to Pratt's bank. Belle was cosignatory of all her father's accounts. When everything was checked and cleared, the total of the cash and of the loan she arranged came to a little over two hundred thousand dollars. She asked for cash. After some delay the bank manager asked her to accompany him to see the Managing Director. They went into a large, bright room overlooking the river and, directly under the windows, the two bronze lions that guarded the famous portals of the bank. The tall, silver-haired Englishman behind the vast desk said gravely, "Miss Pratt, you are cleaning out your father's accounts."

She nodded. She was magnificent: tearless, composed, full of dignity.

"May I ask why?"

"I'm sorry, no."

"I should like to speak to your father."

"If he could speak for himself, I would not be here."

"I cannot reach him?"

"No."

"Where is he, Miss Pratt?"

"Are the papers in order?"

"Yes. But—"

"Then please let me have the money."

"Very well. I shall have a draft prepared."

"I asked for cash."

"Two hundred thousand is a very great deal of cash."

"I must have cash."

"Miss Pratt, are you sure the police should not be involved in this?"

"I am sure."

After a long moment, the banker gravely authorized payment to Miss Pratt of two hundred thousand dollars in cash.

* * *

At nine o'clock precisely, in heavy rain, Didi slitted the gate open. Mei-mei placed the brown paper parcel into a market basket that stood on the sidewalk just outside. Almost before she let go of the bundle, the basket started to move, pulled away by a string attached to it. Then there was nothing but the drumming of the rain and the thrash of leaves and debris blown about by the wind.

And now they waited, sitting at the kitchen table.

It was nine thirty.

Mei-mei said, "Two and a half hours more. Or maybe two hours. Or maybe one hour. The letter said before midnight. Before midnight . . ."

She repeated the words like an incantation. Her eyes were very shiny, her face so pale that it was like glass. Didi watched her, his mouth dry, his heart hammering. Was it possible that Pratt was still alive?

Mei-mei said, "We are like a funeral, so sad and silent! I'm going to tell you a story." She smiled gaily at Belle, a ghastly smile. "Ah-fet doesn't want you to know, but he told a secret, so I will tell one too. The story of my life. I would have no life story but for Ah-fet. I'd have died in the Flower House."

She rose and poured tea, her hands trembling.

"But the Flower House wasn't my first job. My first job was selling flowers. You know those jasmine flower ornaments women wear in their hair? My mother made them, and I sold them. I walked around the streets all day every day with the flowers on a tray that my mother tied around my neck. That's how I met Ah-fet, when I was four or five years old. He was a tallyman in a rice warehouse . . ."

Her voice was too loud, and Belle put a hand on hers. She went on, unnoticing.

". . . and he bought a flower from me every day. When it rained he took me into the warehouse out of the wet, and bought my whole trayful of flowers, and sent me home early. Every day he had something for me to eat . . ."

She turned again toward the clock, and Belle said quickly, "Where was home?"

"A rooming house, but we didn't have a room. We slept under the stairs. We owned a quilt and a towel and a rice bowl and some chopsticks, though we hardly ever used those. Most of what I ate Ah-fet gave me in the warehouse. My mother . . . I can't remember ever seeing her eat. She smoked opium. As soon as I got back from selling the flowers, she'd grab the coppers that I earned and rush out to buy opium. Not real opium—dross. I never earned enough for her to buy real opium, except when she sold me to the Flower House. You can't imagine how I hated opium!"

Her eyes were feverish. She turned again to look at the clock. This time Didi stopped her with a question.

"And then what happened?"

She smiled at him and went on, her voice brightly artificial.

"When I was eleven years old, my mother sold me to the Flower House. She couldn't have got much for me, I was such an ugly, skinny little thing, but she got enough to buy enough real opium to kill herself. Three or four days after I went to the Flower House, they told me she was dead."

Mei-mei shrugged. "Well—I was stuck in the Flower House . . . I tried to think only about the good things. I got two meals a day, and I didn't have to go around in the streets when it was raining, and I had a friend. She came to the Flower House the same day as me. She was my age, but she wasn't tough like me. She was terrified. I took care of her as much as I could. I felt like her big sister . . ."

Didi rose abruptly and went to peer out into the rain. He couldn't bear it. He felt worse than he had when Redface betrayed him, worse even than when Wilson showed him the photo of the limp human remnant that had been his father. Behind him, he heard Belle say, "How did Father find you again, Mother?"

"Oh, he came to the Flower House!" Still that bright, brittle tone. "Ah-fet is very clever. He knew that warehouse job would never get better, so—you know those big hooks the coolies use to shift the rice sacks? Every time they stick the hook in, a little rice dribbles out? Well, Ah-fet swept up those dribbles every day and hoarded the rice until he had a sackful, and sold it, and bought opium. Opium was the quickest way of making money. When he had some money, one of the coolies at the warehouse told him where I was, and he came and bought me out. You see why I say Ah-fet *is* my life?"

Her voice was animated, her face like death. Didi thought,

there must be brandy somewhere in the house. When midnight passes . . .

The gate bell clanged.

Mei-mei was off, running, Belle at her heels. For an instant, Didi's heart swelled with relief. But it wasn't Pratt! It couldn't be Pratt! He dashed after the women, reached the gate before them, slid the bolt, opened it slightly.

Nobody.

Mei-mei pushed him aside and wrenched the gate wide open. Nobody was there. The rain poured down, the wind whistled, the leaves threshed about on emptiness. Mei-mei ran out, head swinging wildly from side to side, shouting "Ah-fet! Ah-fet!" The next instant, she was sprawled on the sidewalk. She had fallen over something. While Belle helped her mother up, Didi, heart slamming like a kicking horse, stepped through the gate to see what had tripped her.

A box.

A large, long, narrow box, lying on the sidewalk just outside the gate.

Seconds passed in screaming crescendo as he stared at it, half blinded by the rain. At last he stooped, found a handle, dragged it into the garden. Mei-mei was quiet now, clinging to Belle, the two of them insubstantial in the darkness, in the downpour, as though they were melting away. He felt their eyes on him. He heard the rain drumming on the box. There was nothing in the world but their eyes, the rain, the box, the pounding of his heart.

He bent and lifted the lid.

Alfred Pratt lay inside the box, on his back, his arms extended at his sides, his face turned peacefully to the drenching rain.

When Belle had taken her mother indoors, Didi shut the box and wrestled it against the gate, where it would be partially protected by the portico. Then he began senselessly trying to wipe it dry with his soaking handkerchief. . . . He had known for ten years that Fish was a criminal. He had done nothing about it, taken no initiative, found no initiative to take, and tonight Pratt lay dead . . . The fearful thought marched inexorably round and round his mind. Bitter guilt nibbled at his foundations as surf nibbles at sand, crumbling it away. His throat, his gullet, all the tubes and channels of his body, felt as hot and raw as his skin felt cold and clammy. He thought that he could not live with the memory of this moment.

Afterward, Belle was beside him, tugging him to his feet, saying insistently, "It's not your fault! It's not your fault! This began when your grandfather bought that valley thirty years ago. Before that! When my father met your grandfather on the ship. Who knows when it began? When the first smuggler smuggled the first chest of opium! It's not your fault!"

He saw that it had stopped raining. A ragged lattice of cloud was racing across the sky before a pale moon. An errant moonbeam flickered over her face. She took his hand.

"Come indoors. We must decide what to do."

He followed her like an automaton. In the kitchen, Mei-mei sat at the table, where she had sat before her world was irrevocably altered. She had not melted, and would not. He marveled at her courage. She had already begun to restructure her life. She said, "Leave Ah-fet where he is. I have a friend who will come tomorrow and take him to a temple until his burial is ready. For now his spirit has gone to his ancestors in England. But when I bury him here in his own garden, it will return and stay with me."

He said hesitatingly, "There is a law that the police must be notified. It is murder. We know that Fish committed it. We can accuse him."

She gave him a scornful glance.

"And what good would that do? Fish has big protection. I know how crooks work—I grew up with them. Besides, Ah-fet broke the law. He kept that opium long after it was supposed to be turned in. Even if the police find the storage receipts, they'd have to turn them in *to the Bureau*, wouldn't they? I thought you and Ah-fet both didn't want that."

He bowed his head.

She said, "So, no police. I'll arrange myself to get the money back. Ah-fet earned it for Belle and me. I can't make Fish give me back Ah-fet's life, but I will make him give me back Ah-fet's money."

She was dreaming, Didi thought. Shock had deranged her mind. Belle put her arm gently around her mother.

"Come upstairs . . ."

She shook herself free and smiled at them grimly.

"You think I'm crazy. You think I can't get the money back. But I can, *and I will*. You'll see . . . I don't want anyone to get suspicious. I want it to be a big surprise when I go to get the money back. So we'll all behave normal. You and I, Belle, will do just like mother and daughter mourning for father. And you, Didi, you'll go back to the Bureau tomorrow like nothing happened. You understand?"

Over her mother's head, Belle nodded at him as though to say "Humor her!"

He said, "Of course, I'll go back to the Bureau like nothing happened."

She nodded. "Good."

And then she left them—her spirit left them and went, perhaps, to seek Ah-fet's—leaving her body still and tiny, as though a puff of breath would blow it away.

Chapter X

1916

THE CHIEF CLERK casually stuck his head into Fish's office. "Somebody to see you." Fish swallowed a wave of anger at the old man's unceremonious manner. He was the only staff member remaining from Julie's day. Fish had had to keep him to maintain contact with the old customers. The old man still looked upon him fondly as the earnest twenty-year-old struggling to replace his gravely ill sister who—the old man had believed without question—was suddenly exhibiting the streak of madness she had inherited from her mother. Now Fish forced himself to assume the youthful, thanks-for-helping-me-out manner he had cultivated toward the old man from the day he took over opium-drugged Julie's office.

"Who is it?"

"A young man called Zung."

Fish's heart gave a little thump of satisfaction.

"Wait five minutes, then show him in."

He began quickly to tidy away the papers on his desk. He had high hopes of Zung, but it was certainly too early to let him catch a glimpse of the careful notations that moved money from place to place and sent opium disguised in a thousand ways to the luxurious private clubs that used to be divans, the brothels, the under-the-counter retail outlets that varied from classy silk shops to dingy wine and money shops—and also, increasingly, to the little attic laboratories where opium was cooked into white powder.

He had met Zung only twice before, the first time when he was recruited to watch Didi, the second time five days ago when he came to report about the Englishman who lived at 507 Bubbling Well Road who had called at the Bureau and invited Didi to his home. Zung had been astute enough to guess that that was important and to come personally to report it instead of sending the usual note. And Zung was personable: a pleasant young man with an easy, friendly manner, well-spoken, knowing quite a bit of English. He would make a fine disciple.

When Zung was shown in, he was grinning just the right kind of grin: hopeful, but modest.

"I'm not disturbing you? I was passing by and thought I'd drop in to see if my report about the Englishman was any good to you . . ."

When Fish said nothing, he covered himself smoothly.

"There's not much else to report. Didi stayed away for a day, but he's back at the Bureau now, same as usual."

Still Fish said nothing. Let Zung demonstrate how well he could handle himself in awkward circumstances.

Zung squirmed a little on his hard chair and said cheerfully, "You're no more comfortable here than we at the Bureau."

It was so unexpected that Fish laughed.

"My father chose these offices and my sister wouldn't have dreamed of changing anything he chose! So now I'm stuck with this. It would cause a lot of talk among our old customers if I were to move, or even get new furniture."

Zung said easily, "Would it cause a lot of talk if you were to get a new staff member?"

Fish smiled, hiding satisfaction. He much preferred Zung to make an approach to him than the other way around.

"You? Don't know if you'd fit in."

"Oh, I'm good at fitting in!" Zung grinned disarmingly, then turned serious. "Frankly, the scope at the Bureau is narrowing. A couple of years ago there was room for . . . private enterprise. But now everybody gets a cut—except, of course, your relative. One of my—er—customers said to me the other day that it's just like paying the opium taxes in the old days, only now it's called 'squeeze' or 'protection.' He admitted it was cheaper when he had only me to pay, but I had to admit in turn that I couldn't give him the kind of protection he gets now that the whole Bureau is in on it. Except, as I said, Didi. He is really a nice fellow, by the way. And it's comforting to know that *somebody* is absolutely honest. But you see my point—he's the only one. Everybody else gets a cut of everything that comes in. It's all regulated. And that's very limiting."

He grinned his pleasant grin, but his eyes were bright and sharp. Fish turned to the window, making up his mind. Zung would not only be a good disciple—he could also develop into a valuable ally against Big-ears. To detect and deflect Big-ears' double deals. The boatman paid to kill whoever was losing. And the storage receipts . . . Fish felt anger boil up again, hot as fire. Big-ears' black-nailed hand had plucked the receipts from Ah-fet's wallet before Fish had even touched them. "You'll get your share in due course," Big-ears had said casually, walking off. Devils take Big-ears!

But Zung . . . Try him out first about getting rid of Didi. Now that Ah-fet was found, Didi was of no further use. Get Zung to stay on at the Bureau, watch his chance, and dispose of Didi at the right moment . . .

Fish turned back to Zung.

"Nice fellow or not, that relative of mine could become a nuisance. A really big one . . . I don't need any new staff members in my office here, but I do still need someone at the Bureau to watch him. Eventually, when I'm sure there's not going to be a fuss about the Englishman, I'm going to have to do something about him."

Zung passed his tongue over his lips. "Fuss about the Englishman?"

Fish shrugged. "About his death . . . Your report about him was useful . . . And there's another reason besides watching my relative why I think you should tolerate the Bureau a while longer. I think the opportunities are going to widen again. Up to now you've been concerned with existing stocks. But with the new taxation that the warlords are inflicting on the peasants, they're starting to grow poppies again. Poppies are the only crop that can pay off those damned warlords and their ragtag armies. So I think—I'm sure—you'll find that *new* stocks of opium will soon be appearing."

"Ah!" Zung nodded, eyes bright.

"You'll stay on at the Bureau?"

"Certainly—since you suggest it."

"Good. And since it seems our association is going to continue—I have a nickname: Little Fish."

"Little Fish . . ." Zung's smile widened.

The door opened and the old chief clerk looked in, frowning anxiously.

"That noise down in the street . . ."

Angry at the interruption, Fish nevertheless realized that for some time he had indeed been hearing some commotion in the street.

"What is it?" he asked impatiently.

"Some people making speeches—about you."

"*Me?*"

Astonishment, then anger flashed through Fish, and he glared at the old man.

"Why haven't you sent for the police?"

"I did . . . They refused to come . . ."

A furious rush of blood invaded Fish's head, thumped in his temples. He shouted, "You idiot!" and watched the clerk's mouth fall open, knew he had ruined the image he'd so painstakingly built up, didn't care. The old dodderer had outlasted his usefulness.

"You should have sent to the police station near my house! I've told you a dozen times! If we ever need police, send to that station!"

"I did . . . Those are the ones who wouldn't come . . ."

Fish cursed viciously. The old fool was losing his mind! His pocket-police from that station would never dare not respond to his call! The idiot must have sent elsewhere!

Zung said placatingly, "I'll run down and see what's really going on."

He left the room quickly. The clerk, ashen-faced, remained, staring at Fish.

"Get out!" Fish yelled. "Get your things and clear out! Don't come back!"

Glowering, he watched the stunned old man creep from the room, then strode to the window. In the street below a big crowd had gathered—so big that traffic was blocked. Rickshaw-pullers, carriage-drivers, cart-pushers, were temporarily abandoning their vehicles and joining the crowd. The mood seemed to be one of intense interest: people were talking to each other animatedly, nodding and shaking their heads, laughing, frowning. Fish leaned out further. Directly below, at the door of the building, three women stood on boxes. He could see only their foreshortened bodies, but one seemed to be young and pretty, the other two older. As he watched, the pretty one began to speak, and the crowd fell silent, craning to hear. Fish craned too, but could hear nothing. He returned to his desk and flung himself into his chair. What the devil was going on?

A moment later, Zung reentered the office, sat down, began to speak, his face expressionless, his tone neutral.

"There're three women down there. You saw them? Well, the young one is saying that she's an inmate of that fancy brothel, the Blue Villa. She's saying that six months ago you went there and fell in love with her. You asked for her to be reserved exclusively for you and promised a lot of money. You visited her every night for a couple of weeks, and then stopped. She hasn't seen you since, and you never paid the money you promised. One of the older women says she's the girl's mother. She had arranged for the girl to be concubine to a very rich man, but called it off when you promised the money, so the family has suffered a big loss. The other woman says she's the manageress of the Blue Villa. She confirms the story."

Fish's anger felt like a bomb about to explode. It was not only completely inexplicable, it was pure fabrication! He never went with the whores in the Blue Villa because Chiang Kai-shek was always around, cavorting with two or three of them together. Big-ears mocked him: fussy, fastidious, d'you prefer boys? But the thought of maybe sharing a girl with that degenerate Kai-shek was too revolting.

He forced his anger down below boiling point.

"Listen, Zung. That's pure invention! Why they're doing it I can't imagine! Blackmail, I suppose! Well, I'm not giving in to it. You know where I live on Mali-lu? Just about a mile down the street is a police station. Go there quickly and get the sergeant here, with a squad of his men. That fool of a clerk of mine must have sent to some other station. The sergeant in that station will jump when you say my name."

Without a word, Zung nodded and strode out.

Seething, Fish went back to the window. The crowd had grown. Zung was having trouble pushing his way through. Devils take it! Who were these damned women? What did they think they were doing? He'd have them thrown in jail for *years*!

His anger swung back to Big-ears. As soon as Zung reported that the Englishman who'd called on Didi lived at 507 Bubbling Well Road, he'd realized that the curio dealer Alfred Pratt must be Ah-fet. He had rushed to Big-ears, and the rest had been easy. Pratt's house had been watched from early the next morning. He'd been followed to the bank and kidnapped as soon as he left it, forced into a carriage, and taken to a Red Gang safe house, where Big-ears and Fish had waited. Ah-fet's wallet had been brought to them—and that devil-cursed garbage Big-ears had simply plucked out the receipts. Fish's father's opium. Part of Fish's inheritance. And that garbage had walked off with it, saying, "You'll get *your share*," leaving Fish fuming

Red-pole had come to deal with the Englishman. Maliciously—or was it by Big-ears' instruction?—Red-pole had said, "Come and see." Had taken Fish's arm in a grip of steel and led him to the room where Pratt was tied to a chair. And Pratt, that mild-looking, common little Englishman, had poured out venom.

"You scoundrel! By God, my poor old friend Jin-see! Scum like you for a son! And to think he was glad when you were born! He should have strangled you as soon as you came from the womb! What did you do with your brother Great Dragon? And your sister Julie? Killed them! Killed them!"

Fish felt his eyeballs straining at their sockets as he stared at the contorted, snub-nosed face, at the faded old eyes in which tears of fury stood.

"You knew Julie?"

"Of course! A wonderful daughter! Thank God Jin-see had her to make up for you . . ."

He saw Pratt's lips continuing to mouth words, but he heard none of them.

Julie had known who Ah-fet was! Julie had fooled him, just as One-eye had asserted!

A kind of bitter sadness overwhelmed him. Julie. Julie. He had loved Julie . . .

"Finish it!" he snarled at Red-pole, hoping viciously to see Pratt's face twist in agony, but Red-pole finished it with a single darting blow of his lethal fingers to the side of the old man's neck.

And then Red-pole, grinning, had walked out! Undoubtedly by instruction of Big-ears. A hint to Fish, in case he should be feeling obstreperous about Big-ears grabbing the receipts. A Red Gang–style disciplinary action. Red-pole does the killing; you do the dirty work of cleaning up.

But—Fish thought, grinning to himself—this time Big-ears had miscalculated. Big-ears was too used to dealing with Red Gang louts who obeyed sycophantically, too stupid to have ideas of their own. But not Fish! Fish had taken a quick carriage ride to his pocket-police station, and his pocket-sergeant had come along with two of his men. One had gone to buy the coffin, the other to stick the note into the widow's front gate. The widow had obeyed implicitly. The daughter had gone straight to the bank in the morning. A man had gone with her, the watching policeman had reported. Fish almost laughed aloud—it must have been Didi!

The door opened. Fish turned from the window. If it was that idiot of a clerk come to beg for his job . . .

It was Red-pole.

Cold fingers tickled Fish's spine.

Red-pole smiled his nondescript smile.

"I have two messages for you, Little Fish. First: give them back the money. Two hundred thousand, wasn't it? Give it back to those women downstairs. Second: there'll be a meeting tonight at nine, you know where."

And nondescript Red-pole slipped out quietly, leaving no impress on the empty air.

The cold fingers grabbed at Fish's heart.

From a small safe installed on one side of his desk, he took the brown-paper bundle: he hadn't even opened it yet, so sure was he that the whole two hundred thousand was in it. He rang his bell and told the office boy who answered, "Go down and give this to those women."

He went back to the window. Watched the office boy appear. Watched one of the older women accept the parcel. Watched the crowd disperse with laughter and jubilation.

Anger overtook him again, dull, all-pervading anger, mixed with dread.

At nine that night, Fish tapped at Jade Flower's door. She bade him enter. She was standing by the closet, so he could not avoid speaking to her.

"Good evening," he said politely.

Usually she answered him with a look of cold dislike, but tonight she smiled, her lips flattening as though savoring a tasty morsel. She was a tall, severe woman with the kind of intense look that inspired caution in the observer. When one knew that she had Pock-marks' complete confidence, it inspired fear. She was the manageress of the Blue Villa.

Now she slid open the door of the closet and waved Fish in. Why the devil was she acting like mistress of ceremonies? He stepped past her, and the closet door shut behind him with a crisp snap. In the dark, he was obliged to fumble along the back wall for the keyhole. He inserted his key and turned it. Without a sound, the secret door swung open and he stepped into the meeting room of the Red Gang's top echelon.

At first he thought the room was empty. Then he saw Tall-short sitting alone on the far side of the round table. A street fight in which he had been crippled gave him his nickname. In the same fight he had suffered a razor slash to the face, the thick scar of which distorted his smile, making it seem menacing. Now Fish couldn't tell whether he meant his smile to be menacing or not. But it didn't matter. He wasn't Tall-short's subordinate. Tall-short might be Big-ears' chief lieutenant, but he, Fish, was unique, beyond Tall-short's domain.

All the same, his heart was beating faster than normal. He took a chair across the table from Tall-short and crossed his legs, trying for nonchalance.

Tall-short's grin widened.

"Well, Little Fish, Big-ears sent me. Be glad that he didn't come himself. He'll cool down in a week or two, but you wouldn't last long if he set eyes on you tonight."

Fish swallowed the burning lump that leaped into his throat and tried for a casual laugh.

"What have I done that's so terrible?"

"A stupid thing. Not just because you acted behind Big-ears'

109

back without his knowledge. The thing you did was in itself the height of stupidity."

Fish shrugged elaborately. Tall-short leaned forward, amusement written all over his ugly face.

"You know that Jade Flower adores Pock-marks like a god, and has his complete trust. What you don't know—what you ran into today, slam bang, headfirst—is that the only other person in the world that Jade Flower loves is the wife of the Englishman Ah-fet."

Fish's throat constricted so painfully that he could not prevent a faint gasp. The amusement in Tall-short's eyes turned to malice.

"This place, the Blue Villa, used to be called the Flower House. When Pock-marks bought it, he built it up a lot, but when it started nearly forty years ago it was a small place with two eleven-year-olds that the owner peddled over and over as virgins. One of them was Jade Flower. The other was Ah-fet's wife, who was called Pearl Flower then. Jade Flower was a timid little mouse, scared out of her wits. Pearl Flower had guts enough for both of them. She protected Jade Flower as much as she could. Jade Flower loves her like life itself."

He grinned again. This time there was no doubt that the grin was menacing.

"When the Englishman bought Pearl Flower out and married her, Jade Flower was left behind. By the time Pock-marks bought the place over, she had gone a little crazy. She was no use as a whore, but Pock-marks took pity on her. Instead of throwing her out, he gave her a job carrying towels and hot water to the rooms. By that act, he bought her love and loyalty. She showed herself competent, and eventually he made her manager. There's a double bonus to that—she's a good manager, and he knows he can trust her with his life . . . Funny world, isn't it?"

Tall-short waited for an answer. Fish mumbled something, keeping his eyes down to hide the rage and dismay that were twisting his guts. Tall-short went on gleefully:

"When Pearl Flower came the other day to ask for help in getting back that two hundred thousand you gouged out of her, Jade Flower was happy to help. Not only does she love Pearl Flower—she also hates you. She says you treat the girls with disdain, you hurt their feelings, and they're human beings after all . . . I didn't see the show they put on outside your office, but I heard it was fine. Lots of people were entertained by it, including some of your *hong*'s best customers. The girl was the prettiest in the Blue Villa. The girl's mother was Pearl Flower. Jade Flower played herself."

He threw his head back and howled with laughter, beating his feet on the floor, gasping through his laughter, "And maybe you don't think you were lucky! You don't know how lucky you were that your pocket-police sergeant had the sense to stay away. In fact, it was he who sent a message warning Pock-marks. If he'd turned up when you sent for him, Jade Flower would have called up some of Pock-marks' men, and your sergeant would have been in the shithouse. And so would you. The foreign papers would have picked it up, and that kind of publicity would have bombed Pock-marks' French police connection. Now d'you see how stupid you were?"

Again, Tall-short laughed uproariously.

"You call yourself 'unique,' don't you?" he spluttered. "You're right! That's the uniquest piece of stupidity I ever heard of! And you've got a unique punishment! Big-ears thought that since Ah-fet has been found you might be thinking of getting rid of your relative. Big-ears doesn't want that! Big-ears wants your relative to stay *alive and healthy!*"

Still roaring with laughter, Tall-short weaved around the table, slapped Fish's back painfully, and let himself out.

For a long time Fish sat still, drained, exhausted, rage smoldering like a banked fire. They must all be laughing at him. Tall-short must have spread the joke far and wide. Well, let them have their sordid bit of satisfaction. How was he to know that filthy brothel gossip about eleven-year-old whores thirty years ago, before he was born? They were all scum, jealous of him . . .

But Didi. Damn that garbage Big-ears. Now he not only couldn't get rid of Didi, he'd have to *watch over him!* Hope that he didn't fall sick or have an accident! Zung's job would be, not to kill Didi, but to tend him!

But even that wasn't the worst of all. Something else was eating at his fundament . . . Julie. By god, Julie sitting there that night on the sofa in the family room, ashen, sweating, staring-eyed, the craving for opium tearing her apart, yet still with the wit to fool him, to make him believe that she didn't know who Ah-fet was! By god, Pratt was right, Julie had been wonderful! If only she would have agreed to the *hong* entering the opium business! She and he together, they could have taken on Big-ears and Pock-marks and mashed them into the garbage they were!

But Julie would never have agreed to go into opium.

He'd been forced to kill Julie.

Tears came to his eyes.

Chapter XI

1917

FIRST CAME THE GEOMANCER, who knew the ways of wind and water and the directions in which the spirits of dragons travel. He roamed the garden, muttering to himself, and finally chose a spot well out of the way of the beaten paths of dragons where Ah-fet would rest peacefully.

Then came the seer, who rattled his bamboo sticks and took the omens and said that the auspicious time for Ah-fet's burial would be the first day of the year's second moon, which was the fifteenth day of March.

Then came the seer's friend, a tomb-maker, who said that that date would allow him just enough time to carve out a magnificent tomb. He stood on the spot chosen by the geomancer and explained his plans, with much gesticulation. There would be a stone-lined vault for the coffin. The entrance to the vault would be a large panel of carved marble, into which would be set the funeral stele. Over the vault would be built a grassy mound. Fronting the mound would be a circular marble-paved courtyard enclosed by a curving marble wall graduated in height from two feet at the entrance to six feet at the back, where it would blend into the panel of the stele. On each side of the entrance to the courtyard would stand a carved marble lion-headed dog, to guard this resting place of Ah-fet's spirit.

Then came the tomb-maker's friend, the funeral director, who had the great, lead-lined, black-lacquered coffin in which Ah-fet lay moved back from the temple where it had temporarily rested to Ah-fet's own study. There it was set up on trestles before a small altar decorated with white candles, white drapes, white flowers.

The funeral director consulted his charts and informed Mei-mei exactly when the policemen of the King of Hell would bring Ah-fet's spirit home to visit. At those times, Mei-mei and Belle must be sure to kneel beside the coffin, weeping and wailing, so that the policemen would report to the King of Hell that Ah-fet was much mourned, and therefore had been a good man.

On other days, certain prayers must be recited accompanied by the lighting and blowing out of candles. On still other days, monks would come in saffron robes to sit cross-legged around the coffin, chanting mantras behind fans held up before their faces.

Mei-mei scrutinized every arrangement, bargaining shrewdly at each step. She had got back Ah-fet's money, and not a dollar of it was to be wasted. When the funeral director said that a ramp must be built from the window of Ah-fet's study to the ground down which the coffin would be carried on the day of burial, Mei-mei said firmly that that would be unnecessarily expensive.

"But," the funeral director argued, "if your husband's body is carried out of the house by an ordinary exit, his spirit will be able to find its way back."

"Let it," Mei-mei said gravely to the shocked director. "I *want* it to come and go freely."

And so, while the stone-carvers worked outdoors in the icy chill of winter, the marble tinkling musically under their tapping chisels, inside the warm house the rituals of mourning went quietly on, channeling grief into orderly conduits. Every evening, Didi came to bow before Ah-fet's altar, and then to sit in the kitchen for a time with Belle and Mei-mei. Belle was as pale and frail as ever. Mei-mei's eyes were less bright, her step less bouncy, but the fountains that fed her spirit had not flagged.

She was very proud of getting back the money.

"Didn't I tell you I would? Of course, I couldn't have done it without Jade Flower. Didi, she knows your relative. She hates him. She says he's not a human being. He goes often to the Blue Villa with someone called Big-ears, who's a friend of Jade Flower's patron."

Belle said, "Big-ears Doo is the king of the Shanghai underworld. Sun Yat-sen's new financier."

"How d'you know?" Mei-mei asked sharply.

"Through *New Culture*."

New Culture was a vernacular newspaper for which Belle was writing passionate editorials. Didi had thought at first that she was burying grief over her father's death, but she was in earnest, and beginning to acquire a reputation.

Mei-mei said, "Belle, through this work that you're doing, that you don't have to do because I got back our money, you're learning about *criminals?*"

Belle said obliquely, "Father knew. I told Father about it a day or two before he died."

"And he didn't object?"

"No."

"Well . . ." Mei-mei capitulated, leaning forward to pat her daughter's cheek. "You're a revolutionist, I know. Your father often said it. 'Our daughter is a revolutionist!' "

Belle smiled a little sadly.

"Only a pen-and-ink revolutionist, so far."

On the day Alfred Pratt was buried, snow fell from a lead-gray sky, a heavy snow that veiled the figures of the mourners, dripped sadly from the bare branches that overhung the tomb, hissed against the red-hot tips of the incense sticks.

The funeral was very simple, as Mei-mei desired. The coffin was carried from the house in procession. First, two men beating gongs; then two others carrying a palanquin on which rested a photograph of Pratt; then eight men carrying the coffin itself, slung with white ropes from white-covered poles; then the mourners dressed in white and wearing overgarments of sack-cloth. They filled the little courtyard of the tomb and over-flowed onto the pathway. The tomb-makers slid aside the stele. The coffin-bearers pushed the coffin slowly into the dark womb of the vault. The stele was replaced. And that was all.

Didi, standing on the periphery of the group, marveled that

so short a time had elapsed between his first sight of Ah-fet behind the counter at the Bureau, and this last sight of his splendid coffin disappearing into its final resting place. And yet Ah-fet's life, from the time before his birth, had already been entwined with his. And with Fish's. Fish, who had killed him.

It was over now. The fated course had been run. For the first time since the night of Pratt's disappearance, since that icy something stirred in his gut, he felt the sweetness of peace. Over the intervening heads he saw Mei-mei and Belle, their profiles etched against the stele, and thought that for them too the turmoil was past.

The funeral director and his staff had left. The servants, murmuring, were kowtowing before the stele, then trailing away back to the house. Soon there were only the three of them left in the little courtyard of the tomb, standing in the trampled snow. Mei-mei brushed snow from her hair and knelt to blow life back into the half-extinguished incense sticks in the bowl before the stele. The sticks began to glow again, the smoke to swirl. The snow stopped. A few last flakes came quietly to rest on Mei-mei's head, and no more fell. A moment later, a crack opened in the leaden sky, and a perfect rainbow slipped out.

Mei-mei drew a tremulous breath.

"Ah-fet sent it! Ah-fet's back home with us! He is pleased with his tomb! He is glad I got back the money! Didi—you must come and stay with us. I know that Ah-fet wants it. He offered you a job. The next thing, he would have asked you to come and stay with us. So you must come."

He felt as though the rainbow had slipped into his heart, but he looked at Belle. She hesitated. Then, "Yes. Come. That is— if it doesn't interfere with any involvements you may have."

He breathed again.

"I have no involvements."

He had had, in Shansi. Nothing heavy. Just pleasant attachments that had seemed part of the courses of nature, that now he knew were not, that now he knew he'd been fortunate to have. Plump, giggling girls who had shared his bedroll on some hilltop. Women in the villages who had welcomed him on his rounds, fed him, petted him, taken him into their beds. Since he left Shansi, there'd been only the few encounters to which he had been driven, that he had kept as brief and *un*involved as possible.

He grimaced as he walked along to the Bureau. He really was some sort of country bumpkin, suited to the rugged mountains and the mountain people. Yet there was something in the life of the Yangtsze Valley that fascinated as it repelled him: some urgency, some vitalness, in the unceasing, furtive, knowing to-and-fro. In the mountains there had been few secrets and little evil. Here almost everything was secret, and there was much evil. Obscurely, he thought of Belle, her frailness, her flashing mind. Belle understood evil, and was unafraid of it.

Why was he still going to the Bureau? He could resign. The whole Bureau was evil, and there was nothing he could do about it—except refuse to be evil. If he resigned from the Bureau, it would be like resigning from his life-duty. Rejecting his inheritance. Throwing up his hands. Saying, "I give up!" It was stupid to stay, but impossible to leave. . . . Perhaps they would fire him. That would make it impossible to stay . . .

Zung fell into step beside him.

"Good morning! How is it that you're walking this way? Your rooming house is in the other direction."

"I've moved."

"At last! That rooming house was a disgrace. Where've you moved to?"

"507 Bubbling Well Road."

Zung stopped short and raised his eyes to heaven.

"My dear fellow! You actually took my advice to chase a rich girl instead of chasing opium!"

"Come on, Zung. We're late . . . It's not that at all. You know the Englishman who came to see me at the Bureau that day, who lived at number 507? He died. The widow asked me to stay—they need a man in the house. And of course I was glad to. If *you* thought the rooming house was a disgrace, you can imagine what I, who lived in it, thought of it."

They climbed up the steps to the Bureau. Zung held the door for Didi.

"Well . . . then . . . maybe it'll work out."

"What will work out?"

"It'll cost you more, won't it? Living at number 507?"

"No. At first they wouldn't take any money, but I've insisted on paying at least what I was paying at the rooming house. It's shameful, but they simply won't take more. Nor, of course, could I afford much more."

"You could, you know. And you'll need better clothes, on Bubbling Well Road . . ."

"Zung, what are you talking about?"

Zung grinned his pleasant grin.

"It's payday. You'll find something extra in your envelope. Perhaps you'll take it, now that your expenses are higher—or should be."

Didi felt suddenly weary.

"You know I won't take it."

"Well, anyway, I'll go with you to the cashier."

They walked down the corridor together, passing one or two agents who, it seemed to Didi, glanced at him speculatively. The cashier slipped an envelope under the grating that protected his window. He and Zung both watched as Didi opened it. Inside was a money order for the amount of his salary, plus a bundle of cash.

Didi riffled through it.

Zung murmured, "That's six months' salary."

The cashier murmured, "It's your bonus for the confiscated opium."

Didi pushed the notes back under the grating.

"What bonus? We don't get bonuses. What confiscated opium? There isn't any."

The cashier shrugged as he put the money back into his drawer.

"We were only trying to share it out equally."

"Share what out?"

"The bonuses for the confiscated opium."

Didi walked away. Useless to argue!

Zung followed him to his desk.

"Listen. When was the last time we got a raise? The oldest man here doesn't remember! And who can live on a government salary? It's impossible, if you want to live decently. Peking knows that. But they can't afford to increase our salaries. So they're glad if we do whatever we can to make our earnings up to a decent level—"

He met Didi's eye and stopped, grininng self-mockingly.

118

Didi laughed. How could a man be such a crook, and at the same time such a nice fellow!

"Why don't you and the others do what you like, and leave me to do what I like?"

"It isn't equitable!"

"You mean we should all be equally guilty."

"You must admit that would be better! It's not so much that you might talk. It's that one fine day you might actually get someone to *listen*!"

Didi laughed again. "You're a funny man, Zung!"

"Seriously—why not cooperate? The only difference is to your own pocket. The money you don't take gets shared out among us venal others. Didi, this is a kind of last chance. If you don't cooperate, they're going to—"

"Fire me?" Didi cut in, something like hope rising.

Zung gave him a surprising look. Was the outspoken, open-mannered Zung *hiding* something? He looked secretive! But a moment later he was smiling his usual joking smile.

"No. They're going to bore you to death by posting you to Lung-hwa, where the main industry is slaughtering pigs. You'll have to leave the widow and move out there, unless you get up at four every morning and take the train."

"Getting up at four won't bother me—I did it all the time in Shansi. But—why don't they fire me? They don't need any-body in Lung-hwa! Why keep on paying my salary, when it could be shared out among you all?"

"A drop in the bucket!"

"I know, but . . . everybody except you hates me, Zung. They hate me for not being 'equitable.' I really can't understand why they don't fire me!"

"It's a mystery," Zung said, laughing.

The mail-boy clattered into the room in his wooden clogs and dumped a box on Didi's desk.

"What's that?" Zung said, his quick curiosity immediately aroused.

Didi lifted the box and held it in his hands, all the aggrava-tions forgotten . . . The soul tablets! Mei-mei had given him a lovely room, large and square, with two windows facing east, between the windows a narrow carved table, intricately fitted together, not a nail or a screw in it. One of Pratt's antiques. It would make a wonderful ancestral altar. He had written at once to the governor of Shansi, asking for his soul tablets. And here they were. He felt overwhelmed. The peace that had touched him at Pratt's funeral, that had been growing timidly ever since, suddenly blossomed. It was like coming home. Pratt's big, solid house. His big, airy room. Mei-mei, kind as his own mother had never been, slowly regaining her cheerfulness. Belle, clever Belle, whose frailness somehow sparkled with the vitality of her mind. And now, the soul tablets of his ancestors.

He smiled, remembering. When he was a child, when something good happened—as, for instance, one of his mother's rare good moods—he had always anxiously examined his conscience. Had he already paid for this good thing by some prior suffering? Or would he have to pay for it later? Surely he had already paid for the good time that had arrived for him now! Surely he could just enjoy it!

"What are you grinning at?" Zung cried. "What's in that parcel? You act like it's sacred!"

"It is!"

He tore off the wrapping and opened the box, the same box in which Donald Mathes had packed the soul tablets more than ten years ago. He took them out one by one and set them on the scarred desk. The pair of marble tablets. The pair of green jade. They glowed as they had the last time he saw them in the Peking house, drawing to themselves all the light in the dingy room.

"They're lovely!" Zung said. Even he sounded reverent.

"They are . . ."

He began to put them back into the box . . . But where was the letter Donald Mathes had written him about his last meeting with Julie? He had packed it in with the soul tablets. He removed the tablets again, took out the tissue, looked into the empty box, felt through the tissue.

"What are you looking for?" Zung asked.

"A letter. I packed it in with the tablets."

"Maybe it fell out."

They looked all over the dirty floor, but it was nowhere. Could the governor have removed it? Perhaps he'd repacked the box, and it had fallen out then . . .

"Is it important?" Zung asked.

"It *was* important! I suppose it doesn't matter now. Anyway, I remember what it said."

"That's all right then."

Didi packed the box again, and rewrapped it.

"There's a table in my room at number 507 that will make a wonderful ancestral altar," he said to Zung.

But Zung was no longer there.

Chapter XII

1918

Z UNG GRINNED at Fish and said lightly, "Nothing that you wouldn't expect from a nice fellow like him."

Fish growled, "I'm not interested in his character! Just in what he's doing."

"Nothing much he can do in Lung-hwa. I hardly see him these days . . ."

"I'm paying you to see him!"

"Well, I can't go out to Lung-hwa to see him—it would make everyone suspicious—even him! As it is, he's wondering more than ever why the Bureau doesn't fire him."

"What did you say?"

"I *didn't* say, 'Because it's easier to keep track of you while you're with the Bureau.' Though I don't know why you still want him watched! I thought you wanted to get rid of him two or three years ago."

Zung looked innocent. Fish said shortly, "That's my business!"

Though Big-ears had gradually taken Fish back into his good graces, he had not relented from his dictum that Didi must be kept alive and well. An angry little gust blew through Fish. Not only was Didi alive and well—according to Zung, he was now living comfortably at the widow's house, had an ancestral altar on which stood the true tablets of their mutual ancestors, not the elaborate fakes he himself had shown off to Big-ears as part of the hallowed aura of his heritage. And the widow had a daughter. Zung said she was plain and scrawny but had a fine mind. Didi would care for her mind more than for her looks. He might marry her. He'd really be well off then, with access to the money Big-ears had forced Fish to return to the widow. Curse it! Fish had liked to think of Didi alone, friendless, poor, living in a dingy rooming house.

With an effort he pushed away his somber thoughts. At least he was once again sitting at Big-ears' table in the Blue Villa, bodyguards at all the surrounding tables, their pistols lying beside their strictly teetotal mugs of tea. Yes . . . and he was also once again making the kind of jokes that Big-ears laughed at, listening to his guffaws, trying not to shrink away when Chiang Kai-shek plumped himself down beside him—he always seemed deliberately to choose the nearest chair. And some night soon the ritual of being in Big-ears' good graces would oblige him to go upstairs with one of the whores, perhaps one who'd just been with Kai-shek. It would amuse Jade Flower to see to that!

"Why so gloomy?" Zung asked, smiling.

Once again he pushed his thoughts aside. What was wrong with him? Between anger at Big-ears and dislike of Chiang Kai-shek . . .

He picked up a square of stiff red cardboard ornate with gold-engraved characters. A Red Gang messenger had brought it that morning, with a message from Big-ears:

Accept. Be prepared for a meeting. Learn what you can about the new Frenchman who's replaced the old chief of the French Town police.

He tapped the card lightly on the desk, his mood lifting. This would be a fine opportunity to spring Zung on Big-ears. His own disciple. Young, educated, well-groomed, English-speaking, fit for any high-society party, not a skulking Red Gang bodyguard type who had to be hidden behind a potted palm.

He grinned at Zung.

"Here's an invitation to a dinner party at the house of Dr.

Kung Hsiang-hsi, the banker. You know—the one the foreigners call 'H.H.' His wife is Soong Ai-ling, sister of Sun Yat-sen's new wife Soong Ching-ling. The party is in honor of Sun Yat-sen and Ching-ling. You'll accompany me to it . . .

The Kung mansion was on Route de Sieyes in French Town, a broad, tree-lined street on which there were no terraces of small houses, no blocks of flats—only gracious homes set in large gardens behind high, shard-topped walls.

Fish and Zung left Fish's chauffeur to park his new dark green Essex around a corner. Fish was not yet sure of what Big-ears would think of his owning an automobile. Big-ears was still enjoying the distinction of being the only person in Shanghai who owned three Packards, one for himself and two for the bodyguards who drove before and behind him, guns bristling.

Side by side, uncomfortable in their foreign-style starched shirts and wing collars, Fish and Zung walked toward the Kung mansion, easily identified by the lights and music that rose from behind its walls. A battery of policemen were trying to control the excited crowd of gapers who seemed not to care if they were hit by a nightstick as long as they managed to get a glimpse through the gates at the fairy-tale world beyond, in which hundreds of tiny lights glimmered in trees and bushes and a tide of golden people moved back and forth over manicured lawns, talking, laughing, taking drinks and food from silver platters offered by white-gowned waiters. The bony, ragged gapers gaped and ooh'd and ahh'd as though these gorgeous sights were filling their stomachs.

Fish and Zung pushed their way through. On each side of the gate stood one of Big-ears' most trusted bodyguards, scrutinizing the guests who passed between them. The display of invitation cards was not enough to allay their suspicions: anyone might have had a facsimile printed. Foreign guests passed through, seemingly unconscious of the scrutiny, but every Chinese found occasion to pause, speaking to his wife or instructing his driver, to give the scrutinizers a good look. When it came their turn to enter, Fish and Zung paused too, Fish's hands in full view fiddling with his bow tie, Zung smoothing back his perfectly combed hair. Fish said something to Zung, pronouncing his full name distinctly—the scrutinizers didn't know Zung by sight, but had his name on a list of additional invitees.

Inside, they joined a group of guests winding slowly toward the receiving line on the raised front porch of the tall brick house. Kung and his wife—Big-ears' helpers in defrauding the public—were remarkably alike, short and dumpy, told apart as male and female only by their dress and hair. Beside them, Sun Yat-sen looked exactly like his many photographs, short, dapper, mustache well twirled, hair brushed in a dip across his forehead. Ching-ling, beside him, was a surprise: taller than her sister, willowy, her hair a dark froth, her eyes hidden in pools of shadow. Zung leaned forward to whisper, "Pretty good-looking for a revolutionist!"

Behind her, Fish made out a shadow who must be Big-ears, standing where he could be easily covered by bodyguards in the bushes beside the porch. He seemed to be wearing a brocade gown, with round frog buttons that glittered in the porch lights. Gold? But nothing could improve that gawky figure, the grotesque ears that even in the dim light protruded angularly from his head.

The line snaked slowly forward. At last, Fish found himself bowing before the host and hostess. They bowed back automatically, their gaze elsewhere. He moved on to Sun Yat-sen, who smiled and nodded, blank-eyed. But Ching-ling looked into his eyes, her gaze clear, without guile. With a sense of shock he bowed to her and passed on. Behind him, Zung murmured, "Didi looks at you like that."

Curse Didi! He swung round to glare at Zung, but his arm was taken in a strong hand and he was pushed into the shadows by the porch. Big-ears' voice rasped in his ears, "Little Fish, the meeting will be during dinner. Eat quickly if you're hungry . . ." Then suddenly, sharp and angry, "Who's this?"

Zung had followed him into the shadows, now stood rigid, a bodyguard's pistol in his side.

"My secretary," Fish said smoothly. "I asked Tall-short to get him on the invitation list because I put him in charge of finding out about the new Frenchman."

"Huh?" As usual, Big-ears sounded stupid, but his hooded eyes flicked over Zung quickly. Then he gestured to the bodyguard, who withdrew.

"What did you find out?"

Zung bowed with his pleasant smile. "I am honored to be here, sir. I found out quite a lot. Actually, the man is not a born Frenchman. He's a Corsican, with connections in Marseilles. Quite a large factory, I was told, for cooking morphine and heroin. And other connections for shipping out of Marseilles, mainly to America . . ."

Big-ears was listening. Fish took a soft breath of relief, cursing himself at the same time. One day he would be unafraid of Big-ears! One day he would curse Big-ears instead of himself—curse him aloud!

Big-ears was nodding. "Good! Bring your secretary to the meeting, Little Fish. What we're going to do is make new arrangements with this cursed new Frenchman. The old arrangements were made by Pock-marks with the old chief, and this new bastard remembers or forgets them as he pleases. He'll have to be taught. I've persuaded Pock-marks to let me handle it. There'll be only five at the meeting—the three of us, the Frenchman, and an Englishman. The English have been licking the honey pot free of charge for too long, profiting by my control of the gangs for nothing. They're going to have to make some commitments now." He grinned his shark grin, snaggle teeth showing. "All right. I'll send a man for you when it's time."

For a while, Fish and Zung circulated. The food was magnificent, and champagne flowed like water, but they both ate and drank sparingly, watching the swirl and sway of the party. There were several hundred guests, Chinese and foreigners, being gracious to each other. The foreigners were there, of course, because of Sun Yat-sen. Ever since the opening of the first Chinese port to foreign trade, the foreigners had tried to bolster centralized Chinese government. They could deal with central government, however weak, but not with a fragmentation between rebels and warlords. Sun Yat-sen was today's best bet for wresting China from the warlords, and the foreigners hovered about him, contemptuous of him, as they were contemptuous of Chinese in general, but paying him court in case he should really one day reunify China and recentralize the government.

And Sun Yat-sen served Big-ears' purposes too. Big-ears controlled the labor market in the Yangtsze Valley, where China's industry was concentrated. Anything that agitated labor, agitated Big-ears. In Big-ears' book, there were far too many despairing peasants being driven by the warlords into the cities to swell the already hopeless ranks of job-seekers, their anger and despair exacerbated by groups like the Socialist Youth Corps who preached better-than-starvation wages and better-than-prison-camp working conditions, all in the vernacular in newspapers like *New Culture*, which even coolies could read. In Big-ears' book, angry and despairing people tended to be reckless. Better for people to have a modicum of hope to make them cautious and obedient. Sun Yat-sen was supplying that modicum, promising peasants the suppression of the warlords, promising laborers something he called democracy.

Big-ears was channeling opium profits to support Sun's shadow government in Canton and his Whampoa Military Academy, where officers of the Kuomintang army that would conquer the warlords were being trained. Kuomintang. The National People's Party. The Red Gang's party.

Someone touched Fish's shoulder. He rose at once, Zung with him. The messenger led them around the house and into a huge kitchen where frantic cooks rushed about. No one paid them attention. In semidarkness they climbed three flights of narrow, uncarpeted stairs—the servants' stairs—to a small landing under the roof. The messenger opened a plain wooden door. Feeling the strong beat of his heart, Fish stepped through it, Zung at his heels.

The room was small—a servant's room—and unfurnished except for a round table and plain wooden chairs. It was quiet—at the back of the house, and too high up for the noises of the party to reach. At the table three men were already seated. Big-ears, at his dullest, hooded eyes half closed. A short, swarthy foreigner, stiff-fronted shirt bulging over a solid belly: the new Frenchman. And the Englishman, thin-faced, with disdainful eyes and a pencil-line mustache over pursed lips.

Fish took the chair beside Big-ears, Zung the chair on his other side. Across the table, the Frenchman leaned forward: "Let's get on with it. I want to get back to the dinner. The wine's excellent."

His English was slightly accented, but fluent. Fish already knew from Zung that his name was Etienne Fiori and his rank

Captain, but Zung now leaned forward respectfully and put a bit of paper before Fish on which the same information was written. It made an impression. Fiori frowned.

"What's that paper?"

Fish glanced at it casually. "Your name and title."

"Hmmm." Fiori jerked his head at Big-ears. "What's his complaint, anyway? I'm satisfied with the way things are going."

Fish murmured a translation. Big-ears smiled vaguely.

"Tell the mother-sticker I'm not!"

So it started, and for ninety minutes it went on, Fiori growing red and angry, Big-ears gently vapid, never letting the venom of his words reach his voice or eyes. The Englishman said nothing, maintaining a demeanor that strongly disassociated himself from Fiori. According to a piece of paper Zung produced, he was Bruce Jones, deputy of Stirling Fessenden, Secretary General of the Shanghai Municipal Council, governing organ of the International Settlement. Fish smiled to himself: to the Chinese, foreigners were foreigners, but among foreigners there were, clearly, distinctions. The Englishman despised Fiori, and Fiori had no use for the Englishman. But much as they disliked each other, they would stand together if they had to against Big-ears.

As the meeting went on, Fish himself grew cooler, more confident, enjoying his command of the English language. He had never before had the chance to exercise it so thoroughly. If One-eye were here now, he would be green with jealousy. Was Big-ears properly impressed? There was no telling from his vacant expression, but he must be impressed, not only with Fish but also with Fish's acquisition of the calmly competent Zung, always prompt with bits of paper or murmurs.

At last Big-ears mumbled, "All right. Summarize. Make that French mother-sticker repeat his agreement on every point."

Fish smiled at Fiori.

"Captain, like you, we'd all like to get back to the excellent food and wine. Let us recapitulate . . ."

Zung placed a piece of paper before him. He glanced at it briefly.

"Yes . . . Firstly: territory. Divans, brothels, and retail outlets for opium operating in French Town will be located in the area south of Rue du Consulat, east of the Boulevard des Deux Republiques, and west of Rue Tenant de la Tour. There will be none along Avenue Joffre, Rue Lafayette, Avenue Petain, Route de Sieyes—the better residential districts. My secretary will draw up a map of which we will all have copies. Agreed?"

Fiori nodded grumpily.

Zung handed Fish another piece of paper.

"Secondly: supplies will be moved to the divans, brothels, and retail outlets between 10 P.M. and 4 A.M. on any weeknight. Not during the day, and not on weekends. They will be moved in closed carriages with a small yin-yang sign painted on the doors. Your men will never stop such carriages. Agreed?"

Fiori nodded.

Zung passed over another piece of paper.

"Thirdly: the river steamers. You have introduced a regulation that they be searched immediately after docking, you say because of gunrunning. But the way it has worked out is that your inspectors have been extorting squeeze on opium they may find while they're supposedly searching for guns. This will stop. From now on, no river steamer will be boarded until a small yin-yang flag is flown over the transom, indicating that the opium has been removed."

Fiori grunted.

It went on, Zung producing bits of paper for each item: location of warehouses, quantities to be stocked at any one time, morphine factories, control of morphine manufacture, movement of morphine stocks, a dozen other details. At last, with a glance at Big-ears, Fish said, "Lastly—the new system of taxation."

Fiori's mouth tightened like a trap. The hardest bargaining had taken place on this point. Under the old system, divans, brothels, and retail outlets had paid "tax" twice—once to the Red Gang, and again to the French police, who shared what they collected with their chief. The old chief had kept a strict eye on his men, in accord with his agreement with Pock-marks, and they had rarely exceeded the amounts they were authorized to collect. But with Fiori's advent, they had so escalated their demands that the whole system was in disorder. The opium dealers were complaining bitterly to the Red Gang, and clamoring for protection.

Now, Big-ears had insisted, taxes would be collected only by the Red Gang. No member of the French police would be authorized to collect from any divan, brothel, opium shop, or other outlet. Anyone who tried would at once become fair game for Red-pole. In return, the Red Gang would pay Fiori a flat monthly fee which it would be up to him to share with his men generously enough to keep them happy. The principle had been agreed, but not the amount of the fee. Now the bargaining began again, sharp and hard as flint. Fish kept his voice cold and neutral. Fiori's eyes flashed, his face grew dark and his voice gravelly. Big-ears grinned his idiot grin and called Fiori every filthy Chinese name. At last, Big-ears stuck at the sum of $150,000 a month.

"Tell the bastard if he doesn't agree I'll remove all controls from the thief, pickpocket, waterfront, and beggar guilds. There'll be riots everywhere. Even here on this shit-holy Route de Sieyes, beggars will be howling and crying, picking lice off themselves to flick onto passersby . . . Tell him, in case he doesn't know it yet, in this city half a million men obey my orders."

Fish licked his lips. The Red Gang was grossing five million a month on opium, most of it through his own *hong*. A hundred and fifty thousand was a drop in the bucket. But the fat-bellied Corsican suddenly gave in, his grin becoming wolfishly ingratiating.

"All right. It's a killer, but all right. Provided I get something—a *cumshaw*, a gift, for making everything so easy for you. . . . The Messageries Maritime steamers sail from Shanghai to Marseilles once a month. I want five hundred pounds of raw opium on every sailing. You just deliver it—I'll arrange the stowing and everything else."

Big-ears shrugged. "That's why he was willing to come without his own interpreter. He didn't want anyone present who could leak to his men what he's getting out of it for himself. A traitor. Betraying his own people. A mother-sticking traitor. Tell him three hundred pounds."

After some more haggling, Fiori agreed.

The Englishman sniffed and rose.

"I take it the meeting is over."

Big-ears grinned stupidly.

"Tell him get his backside back into that chair. I'll let him know when he can leave. Tell him the British have been lucky. The French are greedy for all the take from the opium, so we haven't had to go into the Settlement. They've paid nothing for their peace and quiet. But they're going to have to pay something now."

Fish turned to Bruce Jones.

"You'll appreciate that the International Settlement benefits from our control of the guilds and gangs just as much as French Town. If controls are removed, the guilds and gangs could go just as wild in the Settlement as in French Town."

Bruce Jones sniffed. "What d'you want?"

Fish turned to Big-ears. "What do we want?"

Big-ears smiled sleepily. "A few little things . . . In the next month or two I will nominate somebody to be on the Board of Directors of a couple of banks, one French and one English. These two bastards are to ensure the appointment. Also, there's a new joint English-French committee which is collecting millions for aid to refugees from the warlords' fighting. I want my nominee to be chairman of that committee. No—treasurer. The treasurer has better access to the funds. That's to begin with. In a year or two, when my nominee is well known in the foreign business and society circles, the director of the Shanghai branch of the Opium Suppression Bureau will retire, and my nominee will replace him. I want full cooperation from both the foreign municipalities."

Fish's heart had begun to pound heavily. He had almost given up believing in the dazzles Big-ears had held up to his eyes that night on the launch. But here they were, as bright and dazzling as he could have hoped. Zung laid a slip of paper before him, blank except for the word "Congratulations." He crumpled the paper with a hand that trembled a little, a tiny twitch of superstition flicking him. But there was nobody else Big-ears could nominate to such posts—nobody but himself.

He swallowed, and told the foreigners what Big-ears had said. Fiori nodded impatiently, but the Englishman said in a strangled voice, "Who's he going to nominate? We can't have *trash* on our boards and committees!"

Fish turned to Big-ears. "They want to know who you're going to nominate."

"You, of course, Little Fish." Big-ears spoke as softly as his voice would allow. "Who else?"

Triumph erupted in Fish like steam from a boiling kettle. An inconsequential picture flashed through his mind: his blind old father saying, "The taste of success is sweet and peaceful." For that old dodderer, maybe. For himself, the taste of success was fiery hot. But he kept the shine from his eyes as he turned back to the foreigners.

"The nominee will be myself."

Fiori said, "Of course." The Englishman grunted. They rose. The meeting was over.

When the foreigners had gone, Fish sat still for a moment, the thrill of success still rippling through his veins. But it was no more than his due, after all. It was what Big-ears had promised in that "compromise" on the launch. Still, Big-ears would expect sycophantic gratitude . . .

Big-ears diffused the tension by slapping him on the back and saying coarsely, "Now all you need is a wife. Foreigners always have hostesses. Not Susu of course. Some woman who'd look good hostessing for a bank director."

Fish managed a hearty-sounding laugh. "I'll go down and start looking for one at once."

The atmosphere lightened. Big-ears grew affable and talkative. He was very satisfied with the agreement they had just reached with Fiori, especially as it gave him a handle on that slippery bastard of a Frenchman: he wouldn't like word of those secret shipments to Marseilles leaked to his subordinates! And the new agreement was very opportune, now that the flow of opium from the interior was fast increasing. Fish had done a fine job organizing production in the Yangtsze Valley, and the supply lines into Shanghai. Was Zung helping him? Good! Better to have a backup. What were the prospects of extending production further into the interior? Of course, he understood, it depended to a great extent on the warlords' activities. Fighting could destroy crops or void the planting season. And the devil-cursed warlords were seizing opium in payment of the "taxes" they were imposing on the peasants.

"That seized opium comes back to us eventually," Fish said. "I'm fixing it so there's no one else the warlords can sell to. And I can control prices, since they've got to have money: they can't pay their troops with opium."

Big-ears grinned amiably. "Fine! And how about Yunnan province? That was your own suggestion, you remember? That we might export opium from Yunnan to compete with the British for the Indochina and East Indies markets? You made One-eye shit-furious that night! Just a kid you were, twisting One-eye's tail! Don't think I didn't know what you were doing!"

Big-ears' hooded eyes were gleaming with—*malice?* But the next instant he was guffawing heartily.

"Cheeky kid you were, Little Fish! Full of guts! Well . . ." He pushed back his chair. "As the French bastard said, the eats are good downstairs."

Down in the garden the lights seemed brighter, the people gayer, the music louder, the scene more golden. Soong Ai-ling, Big-ears' financial helpmate, came to Fish. In the receiving line she'd stared blankly over his shoulder. Now she beamed at him.

"You're Little Fish! I want to introduce you to one of my husband's colleagues." She giggled coyly. "Not that I understand a thing about banking, but he's one of the biggest bankers in Shanghai." She beckoned to a tall, silver-haired Englishman she had in tow. "The Managing Director of the Hong Kong and Shanghai Bank."

The Englishman bowed stiffly, bristling with reluctance.

"I understand that one of these days we're to welcome you on our Board of Directors."

Fish bowed to hide his astonishment. Big-ears must have signaled Soong Ai-ling! He raised his eyes to the Englishman's.

"I understand I'm to be offered that honor."

The Englishman goggled slightly. "Your English is excellent, sir!"

Fish smiled.

Chapter XIII

1921

DONALD HEARD JIN-SEE calling and smiled: something had made Jin-see glad. He sounded as glad as on the day Dent had said to him, "Got us by the balls, haven't you?"—the first sign that the British opium traders were feeling the pinch . . . But that was long ago and far away. In Shanghai. It couldn't be that that was making Jin-see glad today.

Donald turned to ask him what it was, but by the time he got his heavy head around, Jin-see was no longer there. Julie had taken his place. Lovely Julie! But she was sick . . . Her face was gaunt and vivid with the colors of fever, her eyes huge and too brilliant. He took her in his arms and she rubbed her cheek against the shoulder of his greatcoat, tears streaming from her eyes. When he asked her what was wrong, she wouldn't answer. Instead, she asked him to take the ancestor tablets to Peking, to Didi, Jin-see's grandson, though it was Great Fish, Jin-see's son, who should have them. Why didn't she want Fish to have them? Fish must have done something terrible! Julie pleaded urgently, "Go, before he comes back and stops you!"

He heard Jin-see call again in that glad voice, and now he could hear what Jin-see was saying. "Come on, Donald! Come on!" But he couldn't go yet because Noelle was there, saying,

"Father." She'd been saying it for some time, he realized, but he'd been listening to Julie and Jin-see and hadn't heard her. He made a great effort and opened his eyes and saw her face bending over him. Noelle, his beautiful, beloved, willful daughter, who had come into his life too late for him to understand. "Noelle," he whispered, wanting to say that he was sorry, but suddenly she disappeared and Jin-see was there at the bedside, young and vital, smiling.

"Come!" he said gaily. "Come on, Donald!"

Donald rose, and he too was young again, his legs strong, his heart springing. They laughed together, he and Jin-see, and went together through the door of the office they had shared for so many years, down the broad marble stairs, out onto the Bund, threaded their way between the crowding traffic to the grass verge that ran beside the Whangpoo River, and strode along it together, delighting in each other.

Noelle waited until the light that had suddenly sprung into her father's eyes faded, until the eyes, once so brilliantly blue, turned a quiet gray. Then she drew the lids down over them and knelt beside the bed, feeling a kind of sad relief. He had been so old—eighty-four, to her nineteen! She remembered him holding her gingerly on his knee, or regarding her anxiously across a table. But for the Chinese lessons, they had never known what to say to each other. He had been puzzled by her stories of school events. She had been bored by his stories of China. They had both always been relieved when Nannie came to fetch her. This last year, when she had returned from boarding school and there was no more Nannie to come between them, had been a kind of loving agony for both of them.

When the nurse came into the room, Noelle rose.

"He's gone."

"Ah!" The nurse sighed, fussed around the bed a little, finally drew the sheet over his face. "A mercy, in a way. That pain in his back would only have got worse, and he had a very long and full life." She smiled comfortingly. "Don't mourn too much, my dear! What are you going to do now?"

Noelle wandered to the window, looked out at gray, drizzly London. "Perhaps I'll take a trip."

"Good idea. They say everyone should spend some time on the Continent."

Not the Continent.

China.

Cousin Gordon Carradine peered at her over his glasses. He was her father's cousin, on his mother's side—she had been a Carradine who had married a Mathes. Noelle hadn't seen him since she was five or six years old. He had looked as old to her then as he looked now, though he was several years younger than her father.

He harrumphed, and she imagined dust flying off the old deed box before him. Her nose tickled, and she raised her handkerchief to it. He rumbled anxiously about there being no need to cry. She sniffled a little to please him. He was sweet. She hadn't been sure he would let her do as she wished, but now that she was with him she knew he would.

He took a fold of vellum from the deed box.

"Your father's will, my dear. Very simple. Everything is left to you, in trust until you reach the age of twenty-five. The manager of his bank and I are the trustees. Until you inherit, you have full use of the interest of the estate. You are, my dear, quite adequately wealthy, though not as wealthy as you would have been had your father not spent such vast sums on the parliamentary campaign against opium. The money then was worth more than it would be today, so altogether that campaign made quite a hole in your inheritance. Nevertheless, you are amply provided for for the rest of your life."

"Thank you," she murmured, smiling, she hoped not too mistily.

He beamed at her. "Now, as to your guardianship. I suggested to your father that he should choose someone younger than I, but he insisted I must assume the duty since I am your only close relative. There are some fourth or fifth cousins in Scotland with whom we lost touch several generations ago . . ."

"And some cousins in China," she murmured. "The descendants of my great-grandfather William Carradine and his son Andrew."

Cousin Gordon looked distressed.

"Er . . . there *was* a rumor that those two gentlemen had

sired offspring in China. Illegitimate, of course. William and Andrew spent much of their lives in China as traders . . ."

"*Opium* traders," she said demurely. "In fact, opium *smugglers*."

Cousin Gordon began to look a little desperate. She went on inexorably.

"Great-grandfather was a murderer too. He killed Charlie Tyson, nicknamed the Red Barbarian, by throwing him down from the fifth story of a pagoda during a battle of the First Opium War. Charlie Tyson was the father of my father's dearest friend, Wei Jin-see. He was an opium smuggler, like great-grandfather William. So Jin-see and my father undertook to stop the opium trade that their ancestors helped to start. That's why my father spent all that money on his parliamentary crusade against opium . . ."

Cousin Gordon had his eyes fixed glumly on his blotter. She watched him for a moment with affection. Then:

"And that's why I'm going to China."

He sat up as though electrified.

"You can't go to China alone!"

"I'm not going alone. I'm going with Phyllis and Hugh Norton, some people my father knew. Mr. Norton is First Secretary of the British Consulate in Shanghai. They're presently on home leave in London. They'll be returning to Shanghai next month on the *City of Bombay* and have kindly agreed to chaperone me. I've already booked passage."

Cousin Gordon was almost gaping. "But . . . but . . . where will you stay when you get there?"

"I'd like if possible to stay with the family of my father's friend Jin-see. I believe his youngest son and his grandson are both in Shanghai. I found an address among my father's papers. Mali-lu. That means Mali Street or Road. I speak Chinese quite well, you know. Father taught me."

His consternation was growing by leaps and bounds.

"Even so, you can't stay with *Chinese people!*"

"I don't see why not. But, don't worry, Cousin Gordon. I can always stay with the Nortons, who have a house in the middle of the grounds of the British Consulate!"

She rose and gathered her things, rounded the desk, kissed his cheek.

"Dear Cousin Gordon, don't worry! Everything will be all

right. The ship stops at Marseilles, Port Said, Colombo, Calcutta, Singapore, Penang, and Hong Kong before getting to Shanghai. I'll send you a postcard from every port and I'll write at least twice a month from Shanghai. I'll be a model ward!"

Phyllis Norton gaped. "You can't stay with *natives!*"

"They're not quite *natives!*" Noelle lightly aped Phyllis' emphasis. "One of their forefathers was English. They're awfully rich. They live on a street called Mali-lu . . ."

"There's no such street! At least, not in the Settlement or French Town! If such a street exists, it must be in the *native quarters!* You can't go native, Noelle, not if you want to travel with us! The gossip would be horrendous! It would get to the Consul General's ears, perhaps even the Ambassador's, and Hugh's career would be finished! He'd be tucked away at some dusty desk in London and *forgotten!*"

Noelle laughed. "It can't be as bad at that!"

"Oh yes it can!" Phyllis snapped. "You've no *idea!* I know your father was there for many years, but he had no idea either. Latching on to that Chinaman . . ."

Noelle flared.

"My father and that 'Chinaman' were the best of friends!"

Phyllis sniffed and Noelle bit her lip. If only there were someone else to go to China with! But she knew no one else who was going, and even if she found that address on Mali-lu, she had no idea whether Jin-see's son and grandson still lived there—or whether they would even want to make her acquaintance.

She swallowed her temper.

"Of course, I'd *like* to stay with you, Phyllis, if you're sure I won't be imposing."

Phyllis laughed, a little shrill with relief. "My dear, of course not! Our villa is the largest next to the Consul General's, and we have a *crew* of servants, of course. We'd *love* to have you!"

Why? Noelle wondered. The Nortons had been no more than acquaintances of her father's. Phyllis supplied the answer.

"We'll have a marvelous time! There'll be loads of invitations! I'll be kept on the go, chaperoning you! Don't forget, dear—the most eligible young men are those on their *second* tour. First tour people—well, one can't be sure. But second tour—it's practically certain then that their firms will keep them on. Promotion, profit-sharing, pension plans. They might even end up on the Board of Directors! Play your cards well, and. . . !"

Phyllis laughed archly.

And you'll be my matron of honor I suppose, Noelle thought disgustedly. It was too bad she couldn't find someone else to travel with. Or perhaps they were all the same, these self-styled "old China hands." Her father hadn't been like that *at all* . . .

Hugh Norton said, "We're turning into the Whangpoo River. See that line, just under the surface of the water?"

Noelle peered down from the top deck of the *City of Bombay*. There was indeed a vague line stretching under the water, one side dark yellow, the other side almost blue.

"What is it?"

"It's where the muddy Whangpoo waters hit the current of the Yangtsze almost at right angles. The waters churn against each other before mingling. It's quite a famous sight. And over there . . ." He took her arm and turned her, pointing. He enjoyed playing tourist guide. "See that ruin? It used to be Woosung Fort, guarding Shanghai when Shanghai was a little walled city with six gates and twenty arrow towers. Three or four hundred years ago, long before we took it over. Now Woosung Fort is mainly used by the opium smugglers."

"Opium?" she said, and heard the sharpness in her voice. "There's no more opium trade!"

He smiled condescendingly. "Oh, I forgot—your father was a prime mover in getting Parliament to condemn the opium trade. For a while, I understand, there really was no opium in China, or hardly any. But they've started up a flourishing black market, of course. Entirely on their own, this time. No wicked British forcing opium down their throats."

She knew she looked shocked, and she turned her face away, but he laughed.

"It's the truth, my dear. A lot of opium is being grown up-country, and there's also quite a bit of smuggled stuff—Indian, Persian, Turkish, take your pick. And, of course, Jesus Opium."

From a tight throat she said "*What?*"

139

"Morphine," he answered. "When morphine was first discovered, the missionaries jumped on it. Thought they had the ideal medicine for curing opium smokers! Needless to say, they had a tremendous increase in conversions! By the time they were disillusioned, their medicine had become famous as 'Jesus Opium.'"

Noelle felt sick.

Unnoticing, Hugh went on pointing out the sights.

"Over there is one of the Yangtsze River steamers. They take seven days to steam up to Hankow, and only five days back, the Yangtsze current's that strong. Quite a lot of opium comes down from up-country on those steamers. They used to search them when they docked, so the opium used to get chucked overboard at Woosung sealed in watertight packages. Swimmers would go out to retrieve them. Lots of murders over that. Chaps who got the packages weren't always the chaps who were supposed to."

"And we didn't do anything about that?" Noelle's lips felt stiff.

Hugh laughed again, both amazed and amused by her attitude. "Why the blazes should we? It's all Chinese business now. The silly buggers! When opium was legal, everything was orderly—proper tariffs, proper licensing of shops and divans, proper price control, proper tax collection. Now it's a mess. Murder, hijacking, gang fights—and opium as plentiful as ever!"

Noelle felt her breakfast creeping back up her gullet. She had shed tears at her father's funeral and wiped her eyes with a perfumed handkerchief and thought she was grieving. Now her hands on the rail whitened as real pain flooded her heart. Had her father known about this before he died? God, please let him not have known! He'd been very withdrawn and vague in the past few years, and very silent. Perhaps he hadn't known . . . God, why hadn't she listened more patiently to the stories he'd so loved to tell? She'd give anything now to take back her little sighs and fidgetings, calculated to make him pause and say ". . . Well, then, run along Noelle, if you'd rather . . ." Hot tears came to her eyes. She wiped them away surreptitiously, but Hugh was obliviously pointing across the river.

"That's Pootung, where the factories are located. Horrible

conditions. Poor little devils of kids standing for hours in the silk mills dipping cocoons into boiling water. Tips of their fingers get like nail-heads. They sleep on mats under the cauldrons. No time wasted—one shift of kids falls to the mats while the next gets to its feet."

"And we don't do anything about *that?*"

"Not our pidgin!" Patronizingly, Hugh used the "old China hand" expression for "not our business." "Pootung's not in the Settlement. Up to the Chinks, what happens in Pootung."

"Who owns the factories?"

"Oh—Japanese, British, Chinese. There's British capital in most of them."

"Then why isn't it our 'pidgin'?"

"*We* don't put the kids to work in the factories! It's the parents—destitute refugees from the warlord areas. We can't do anything about that."

"We might try seeing to it that the adults are paid enough so they don't have to put their kids to work. We could forbid child labor . . ."

"My dear!" He laughed tolerantly. "All that's *not* our pidgin! You'll understand when you've been here a while. *Our* pidgin is what happens in the International Settlement. We make the laws there—"

"I know," she cut in icily. It was one of the things she remembered that her father had told her. "It's called extraterritoriality. If a Chinese wants to sue a Britisher, he has to do it in the British Consular Court. Chinese laws don't apply—doesn't seem quite British-fair-play, does it? A Chinese in China subject to British law?"

He stared at her in astonishment.

"I say! You sound positively *anti!* It's our *right,* y'know. Our *right* by the treaties that ended the Opium Wars—"

"I know," she cut in again. "The Chinese call them the Unequal Treaties."

The steamer's deep-throated siren drowned out his reply. Noelle turned away to gaze over the rail. The steamer was slowing, its propellors churning the thick yellow water. Dozens of small craft bobbed busily around. To her left, the chimney stacks of Pootung belched filthy smoke. To her right, ghostly in the distance, rose the skyline of the city.

Her heart rose. The city of Shanghai, where her father had been happy. In England he had been content—even joyful, when the fight against opium was succeeding. But *happy* . . . With the insight that her sudden grieving for her father had brought her, she knew now that her father had been happy only here in this city, with his friend Jin-see, Jin-see's beautiful wife Olan, his son Great Dragon, his beloved daughter Julie. Only when he spoke of them had the light come to his eyes that had come for the last time at the moment of his death. She watched the skyline of the city sliding out of the distance, becoming clearer . . . She would find out what it was that had made her father happy in this city.

But at first she couldn't find a trace of him. She went to Jinsey Mathes, the company her father and Jin-see had opened together, that was now a conglomerate financial empire from which most of her income still came. She entered the stately five-story building that overlooked the Whangpoo River and climbed broad flights of marble steps, shining with polish and pocked with age. Her father had walked up and down these steps thousands of times. The office he had shared with Jin-see was on the top floor. But the top floor was now one huge room in which a hundred people worked busily. A clerk came to the counter to ask what she wanted. "I think I'm in the wrong place," she said. It was the wrong place: there was nothing left of her father here.

Nor was there at the Shanghai Club. On Ladies' Night she peered into the famous "longest bar in the world" and couldn't imagine her father in it for a moment. She tried to find the house he had lived in: where once had stood the London-style red brick house he had described to her, there now stood a block of apartments. He had spoken of carriages: there were a few left, but mostly now motorcars polluted the air. He had spoken of the pretty grass verge that bordered the Whangpoo River along the Bund: a verge still existed but it was just littered dirt now. She bought a map of Shanghai from Kelly & Walsh, booksellers that she remembered her father mentioning. The map showed the International Settlement and French Town in full detail, all the foreign street names printed plainly in English. But there was no Mali-lu, and the Chinese areas of the city, Nantao, Chapei, Pootung, and the Chinese City, were represented as irregular blank shapes.

She tried to imagine her father at the unending series of dinner parties, and she couldn't. He wouldn't have had patience for the ritual gaiety, the pretentiousness. And there were so many parties! Shoals of invitation cards washed over the hall table. Of course, there were two invitations to each party, one for Noelle, one for the Nortons. "Missee Phyllee vellee happy," her amah said, grinning. Put together with what Phyllis had said before they left London, that seemed to mean that Phyllis, as chaperone, was being invited to more parties than she had ever before attended. Noelle shrugged: at least she was paying her keep!

The frequency of parties necessitated many new dresses. Phyllis bought poplin and taffeta from Lane Crawford, proper British stuff from a proper British store, and sniffed when Noelle went to the Chinese silk shops. Noelle stroked lengths of decadently gorgeous silk and brocade, and thought she had found a little of her father: he must often have seen Jin-see's wife and daughter in fabrics such as these.

The tailor who made up their new dresses was a jolly, fat Chinese who had somehow cornered the market on dressmaking for British Consulate ladies. He came with an enormous cloth-wrapped bundle of fabrics, fashion books, and half-sewn dresses, and talked unceasingly, his mouth full of pins, as he marked and fitted. He spoke his own brand of English fluently, calling his customers "Mississy" instead of the usual "Missy." Perhaps, Noelle said, he thought it a translation of the polite Chinese form of address, a kind of double-barreled "Sir-Madam." Phyllis sniffed: no self-respecting member of the British Consular staff admitted to knowing more Chinese than "maskee" and "chop-chop."

On their arrival in Shanghai, Phyllis had turned into a duchess. Phyllis Norton, who lived in a mews in London and did her own cooking and cleaning, was transformed into a duchess as soon as she stepped into the second-largest house after the Consul General's in the parklike grounds of the British Consulate. She was languid. She sat at breakfast at eleven in the morning and picked at her food and complained. Of the weather. Of Cook's carelessness—"Don't you think the potatoes were *burned* last night?" Of her amah's negligence: "The silly twit let my bathwater get *tepid* this morning!" Of the city: "My dear, the *smells* on Nanking Road! In dear old London one does *forget* what it can be *like* on tour!"

One morning, between Hugh's departure for his office and Phyllis' eleven o'clock rising, Noelle, alone at the breakfast table, tried out her Chinese on the Number One Boy. His eyes suddenly lost their formality and became human. He answered her in a dialect which, to her joy, she understood. They conversed happily until they heard Phyllis on the stairs. After that, whenever possible, Noelle rose before Phyllis and chatted with Number One Boy as he served her breakfast, feeling that she had found a little of what had made her father happy in this city.

She couldn't talk to her amah in Chinese because amah spoke a dialect she didn't understand. All the same, in pidgin, she tried to explain to her amah: "Long-time before, my papa stay Shanghai-side. My papa love Shanghai-side. When I talk Number One Boy, when I talk you, I think of my papa."

Amah, who was of indeterminate age, but not young, chuckled.

"Maybe you all-same you papa. You likee Chinee peoples, Chinee peoples likee you."

"My papa velly-good flend name Wei Jin-see. You savvy? You savvy Wei family?"

"How I savvy Wei fambly! Have got plenty, plenty Wei!"

"Wei family live Mali-lu. You savvy Mali-lu?"

"I flom Ningpo! How I savvy Shanghai-side Mali-lu! More better you sleep now, missy. I lub-lub back."

So Noelle fell asleep to the rhythmic rub of amah's hands up and down her spine and dreamt that she walked a wide avenue that was sign-posted "Mali-lu" every ten yards.

Phyllis dropped a gold-engraved invitation card on the breakfast table.

"It's for the once-a-year dinner-dance that the Municipal Council gives for the principal ratepayers. Diplomats don't pay rates, of course, but we're always invited too. It'll be boring, I'm afraid."

Noelle said demurely, "I'm sure Helen's family are invited. I'll arrange to go with them so you can stay home."

"Oh, Hugh and I couldn't let you go with other people!"

"Then let's all stay home."

"I'm afraid we can't do that. As diplomats, we do have *obligations*."

In the lobby of the Palace Hotel a long line of guests wound slowly toward the Grand Ballroom at the door of which the Secretary General of the Municipal Council and his wife, Mr. and Mrs. Stirling Fessenden, were receiving. Phyllis and Noelle, shepherded by Hugh, joined the line behind Helen and her family. The two girls threw themselves into each other's arms, giggling, each declaring the other looked divine. This was going to be a *real party!* Not one of those stuffy imitations where tough beef was served on fancy platters and chairs were pushed back and dusty carpets rolled up for dancing to cracked gramophone records. Inside the ballroom, ranks of tables around the walls sparkled with damask, crystal and silver, and tray upon tray of food. Beautiful people, beautifully dressed, swayed beautifully to the music of real violins. White-gloved waiters offered champagne. Groups of young men stood about, trying to look nonchalant, eyeing the girls. Tonight was going to be *different!* Tonight was going to be *fun!*

"Hugh!" Phyllis sounded as though she had bitten into an unripe lime. "Are those people ahead there *Chinese?*"

"Er—yes." Hugh looked uncomfortable.

"At *Stirling Fessenden's* party?"

Noelle squeezed Helen's hand. "Horrors, Phyllis! Hadn't we better *leave?*"

Phyllis glared. Helen's mother said pacifically, "You diplomats haven't caught up yet, Phyllis. We bankers have been having mixed parties for some time now. More enjoyable, really. Some of those all-British parties *do* get *stuffy*."

Hugh said unhappily, "Move on, dear. You're letting the line sag."

Noelle and Helen hugged each other behind Phyllis' back. Tonight was really going to be special!

They reached the receiving line, murmured, shook hands, bowed, passed into the kaleidoscope of the great hall. A resplendent maître d'hôtel offered dance cards with tiny, tasseled pencils. Young men presented themselves, murmuring their names, asking to be registered for dances. "The waltz, please?"

"The fox-trot?" Noelle was whirled away. Time dissolved into a joyous flurry of floating about in the arms of admiring young men, feeling beautiful, being desired, knowing herself desirable. The music was better than ever before, the young men handsomer, herself more glowing. At some magic time she looked up to see yet another man bowing before her, not a young man, a middle-aged one with wrinkles around his smiling eyes. How delightful! She beamed at him. His deep voice came pleasantly to her ears under the decibels of sound: "Miss Mathes, I am Dr. Macpherson. I'm sure your dance card has long been filled, but perhaps you'll make room for an old man whose father knew your father?"

The lights and music faded. She could say nothing: her breath was snatched away. He went on: "My father practiced medicine here for almost fifty years. He was a bad-tempered grouch with few friends, but your father was one of them."

The band struck up a waltz. The doctor held out his arms, and she stepped into them. An approaching young man stopped short, looking angry. She didn't notice.

"Dr. Macpherson, please tell me about my father and yours."

He swung her smoothly out onto the floor, his kind eyes smiling.

"I hoped you'd want to know . . . They met in 1860, or thereabouts, just after your father returned from Peking where, because of his excellent Chinese, he'd been chosen to help with the signing of the Treaty of Tientsin. Everybody was congratulating him, and my father thought he'd be the typical cocky young Englishman, basking in his moment of glory. But when he learned that my father was donating three evenings a week to a clinic for opium addicts, he told my father how much he hated opium. That made them a minority of two in a community of enthusiastic opium traders, so naturally they became fast friends. They worked together, your father contributing funds for shelters for opium addicts, and my father caring for the addicts. There's not much that can be done for addicts, you know. Most often it was a matter of helping them die with some dignity under a roof instead of sprawled in some gutter . . ."

She remembered her father saying the same words. She had been ten or eleven years old, fidgeting, trying not to show impatience . . . Her heart lurched, and tears came to her eyes. He led her off the floor.

"Too much dancing, and no food!"

He commandeered a waiter who found a place for them at a table and brought them platters of food. She forked up a mouthful of something that she was sure she couldn't swallow, but it tasted wonderful and she ate it all while he watched her. When her plate was empty, he said gently, "It wasn't only hunger that made you feel faint . . . You were upset about your father."

She nodded like a child. "Yes. He was so much older. I never listened to him properly. Ever since I arrived here, I've been trying to *find* my father. To find out what made him happy here. But I found so little. And then suddenly tonight, you came . . ."

Tears came to her eyes again, and he handed her his handkerchief, smiling very kindly.

"I understand," he said, and for a while spoke to her gently, not mentioning opium, telling her little anecdotes of life in China fifty years ago that he had heard from his own father. She listened dreamily, feeling that she was living on two levels, hearing and seeing the gaiety of the party, hearing and seeing too her father—able for the first time to hear and see him clearly in the setting that the doctor was creating.

She said, "I know now why I couldn't find my father. He lived in an in-between world. There were the foreigners, the English, French, Americans, all the others who came to make their fortunes in this new bonanza city. And there were the Chinese who had always lived here. And my father—yours too, I suppose—lived somewhere between them."

He nodded. "It's only recently that Chinese and foreigners have begun to mix socially. In the time of your father and mine the foreigners thought it a disgrace to have more than minimal business relations with the Chinese. My father was considered a sort of mad eccentric, working with Chinese drug addicts. But your father, whose best friend was a Chinese—the foreigners considered him a traitor."

"Did your father know my father's best friend, Wei Jin-see?"

"Yes. He served him twice. He delivered one of his children. That might have been the very first time that a Chinese asked a foreign doctor to attend his wife in childbirth. It was a very difficult birth. The baby, a girl, was born deformed and died soon after. Many years later Jin-see had an accident to his eyes. My father managed to save the sight of one of them."

She cried out, "How strange! You know, my father came back to China in 1900. That was the last time he saw Jin-see, who died shortly after. But Jin-see still had enough sight left actually to *see* my father. And it was your father who saved Jin-see's sight!"

He smiled. "To coin a phrase—it's a small world!"

She said with a laugh, "Do you know Jin-see's family? There were a son and a daughter of whom my father often spoke, but they are dead now. I believe there was a younger son, though my father never spoke of him much, and a grandson. I think they're both living in Shanghai now."

"I don't know about the grandson, but there is a second son who was much younger than Jin-see's other two children because their mother was not his mother—he was the son of a concubine . . ."

Perhaps that was why her father had hardly ever mentioned him. Her father had loved Jin-see's wife Olan. Perhaps he'd been distressed when Jin-see took a concubine . . .

". . . here tonight," the doctor finished.

"What?" she said. "I'm sorry, I was thinking of something. What did you say?"

"I said the younger son is one of the new breed of Chinese who are prominent in the foreign community. On the Board of Directors of the Hong Kong & Shanghai Bank and the Banque de l'Indochine. Treasurer of the International Refugee Relief Committee. Speaks excellent English. A fine-looking young man. He's here tonight."

Her heart leaped.

"Oh, Dr. Macpherson, will you introduce me?"

"Of course, if you wish. He has a strange name: Great Fish, though they call him 'Little Fish.' Come along, we'll go and find him . . . though I believe that's your chaperone Mrs. Norton waving to you over there."

Noelle jumped up, laughing, turning her back.

"I don't see her! Come on, Doctor!"

They found Great Fish in the alcove of a red velvet–draped

French window, in discussion with a group of men which included Helen's father who was somebody in the Hong Kong & Shanghai Bank. As they approached, the group was breaking up. Helen's father said to Noelle, "My dear, Phyllis has been looking for you for an hour."

Noelle didn't answer—didn't hear him—for she was looking at Great Fish. In an eerie kind of way she recognized him for he fit so well the description she had heard her father give of Great Fish's father Jin-see. The roundness of his eyes and the fairness of his skin came from that English ancestor. Indeed, he was handsome. And bold. And challenging.

Dr. Macpherson said, "Miss Mathes—Mr. Wei Ta-yu. Mr. Wei, Noelle Mathes is the daughter of your father's old friend Donald Mathes."

His eyes on hers became deep and glowing. She laughed with pleasure and said in Chinese, "Great Fish, our ancestors were the best of friends."

He answered her in Chinese, "So our spirits, yours and mine, must already know each other." And then, in English, "You are very beautiful, Noelle Mathes."

Chapter XIV

1922

ZUNG SHOOK HIS HEAD at Didi in mock exasperation. "Did you have to take him to the chief of police?"

Didi answered stolidly, "It's bad luck that the chief happened to be present. Where I took him was police headquarters, which is what it says in the book—which I'm sure you've never read. Smugglers are to be taken to police headquarters. Zung—it's simple. They posted me to Lung-hwa because there's no opium there to speak of and they thought I couldn't make a nuisance of myself, but I caught a smuggler with ten pounds of opium in the bottom of a rice sack and I took him to police headquarters, like it says in the book."

"And the smuggler had already paid protection, so all you did was give yourself and the police a headache. What did they do with him?"

"Lugged him off somewhere while I was making my report. He was probably back on the street before I finished. At least I destroyed the opium before taking him in: if that got to police headquarters, it would have been like putting it in the bank."

"How did you destroy it?"

"Made him dig a trench beside the river. It filled up with water as he dug and I dropped the opium into it and mashed the whole thing into a muddy mess."

Zung sighed. "Destroying ten pounds of opium is like taking a cup of water out of the sea!" He glanced around. Then, in a low voice, "Didi, why don't you resign?"

Didi didn't trouble to lower his voice. "Why don't they fire me? They hate me. I'm a damned nuisance. But they don't fire me. Why?"

Zung stared at him for a moment, eyes blank. Then, with a quick return to his usual tones, "Did you get your invitation to the reception next week?"

"I threw it away."

"But you've got to be there. We've all got to be there to say good-bye to our old director and greet the new one."

"Is the new director going to stop the bogus bonus system? If so, I'll attend the reception."

Zung flicked a sardonic eyebrow. "He'll probably *extend* the bonus system . . . In any case, you've got to attend."

"Will they fire me if I don't?"

"That's a question with no answer because you *are* going, like all the rest of us."

"Who's the new director?"

"His name hasn't been announced yet. Didi, will you please stop arguing? You can't get out of it."

Didi grinned suddenly. "Oh all right! The things I do for you that I wouldn't do for anybody else!"

"And the things *I* do for *you*—or try to—that you don't even realize!" Again the glance around, again the low tone. "Don't forget that I asked you to resign . . ."

He walked away. Didi watched him, puzzled for a moment. What did he mean? Whatever—his friendship was the only thing that made the sour joke of the Bureau tolerable. He grinned wryly. Here was Zung trying to get him to resign, and if not for Zung things would be so awful that perhaps he *would* resign.

He dressed up for the reception. Zung and the other Bureau agents would be wearing foreign-style suits which, with their bonuses, they could well afford. He had nothing but his threadbare long gowns, so he decided to wear one of his father's mandarin robes: ankle-length silver-gray satin split to the waist in front to show an underskirt of knife-pleated white silk.

151

Neat, round, white silk collar. Sleeves long enough to hide his hands. He inspected himself in the mirror and thought that he looked rather exotic. It must be ten years since the last mandarin put on the last mandarin robe!

On his way out of the house, he stopped at the door of Ah-fet's study to look in on Belle. As usual, she was absorbed in a mass of papers. She was now chief editor of *New Culture*. After a moment she looked up and exclaimed admiringly, "You look very fine! Where are you going?"

"To a reception at the Astor House Hotel that all the Bureau agents are required to attend. We're getting a new director."

She frowned. "I should have thought a new director for the Bureau would be the last thing on Peking's mind. Warlords creating havoc, the country in chaos, and Peking bothers to appoint a new director for the Bureau?"

He didn't answer. He hadn't given that a thought, but she was right. How sharp she was!

She went on. "It's very curious! Do find out what you can at the reception and let me know. Might be useful for *New Culture*. And you look splendid. Don't go and hide behind a curtain or something. Walk around. Talk to people."

He smiled at her. "I will!"

Her hair was tangled where she'd pushed her fingers through it. She had a smudge on one cheek. She was pale, as usual, her face too thin and bony. She flashed her remarkably lovely smile at him and returned to her papers.

He decided to walk the three or four miles to the Astor House Hotel. It would make him late for the reception, but he didn't care about that. The evening was too fine to waste. Sunday peace reigned over uncrowded streets. For once, the city seemed to be an abode for human beings. But soon a squad of newsboys raced around a corner, waving papers, singsonging headlines. *Wu Pei-fu battles Feng Yu-hsiang and Chang Tso-lin.* Warlords! Last year Wu Pei-fu had defeated Chang Tso-lin and forced him back into Manchuria. This year, Chang Tso-lin had emerged to join Feng Yu-hsiang in trying to wrest control of the Yangtsze Valley from Wu Pei-fu. More millions of refugees were being thrown off like scum from the violent waves of fighting, were pouring into the cities to eke out their lives until the day their wasted bodies were picked out of the gutters by the early-morning mortuary crews. It was cosmic madness. It was as though the world were made, not for life, but for death and dying.

And refugees weren't the only people pouring into the cities. On the Bund, along the dirt strips beside the river that used to be green with grass and flowers, the rich, fat wives of rich, fat provincial merchants took the air, their children playing about them. The same provincial merchants who protested the Unequal Treaties and demanded the return of Shanghai to Chinese control, secretly sent their families scurrying to Shanghai, with all their transportable wealth. The foreigners were hated imperialists—but they had law and order. Inside the Settlement and French Town, rich people could live in safety.

The shrill voices of the gamboling children echoing in his ears, Didi crossed Garden Bridge that spanned the Soochow Creek where it joined the river, traversed Whangpoo Road, mounted a broad flight of marble steps, and entered the lobby of the Astor House Hotel. Rich, gold-colored drapes and carpets, gold upholstered armchairs, golden sconce lights against molded plaster walls. Everything rich and golden, including the people who moved about, their tinkling laughter like an aura around them. An eddy of people was heading for the entrance to the reception hall. Didi fell in behind a group of English people, who were chatting in their penetrating English voices.

"Phyllis was simply *mortified*, my dear!"

"Is she here this evening?"

"Oh *no!* She wouldn't even go to the wedding! Can't say I blame her. She brought the girl out from England, introduced her everywhere, chaperoned her—and the next thing you know, she goes and marries a Chinaman! Rich, I'll grant you, and quite handsome, rather European-looking in fact, probably has some foreign blood. But all the same—I ask you!"

The voices faded as the group entered the reception hall. Didi followed them. There was no receiving line at the door. Instead, there was a dais at the end of the long room on which stood the guests of honor. Toward the back, the retiring director and his wife, looking neglected. Captain Fiori of the French police—Didi had run foul of him on two or three occasions. Fessenden of the Municipal Council. The Chinese Mayor of

Greater Shanghai. The chief of the Chinese police—Didi winced, thinking of the confrontation a few days ago when he'd brought in the smuggler. There were also a couple of older foreign women, ropes of pearls overhanging their clifflike bosoms, and a very young girl—Didi had an impression of fair-haired beauty, but she was partially hidden behind a tall, slim, black-haired man in foreign-style striped trousers and tailcoat, who was standing with his back to the room. He must be the new director. And . . . was that *Zung* standing beside him?

Didi was suddenly conscious that people were staring at him. Staring, then turning to whisper behind their hands to their companions. Was it his mandarin robe? It wasn't . . . The people were staring at his face . . . He took a glass of champagne from the tray of a passing waiter and made toward the alcove of one of the French windows, remembering wryly what Belle had said about hiding behind a curtain. But this was some kind of emergency. Why on earth were people staring at him?

The alcove was already occupied by one of his colleagues from the Bureau holding a bottle of brandy—no genteel champagne for him. Red and unsteady, he sniggered at Didi, "You really do look like him!"

"Like who?"

"The new director! You could be his brother! And he has the same surname as you!"

The solid floor beneath Didi's feet seemed to quake.

The man sniggered again. "Go on! Go up to the dais. Zung left instructions that as soon as you arrived you were to go and meet the new director."

Didi's heart began to bang around in his chest, sending the blood charging through his veins in uneven spurts, hot as fire, cold as ice. He began to push his way toward the dais, unconscious of the stares and murmurs that trailed behind him like a ship's wake, dying away into hushed stillness. On the dais, talk began to fade as, struck by the abnormal quiet, the guests of honor turned to seek the source of the unease. Soon, total silence reigned. In a throbbing void, Didi reached the dais and stepped up onto it. The new director slowly turned to him. They stood face to face, a foot apart, looking into each other's eyes: two men of the same height, the same coloring, the same features; two men born within an hour and a hundred yards of each other, of the same blood, the same ancestors. Two enemies.

For what seemed a long time, no one moved or spoke. Then the golden-haired girl put a hand on Great Fish's arm.

"Darling . . ." Her high English voice carried clearly around the hushed hall. "He looks just like you! He must be your father's grandson!"

Fished smiled at Didi, a small, amused, infinitely cruel smile. "He is. The *scoundrel*."

Didi smiled calmly back. Now Zung would laugh and say, "*Didi* a scoundrel! He's so honest that he's stupid!" Or the chief of police would say, "He's that idiot who arrests smugglers who've already paid protection!" Or Fiori would say, "He's that damned nuisance who's forever poking about where he's not wanted!" And everybody would know who was the real scoundrel.

No one said anything. After some tearing, pulsing moments, Didi snatched his eyes from Fish to glance at Zung. Zung merely shook his head slightly and flicked an eye toward the door. Didi's chest swelled to bursting. A great hand snatched away his breath. Gasping, he turned back to Fish. But the girl stepped forward, her eyes flashing blue as turquoise gemstones.

"Why did you come?" she said contemptuously. "Isn't it enough that you're ruining the work of the Bureau, and betraying your ancestors? Did you want to ruin this reception too? Ruin my husband's big day? Well, it doesn't matter! Now that he's director, he's going to *crush* you and your filthy kind!"

He was astounded. He stared at her, open-mouthed, and spoke wonderingly, "You've got it wrong . . ."

Fish pushed him. Laid a hand against his shoulder and shoved hard. A turmoil of things began to happen all together. He went flying backward and landed with a jarring thud on his back on the floor. The chief of police grabbed him, shouting out an order. Secret service men who had been dotted around the room came surging forward. Zung took the chief's arm, murmured soothingly in his ear. Fish said loudly, in a tone of forbearance, "Let him go! Zung, get him out of here!"

Zung left the chief and helped him up, murmuring urgently, "Let's go, Didi . . ." He wrenched away from Zung and staggered dizzily toward the dais. Secret service men grabbed his arms and rushed him past a blur of gaping people, through the golden-colored lobby, out into the street. Then he was in a fast-moving carriage, swaying along, blinded and deafened by a roaring wind that whipped and tossed his spirit as the great storms of the Shansi mountains whipped and tossed trees as though they were grass.

Afterward, he could never remember much of that ride. At one point he became conscious that Zung was in the carriage with him, an unfamiliar Zung, unsmiling, looking somehow agonized.

Zung mumbled, "I'm sorry, Didi . . . I'm sorry . . . I did try to get you to resign . . . You weren't fired because he had to keep track of you, and it was easier to do so while you were employed at the Bureau. But I did try to get you to resign—"

"You mean he's behind it all? The bonuses? The squeeze? Everything?"

"No . . . He's high up. But he's not at the top. At the top is Big-ears Doo. But it's Fish who pays me. I like you, Didi. In a way, I *love* you. But he pays me . . ."

When the carriage stopped at Pratt's gate, Zung said painfully, "Don't suppose you'll want to see me again."

It was nearly dark and he couldn't see Zung's face, but he heard the pain in his voice and thought how strange it sounded. Zung's voice had always been gay and friendly. Zung had been his only friend. He mumbled, "Don't suppose we'll meet again . . . I like you too, Zung."

He stumbled out of the carriage and stood on the curb and looked up at the dark blob that was Zung's head.

"Who was that English girl? Fish's wife?"

He felt the reluctance in Zung's voice.

"Noelle Mathes."

He watched the carriage rattle away into the darkness and heard himself give a short, sharp, bitter bark of laughter. Hadn't her father told her about Fish? If her father's letter were not lost . . . He was sure he'd packed it with the soul tablets, but where was it now? If he had it, he could show it to her, show her, all written out in her own father's handwriting, what her father had thought of Fish.

But it wasn't worth the trouble. Nothing was worth the trouble anymore. He turned wearily toward the house.

As he let himself in the front door, Belle called, "You're back early!"

He stopped in her doorway.

"You were right. It wasn't Peking that appointed the new director of the Bureau. It was Big-ears Doo. And the new director is my relative Great Fish. You know—the murderer."

He ran up to his room. As he flung open the door, the light from the hallway glinted on the tablets on his ancestral altar, making them glow. He thought that the ancestors were alert, waiting, listening for what he had to say. He knelt before them and kowtowed.

". . . I am sorry, Father. I tried to be like you, but I didn't know how. I have failed. I am sorry that you have a fool and a failure for a descendant."

He slumped to the floor, too drained, too hurting, to do more than endure the moments as they passed slowly, one by one. He heard Belle enter the room, felt her sit on the floor beside him. Her presence was familiar, undisturbing, and he did not move.

She said, "What did you say to your ancestors?"

He said dully, "I apologized for having failed."

"You haven't failed!" she said crisply.

He said nothing. Hadn't she heard what he'd just told her downstairs?

She said again, "You haven't failed! Listen to me, Didi. What, exactly, was the 'life-duty' that your forefathers undertook?"

Still he said nothing. She knew. He'd told her before.

She answered herself. "They undertook to force the British to stop shipping opium to China, to stop the cultivation of poppies in China, and thus finish off the opium trade. That was it, wasn't it? Well, *all that has been done.* You yourself did a great deal by getting rid of poppies in Shansi in only five years. By 1913 there were virtually no more poppies being grown anywhere in China. In that year the British stopped their opium shipments to China. The trade was finished."

He said nothing. She didn't understand! It had never really stopped! It was all still going on!

"It started up again," she said, "and it's roaring on again—but now it's something entirely different. Opium today is far from the single, straightforward objective of the life-duty your ancestors formulated. Opium today is many different things, a means to many ends. It finances the warlords, and Sun Yat-sen who has vowed to subdue the warlords, and the great criminals like Big-ears Doo who pull the strings that control everything. What you think of as your 'life-duty' isn't even relevant anymore!"

He realized at last that she was saying something vital. He sat very still, cross-legged on the floor, feeling virtue emanate from her, straining for her next words.

She went on. "Now there's only one duty that's relevant to all of us: to save our country. Our country is deathly ill, the government in such disarray that it cannot govern, criminals preying on the cities, warlords tearing the countryside apart. We can no longer wait for Sun Yat-sen to save us. He's been bumbling along for nearly thirty years. The 'First Revolution.' The 'Second Revolution.' The 'Three Principles of the People.' Now the Great Northern March that'll subdue the warlords and unite the country. But he's still training officers for it at his Whampoa Military Academy, while the mess gets bigger and bigger. We can't wait for him any longer!"

Her thin face was rapt and vibrant with passion.

She said, "I've joined the Communist party. We're still tiny, about two thousand members, but there were only thirteen when the party started last July. We work very hard. When you left for the reception, you thought I was writing another editorial for *New Culture*. I wasn't. I was drawing up lists of factory workers I've trained to lead their own groups and recruit others. When we're ready, we're going to organize a general strike of all the factory workers in Shanghai, against starvation wages, child labor, foreign domination—the ancient evils. It'll be our first big undertaking. We hope it'll fire up the country."

She had been sitting on the floor beside him. Now she knelt so that her face was on a level with his and her dark eyes could look directly into his.

She said, "Didi, you could help . . . The way you organized the Shansi farmers was marvelous. You have a talent for it. Will you join us? It would be a new kind of life-duty."

"Yes," he said at once. "Of course I'll join."

He felt a great surge of elation. He was thirty-five years old. Nearly all his adult life he had pursued the life-duty without noticing that its rules had become shibboleths that today she had demolished. It was right, it was fitting, that a new life-duty should rise from the ruins. His ancestors approved—he saw that their tablets were no longer glowing; they rested in shadow and were tranquil, benign.

And there was something else. Once he had said to this woman, "I have no involvements." But he did have one. Not an easy one, as with the plump girls of Shansi. A hard, demanding one with this woman herself. This thin, frail, strong, passionate woman.

He said, "Belle, will you marry me?"

She was startled. She bowed her head and the black wings of her hair fell forward to hide her face. She murmured, "I've not thought of being married. No—that's not true. I've thought that I would not be married. I'm not the type of woman that men want to marry."

He said gravely, "There's a type of man that women don't want to marry. A type like me—a fool who blunders about trying to do his best, never knowing how till someone like you tells him. Shall we two unmarriageable types marry each other?"

She laughed and raised her head and said, "All right. I'd like to."

Chapter XV
May 30, 1925

NOELLE PAUSED in her letter writing to gaze around her living room, which was really a bright and airy glassed-in porch, exquisitely appointed with silken carpets, brocade drapes, deep armchairs, rosewood furniture. The house on Mali-lu had turned out to be absolutely lovely! Smiling, she returned to her letter. She was trying to describe to Cousin Gordon of the dusty deed boxes the kind of life she was living, but she was afraid he wouldn't be able to conceive of it! She paused to think of a new adjective, heard someone shouting out in the courtyard, paid no attention: Chinese servants in Chinese households were not nearly as well trained as in the British Consulate. When more shouts followed, she leaned to peer from a window: out in the pink marble courtyard a number of people were running toward the reflecting pool . . . With a sharp stab of fear, she glanced at the corner of the room where Donnie had been playing, and the next instant, mouth dry, was running too.

She reached the pool as the gardener stepped out of it, the limp, dripping little body in his arms. She snatched the child from him and put her ear to the slack lips. He was breathing! Thank God, he was breathing! She rushed with him back to the house, servants streaming behind her. Indoors, she thrust the child into baby-amah's arms and flew to the telephone, cranked the handle, jammed the receiver to her ear. Nothing but humming and crackling! Again and again she cranked, her mind screaming at the operator *Answer! Answer!* At last the answer came, faint and harried, and she gave Dr. Macpherson's number. Please God, let him be home! It's only five o'clock, please let him not have left yet for a party! At the other end someone lifted the receiver and said "Hello," the voice as faint and harried as the operator's. Dr. Mac's wife Mary! He must still be at home! Relief constricted her throat so tightly that she had to swallow before she could speak.

"Mary, it's Noelle Wei. Please put Dr. Mac on quickly!"

Mary said something that was drowned out by static. She began to panic.

"Mary, I can't hear you! Just get Dr. Mac, Mary! Donnie fell into the pool . . ."

The line suddenly cleared and Mary's voice boomed in her ear.

". . . at the hospital. He phoned that he can't get back . . ."

"Then I'll take Donnie to the hospital . . ."

"Wait, Noelle! You can't get there! There's a strike on! The streets are jam packed . . ."

The line went dead.

Noelle banged down the receiver. She had to try and get to the hospital! She couldn't just sit here with Donnie looking dead! She turned to the servants clustered in the doorway.

"One of you, run and tell the driver to bring the car round. Baby-amah, you come with me. We're going to take Donnie to the hospital."

None of them moved.

What was wrong with them?

She stamped her foot and shouted, "GO!"

Baby-amah gulped. "We can't get out of the courtyard."

"Why not?"

"The gate is locked."

Wild anger flashed through her. Donnie dying perhaps, and these idiots making difficulties!

"Get the key then! Unlock the gate!"

They stared at her, frightened but unmoving.

She rushed to the nearest amah and shook her.

"Get the key! Where is the key?"

"Susu has it," the woman muttered dazedly.

"Who's Susu?"

Someone behind her said quietly, "I am Susu."

Noelle swung around.

A woman had entered from the courtyard door, an ordinary-looking woman who bowed to her, neither timid nor assertive, then went to the sofa where baby-amah was sitting with Donnie. The servants evidently knew the woman, for their eyes turned with relief from Noelle to her, and baby-amah sat back as though offering Donnie for her inspection. Noelle rushed forward furiously, then stopped, stricken. Donnie too seemed to be responding to the woman! He was stirring. His eyes were flickering.

The woman turned to Noelle and spoke warmly, in a lilting dialect that Noelle had no trouble understanding.

"It's not serious! He got a fright in the water, so his spirit left his body, but it's coming back now."

Donnie opened his eyes—his great, blue Carradine eyes that were all the more startling against his black brows and hair. With a sob she rushed to him and gathered him up in her arms. For a moment he was quiescent, then he began to wriggle and giggle, suddenly well again, her beautiful, blue-eyed son.

"Donnie falled down!" he shouted. "Donnie falled in the water!"

Laughing with joy, baby-amah reached for Donnie: it was her turn to kiss and hug him. The woman nodded to the other servants, who withdrew quietly, murmuring. The woman held out to Noelle a bowl she had brought with her.

"It's tea made from dried orange peel and herbs. It soothes the blood. Will you taste it?"

Noelle found herself reaching for the bowl. She sipped, and her mouth was filled with a strong, bitter taste that an instant later turned wonderfully sweet. Involuntarily, she sipped again. The woman said, "It's good, isn't it? Shall we tell baby-amah to give it to Donnie and put him to bed? He needs rest after his fright. Then you and I can talk."

The woman was watching her intently. Her eyes, ringed in arcs of short, black lashes, seemed to be sending a message that knocked at Noelle's mind. She nodded slowly. Baby-amah left the room with Donnie, taking the bowl. The woman sat down on the sofa and Noelle sat beside her, knowledge rising in her mind like yeast. She said, "Susu, who are you?"

Susu said slowly, "I am his concubine. I have been with him for fifteen years."

Noelle closed her eyes. Now that it was said out loud, she knew that she had known it ever since the servant first said the name Susu. She was still too stunned by her fright over Donnie to feel deeply, but soon the outrage, the fury, would come rushing in. She waited tensely . . .

Nothing came. She began to feel calm. In a strange way, relieved. In the midst of the joys of marriage, every now and then she had felt uneasy, wondering with a little stab of dread if she was living in a fool's paradise. There was so much she didn't know about Fish. He spoke so seldom of his past, and when he did she always had the feeling that what he said had been carefully selected. He never said spontaneous things like "My father and I used to . . ." He was secretive and watchful.

But now she had learned something about him. Something very important. And it wasn't dreadful. And, not being dreadful, it was in its own way—good.

She opened her eyes. Susu was watching her anxiously. She said earnestly, "Noelle, he hasn't been to me since you were married. I'm a kind of fixture here. The manager. I run the whole compound for Fish. It would be most inconvenient for him to send me away. Please believe me!"

Susu's face was warm, honest, aging, ageless. The light in her eyes was sincerity itself. It was impossible not to believe Susu. Susu read her expression and laughed in relief.

"Oh, Noelle, you and I will be friends! But we must never tell him. He is too prideful to bear it!"

Noelle laughed too. Susu was right! If Fish knew that she knew about Susu and was not jealous, he would be utterly furious! Try explaining *this* to Cousin Gordon!

Susu rose and poured tea from the ever-present teapot, kept warm in its cosily lined basket.

"Noelle, I know all about you, so I want you to know all about me . . . I met Fish when I came to this compound one day about fifteen years ago with my father. Fish had ordered four ancestor tablets from my father, who is a stone carver.

When he came to deliver them, I came with him because he wasn't well that day. I sat in the room while Fish and my father talked. A few days later, we were astonished to receive an offer from Fish for me. He wrote my father that he had found me attractive, quiet, and well-mannered. Frankly, he said, he hated brothels and he also hated lying with the housemaids because that made them giggly and demanding. He offered me the position of concubine—the only one, he said. He might marry one day, but until then there would be no other woman. He was fastidious, he said. He offered my father a fine price for me. My father wouldn't have accepted if I had objected, but I didn't object at all. I was already twenty-five years old—Fish was twenty—and there wasn't much prospect I would marry. Fish is handsome now, but you should have seen him at twenty! And I wanted a man, I wanted children."

Noelle felt a little stab of pain.

"You have children?"

"Four—three girls and, five years ago, a son."

So Fish had children other than Donnie! A son three years older than Donnie!

Susu put a hand on her arm. "Don't feel bad, Noelle. My son's name is Lonnie—Lonnie and Donnie!—and they are brothers. That makes us sisters, you and me. From now on I will send Lonnie to play with Donnie in your courtyard every day, and you will be the chief mother of them both. I'll tell Fish that you think Lonnie is a servant's child. And when you and Fish are out in the evenings, I'll do as I have done all along, I'll come in and look after Donnie if baby-amah can't manage."

Again, distress stirred Noelle's heart.

"You can come and go as you like, but I can't. You lock me in."

Susu made a wry face.

"I'm sorry! Fish insists on it when he's going to be gone for a while. He doesn't want you wandering around the compound. He doesn't want you to see me, of course, and wonder who I am. But also, people are constantly coming in and out to see him on business, and I suppose he doesn't want you to see them either. Sometimes he even orders me to stay indoors."

Noelle felt guilty. Fish's job was very dangerous—he said so frequently. He was having Susu lock her in for her own protection. But . . . her guilty feelings fled.

164

"Susu, what d'you mean—'the compound'? People don't come in here to see Fish on business!"

Susu stared a moment, then shook her head sadly.

"I *knew* Fish was lying to you! I've wanted for a long time to come and see you . . . Noelle, the *whole compound* belongs to Fish. The outer courtyard and all the houses in it as well as this little inner courtyard and this house."

Astonishment almost took Noelle's breath away.

"I thought he owned just this house and courtyard!"

Susu looked as grim as someone as warm as she could look.

"That Fish! Noelle, Fish is a liar. And even when he does tell the truth, he never tells all of it."

Noelle closed her eyes again . . . She had known Fish was a liar. She had guessed it, in those careful little tales he told when she asked him about his childhood . . . She felt tears rising fast behind her eyes and blinked them away.

"Susu, tell me about the whole compound. We don't have to worry about Fish coming back. He phoned me that he's at a meeting and won't be back till late."

"He didn't tell you about the strike?"

"No . . ." Another lie, another omission. Oh God, how many were there! "But I do know there is some kind of disturbance. The doctor's wife told me, when I tried to get him for Donnie."

"When Fish phoned me to lock you in, he told me that there's a big strike on in the city." Susu took Noelle's hand and pressed it, her eyes warm with sympathy. "Oh, Noelle, I'm so sorry! I could just keep quiet and not tell you anything, but Fish is fooling you and I hate it! Fish isn't a good man, Noelle."

Not a good man! But I love him! Noelle thought. I'm *not* living in a fool's paradise! I'm not! I'm not! There's some explanation. His job is dangerous. He's trying to protect me from dangerous knowledge . . .

She clamped down on her tumbling thoughts.

"Susu, tell me about the compound."

"Yes . . ." Susu nodded understandingly and turned to gesture. "Here, this house where you live, used to be the house of Olan, wife of Jin-see, Fish's father. This house can be isolated from the rest of the compound by locking that one gate, which is its only access. Jin-see built this house to confine Olan because she was mad. She had a child who was born with only one leg, and she killed the child. Couldn't bear the thought of

165

how unhappy the child would be growing up in this world with only one leg, so she sent her to the other world, and on every anniversary of her death burned a wooden leg for her, so the spirit of the leg would join her spirit in the other world and she would grow up whole and happy. Olan was quite mad."

Noelle remembered Dr. Macpherson . . . "It was a very difficult birth. The baby, a girl, was born deformed and died soon after . . ." Had he known that Olan killed her baby? And why had her own father never mentioned the baby? Of all the hundreds of stories he had told of Jin-see and Olan, he had never told this one. Because he had loved Olan almost as much as he had loved Jin-see, and hadn't wanted to say that she was mad . . .

Noelle rose slowly and switched on a shaded lamp whose soft glow turned Olan's lovely living room into a warm, mysterious world set in the blackness of nightfall. An eerie sorrow touched her. She caught sight of her own reflection in the dark glass of a window and thought it might be Olan standing out in the courtyard, peering in, pleading for admittance. She shivered. Tears rose again to her eyes, and she hurried back to Susu.

"And the other houses?"

Susu gestured. "The big house, to the right of the main courtyard as you enter the big gate, used to be the family house. The whole family lived in it until Olan did what she did. Fish lived in it before he married you and came to live in this house. Now he uses that house for meetings and business . . . Next to the big house is the ancestors' house—that beautiful little house with the golden moon door. Then comes the cluster of trees and shrubs that form the lane leading to your gate . . . On the other side of the lane is my house, that used to be Fish's mother's house, where Fish was born—"

"Fish was born in this compound? I thought he was born up-country! He told me his father found his mother in a village up-country!"

"And he brought her here, and built that house for her! I suppose Fish couldn't tell you because he hadn't told you that the whole compound was his, because he didn't want you wandering around and maybe meeting me . . . It must be very difficult for Fish, remembering all the different stories!"

Noelle felt light-headed. Involuntarily, she giggled. Susu said emphatically, "Good! Don't let all this distress you too much . . . On the other side of my house is the last house in the compound—the 'teacher's house.' It's the house that Jin-see built for the teacher of his eldest son Great Dragon, who was a mandarin. . . . Did Fish tell you that Great Dragon married his teacher's daughter, and lived in that house with her until he went to Peking? Did he tell you that their son Didi was born in that house, within the same hour that Fish himself was born, not a hundred yards away?"

"No . . . ," Noelle breathed, "he never told me. I know that he has a relative, Didi, his father's grandson . . ."

"Well," Susu said, "he was born right here, he's exactly the same age as Fish. Fish stayed on here with his father and his half-sister Julie, but Didi was sent to his parents in Peking when he was four years old, and never came back."

Noelle's heart thumped heavily. "Oh yes, he came back! *He's here now!* He was at the reception when Fish was appointed director of the Bureau. I spoke to him!"

They stared at each other. Noelle went on slowly.

"Fish says he's still here in Shanghai black-marketing opium. He used to work for the Bureau. He was one of the most corrupt agents the Bureau ever had. When he was the Opium Suppression Officer in Shansi he was buying opium from the farmers instead of suppressing it. His father, Great Dragon, Fish's brother, was so distressed that he went to Shansi to try and stop it, and somehow got killed in a riot over opium. Fish says it wasn't accidental . . . Fish says that's why he has all the family inheritance. Didi hasn't dared to claim his share of it. Fish says Didi also killed his aunt, Fish's sister Julie."

It was Susu's turn. She spoke as slowly as Noelle.

"That can't be true. I don't know how Great Dragon died, but I do know that Julie died right here in the family house, shortly before I came to live here. She's buried in this very courtyard. You know that little pink marble house at the far end of your courtyard? It marks the grave of the baby Olan killed. Fish had Julie buried in the same grave. Didi couldn't have killed her."

Noelle leaned back, staring into the dimness, seeing Didi's eyes, so like Fish's, on the night of the reception, hearing his wondering voice, "You've got it wrong . . ."

Oh God!

She felt Susu's arms encircle her. Wordlessly, they embraced. Then Susu rose.

"I'd better go now. Go to sleep, Noelle. If there's more of that orange-peel tea, ask baby-amah to warm it and drink it. Don't worry too much . . ."

At the door, Noelle's jumping thoughts lit on something inconsequential.

"Susu, did you say that Fish ordered four ancestor tablets from your father? All at the same time? I thought ancestor tablets are made one by one, as the ancestors die."

"Yes. But Fish said that the four originals had been lost and he wanted replacements."

"So the ones your father made are fake?"

Susu looked startled. "Yes, I suppose that's what they are. Fake."

Fake.

Noelle sat at Donnie's bedside waiting while baby-amah warmed up the orange-peel tea. At least Donnie wasn't fake. He was sprawled in his cot like a young prince, fast asleep, the blue eyes hidden under long, black, curling lashes.

Was everything else fake? Her marriage? Fish's love for her? Staring over Donnie's head she admitted to herself, rigidly honest, that her love for Fish might be the tiniest bit fake—it had been influenced by Phyllis' horror at the thought of it.

But—her heart turned over. If everything was fake, that would mean that Fish was absolutely evil and, of course, that was impossible! There were explanations. Misunderstandings. She would find out what they were. She would ask him . . .

Baby-amah came back with the tea. Wearily, she kissed Donnie and took the cup to her bedroom, undressed quickly, slipped into the big bed. She would never get to sleep tonight! Her thoughts tossed about, flip-flopping, prickling, hurting. She remembered the tea, sat up to sip it. Extraordinary, how the taste changed from bitter to sweet. It was marvelously soothing. Her eyelids began to droop of their own volition. She put the cup down, lay back. Sleep was creeping in deliciously . . . One thing was certain: she couldn't judge Fish out of hand on the strength of unexplained suspicions. She loved him. Yes, she did love him, in spite of Phyllis . . .

He woke her by flinging himself onto the bed and almost bouncing her out of it. She sat up, startled, glancing at her little clock. Midnight. The night light showed him lying on his back, scowling at the ceiling. Waiting for the solicitous attention she'd be showering on him on any night, except tonight . . . She hesitated. Then she switched on the bedside lamp, stretched, yawned.

"You're awfully late, Fish! I had a terrible fright today . . ." His scowl became blacker, but she ignored it. ". . . Donnie fell into the reflecting pool. The gardener fished him out quickly, but he was unconscious. I tried to phone Dr. Macpherson—"

He said sharply, "Did you try to leave the courtyard?"

She evaded a direct lie. "Well, he got better fast."

She felt him relax. Nonchalantly, she plumped up her pillows.

"When I phoned the doctor, Mary said there was a strike on in town today."

He leaped up and began to pace the room like a prowling tiger, spitting words harshly at her.

"Yes, there was a strike on! A goddamned bloody strike!"

She was taken aback. Alone together they always spoke English, for his English was better than her Chinese, but he rarely cursed in English . . . He was still cursing.

". . . god-blasted disaster! Every factory worker in the city on the march! Those damned coolies! Those cursed peasants! Good for nothing but trudging behind water buffalos! Whatever they're paid at the factories is too good for them, and they've got the bloody cheek to demand better wages! And students marching too, carrying banners, yelling for the Unequal Treaties to be abrogated! And delegations from the Chinese Chambers of Commerce, old men who should have some dignity, marching along with the coolies and the students, protesting because they're paying the foreigners' taxes without representation on the foreign municipal councils!"

She felt confused and a little afraid. He was really angry. Something deep inside him was raging. Yet, though they had never talked about it, she had assumed that, like herself, he was on the side of the factory workers whose plight had been the protest of humanists for years. And every Chinese in China hated the Unequal Treaties . . .

He stood at the foot of the bed, glaring.

"And it would still be going on if the police hadn't fired!"

"Fired on the strikers? The strikers were *armed?*"

"Of course not!"

"Then . . . how . . . Who fired?"

"The British police. Killed fourteen of the buggers!"

She felt horror. "The *British police* fired on *unarmed* men and *killed* fourteen of them?"

Suddenly, he covered his face with his hands and slumped down on the bed beside her in a gesture of abandon.

"Oh God, darling, you don't know how I feel! I know it was terrible to fire on unarmed men, but they had to do it. They had to end it somehow. This wasn't one of the haphazard strikes we've had up to now that the police could control with batons and nightsticks. This was organized, planned to the last detail, brilliantly executed, *by the Reds*. My own relative, that devil-cursed Didi, was one of the chief organizers. He and his wife are high-up Communists."

He sat up and took her in his arms, looked deep into her eyes, his own eyes holding anguish.

"Can you imagine how I feel, darling? Fighting so hard against opium, fighting for the life-duty I inherited from my ancestors, and my own relative thwarting me at every step. And now, to find out that he's a damned, degenerate *Red!*"

With relief, she drew him to her breast, kissed his brow, stroked a soothing hand over his back. That was it, of course! He wasn't against the factory workers, he wasn't glad that the British police had killed fourteen unarmed men. He was simply hurt and furious because Didi had become a Communist, because Didi had helped to organize the strike.

He sighed, and his body grew heavy, slid sideways. She eased him down onto the bed, hearing his breathing deepen. He must really be exhausted, falling asleep so fast . . . Or pretending to, in order to avoid further questions? She lay back, hating herself.

He had left the house at eight in the morning and returned at midnight. A long meeting, he'd said when he phoned. As long as all day and half the night? Why hadn't he told her about the strike, as he had told Susu? How long had he known that Didi was a Communist organizer? If he'd known earlier, why hadn't he told her? If he'd found out only today—how, while he was supposed to be at a meeting? And he had never really explained what it was he was doing for the life-duty. Whenever she asked, he said it was too dangerous to talk about . . . Oh God, what was she thinking!

She switched off the light and immediately, in the darkness, saw Didi's eyes again, heard his voice: "You've got it wrong . . ."

But if she had it wrong, Fish was absolutely evil, and of course he wasn't!

All the same, he was like a real fish in the water, moving in and out of sight, and when he was out of sight there was no knowing where he was or what he was doing.

The tears that she seemed to have been holding back all day rose again, and this time she let them come, turning her face into the pillow to sob quietly, wretchedly.

Chapter XVI
April 10, 1927

D AWN WAS BREAKING as Fish left the pink marble courtyard.
Zung, who now lived in the family house in the main
courtyard, was waiting beside the new German car. He
held the door open for Fish and jumped in after him. Immediately, the driver started off.

"What's this about?" Fish growled.

Zung shrugged. "Don't know. One of Tall-short's men woke
me with a message that we're to be at Big-ears' house within
the hour. Wouldn't be surprised if he wants more money."

Anger nipped at Fish's spirit. He and Zung had expanded
the opium supply lines well beyond the Yangtsze Valley, with
tentacles stretching as far as Yunnan. They had even made a
trial of smuggling out of Yunnan into the wild, unpoliced,
unpoliceable land where China meets Burma and Laos, so ideal
for smuggling Zung had nicknamed it the "golden triangle."
Opium money was rolling in like a flood tide under a spring
moon, but Big-ears was pouring it out almost as fast. And the
beneficiary of all those hard-earned opium dollars was that
damned, peanut-headed, crazy-tempered madman Chiang Kai-
shek!

Fish stirred restlessly, his anger a torment. He had disliked
Chiang from the moment he first met him in Big-ears' entourage at the Blue Villa. A braggart with no credentials but a few

years training at some Japanese military school. An unreliable, drunken debauchee given to hysterical outbursts of irrational fury. He had been surprised when Chiang was entrusted with a regimental command, then with a series of more important assignments. He had been incredulous when Chiang was sent to Moscow, where he addressed the Executive Committee of the Comintern on behalf of Sun Yat-sen, toured the Kronstadt Naval Base, had talks with Trotsky. When Chiang was appointed commander of Sun Yat-sen's Whampoa Military Academy, he had finally realized, with grinding anger, that Chiang was being groomed for something, probably understudy for Sun Yat-sen.

When Sun Yat-sen died in 1925, Big-ears, Pock-marks, and other core members of the Red Gang had rushed to the Temple of the Azure Cloud in Peking to pay respect to his remains—and to confer with the Kuomintang leadership as to the transition of power. From that conference had come headlines that made Fish want to vomit.

CHIANG KAI-SHEK NEW HEAD OF KUOMINTANG
CHIANG KAI-SHEK INHERITS SUN YAT-SEN'S MANTLE

The headlines hadn't stopped since then. The Great Northern March had got under way and swept triumphantly across the country from Canton toward Shanghai, the warlord armies hastily turning coat to join it, the peasants hailing it with fierce and terrible joy, rising in their millions to hack to death the magistrates and landlords who were their traditional oppressors. At last, at last, liberation was at hand! The whole country was wild with jubilation. And the hero of it all was Chiang Kai-shek!

Zung nudged Fish, pointing out of the window at a group of newsboys arranging piles of papers, setting up placards. More headlines!

NORTHERN MARCH REACHES OUTSKIRTS OF CITY
HERO CHIANG KAI-SHEK WITHIN FIFTY MILES OF SHANGHAI

Fish let out a vicious oath.

"It's incredible! The man's a maniac! What possible qualification has he got to lead the Kuomintang?"

Zung grinned. "The best qualification of all—the Red Gang chose him. There were other contenders for Sun Yat-sen's mantle. Some were liberals—the Red Gang is conservative. Some were warlords, who have provincial power bases—the Red Gang is ecumenical. Hence: Chiang Kai-shek."

Fish glowered. "When did you take up fancy language?"

"I read that in *New Culture*. You should read it. It's a good paper."

"It's a Communist paper!"

"That doesn't prevent it from having excellent editorials"—Zung glanced slyly at Fish—"written by the wife of your relative Didi. She's a wonderful writer."

Fish's anger flared higher. He should have got rid of Didi right after he was appointed director of the Bureau. But Zung had pooh-poohed it. "You're so big now, what d'you care what Didi does? Big-ears has forgotten him. Why don't you forget him too? Why run risks?" So he had let it go—and before he knew it, it was too late. Didi was a high-up Communist, protected by watchful comrades and the high, shard-topped walls of his wife's father's house . . .

The driver brought the car to a halt outside an ironclad gate. An armed guard peered at them, made a sign to another, who slid the gate open on well-oiled hinges. The driver manuevered the car into the courtyard of a large brick house, barred and armored like a fortress. Big-ears' home.

They got out of the car. Another armed guard led them into the house, down a long hall, to a small room that was sometimes used for Red Gang meetings. It contained nothing but the usual round table and wooden chairs, at which Big-ears was already seated opposite the Frenchman Fiori. Big-ears had dropped his usual expression of amiable stupidity: he was looking tough and dangerous. Fiori was frowning coldly. The atmosphere suited Fish's mood. He sat down with grim anticipation, Zung beside him.

With a brutal gesture, Big-ears indicated Fiori.

"For a month, this bastard's been shitting around a proposal for me to help the foreigners get rid of Reds inside the city. Now that Chiang Kai-shek's almost here, he's got to come out with it plainly. I know what he wants, but I'm not going to let him get away with hints. I want him to ask out loud, word for word, for what he wants. I want it to go down that the foreigners invented this, and I'm just doing them a favor. So no nice-nice manners. Just make him spit it out."

174

Fish turned to Fiori. "Well? What d'you want?"

Fiori's eyes flashed fire at Fish's manner, but he swallowed his anger and started abruptly.

"All right . . . We all know that the Reds are becoming too damned dangerous. That strike they engineered two years ago was a masterpiece. Of course, the British helped by firing on an unarmed mob and creating fourteen martyrs, but even without that, it was superb. It has increased Red membership to hundreds of thousands. It has been copycatted in a dozen cities and stirred up a mountain of unrest and antiforeign feeling. There's been unrest in this country for centuries—but now it's not only more, it's better. For the first time, it's got good leadership. The Reds are dangerous to everybody, not just to foreign capital and foreign investment. I know damned well that every new labor union in the Yangtsze Valley sticks a knife in the side of our ugly friend here."

He sneered, reciprocating Big-ears' gesture, and paused for Fish to translate. Then:

"All right . . . Before Sun Yat-sen died, those Moscow advisers of his fixed it for the Chinese Communists to join the Kuomintang, so Chiang Kai-shek inherited the Reds as his partners. For the time being, that's all very fine. The Reds organized those peasant demonstrations along the route of the Northern March that made Chiang look like such a hero. The Reds are organizing a great big welcome for him in Shanghai . . ." He paused, and his tone grew heavily sarcastic. "But it's my guess that this partnership isn't going to last much longer. The Kuomintang is interested in big business, and the Reds have these quaint ideas about justice and the welfare of the people."

Fish translated. Big-ears remained imperturbable. Fish signed to Fiori to resume.

"All right . . . Now, here's what I think is going to happen. I think that as soon as Chiang gets here, Shanghai's wealthy merchants are going to line up to pour loans and grants into his pockets. It stands to reason: they don't like what the Reds are doing any more than we do—why not pay Chiang to get rid of them? And who better to line up the merchants than our ugly friend here, of whom they're all dead scared? Him and those miniature coffins he sends around to people who resist him . . . Am I right? Our ugly friend has sponsored a nice new partnership between Chiang and Big Business, and Chiang is going to get rid of his old Red partners as soon as possible. Probably within the next two or three days. An all-out surprise attack as soon as the main Kuomintang army gets here, while the Reds still think there's cause for celebration. Am I right?"

His bright, bold eyes glanced from Fish to Big-ears and back to Fish. Fish swallowed heavily. Fiori must be right. Big-ears was going all out to boost Chiang into the presidency. Fury blurred his vision and clogged his throat. He felt Zung stir uneasily beside him and, with effort, kept his tone expressionless as he began to translate what Fiori had said.

Big-ears yawned. "Let him go on."

When Fish nodded at Fiori, Fiori laughed shortly.

"Of course I'm right! Well—there's Reds both outside and inside the city. Chiang attacks the Red regiments outside the city. Even if he wipes them out completely, that won't help us inside the city. We can't let Chiang's troops into the foreign sectors. That would be the end of extraterritoriality—we'd never get them out again. We can't use our own forces to attack the Reds inside the city—the whole world would condemn us. So—here's my proposal: We, the French police, will provide rifles, machine guns, ammunition, and trucks for five thousand men. Our ugly friend will provide the five thousand men. They will attack the Reds inside the city and wipe them out, while Chiang does the same for the Reds outside the city."

In the midst of his anger, Fish felt a cold core of awe. They were talking of slaughter. Inside the city, the Reds were scattered throughout the most densely populated areas. Outside the city it would be Kuomintang regiments attacking Red regiments. Inside, it would be gangsters attacking civilians. No wonder Big-ears was forcing on Fiori the responsibility of proposing it!

He became aware of silence—they were waiting for him to translate. He turned to find Big-ears' mocking gaze on him. Big-ears' droopy eyes mocked him steadily as he talked. When he finished, Big-ears mumbled, "Too raw for you, Little Fish?"

He summoned contempt to his aid. "Too revolting! A really colossal back-stabbing, worthy of Chiang Kai-shek!"

"Well," Big-ears said casually, "we'll eventually have to get rid of those Red peasant-lovers, and now's the best time."

Fish shook with the force of the anger that gushed through him. "We." Big-ears and Chiang Kai-shek, the basic twosome. He himself on the periphery, purveyor of opium, supplier of funds! He felt Zung's steadying hand on his arm and once again took hold of himself, the effort this time enormous.

". . . you can tell him I'll do it," Big-ears was saying. "But there're Reds in both foreign sectors. If this bastard thinks I'll move in the Settlement on his say-so, he's wrong. I've sent for Fessenden. I want Fessenden to give me permission to move my men in the Settlement. He won't like it, so the Frenchman'll have to persuade him."

Fish said to Fiori, his voice sounding tinny in his own ears, "He'll do it. But he wants Fessenden's formal permission to move in the Settlement, and he wants you to persuade Fessenden."

The door opened and Fessenden entered, his face stiff with anger and caution. With a poisonous glance at Big-ears, Fiori beckoned Fessenden to the seat beside him and began quickly to repeat what had been said. Fessenden's face became grimmer by the moment. When Fiori finished he rasped, "With five thousand men and all that weaponry, why does he need permission? How could I stop him?"

Fiori said coldly, "Don't you see, he's rubbing our noses in it. If we do nothing, the Reds inside the city will panic when Chiang starts his attack, and many more Reds will come running into the city. They could take the foreign sectors and hold us for ransom to force Chiang to stop his attack. They might even find those five thousand weapons and use them against us. Or, of course, we could let Chiang's troops into the foreign sectors. D'you want to go down in history as the man who lost extraterritoriality?"

After a moment, Fessenden said stiffly, "It seems I have no choice."

Fiori sat back. "All right. Tell him it's agreed."

Fish nodded at Big-ears. Big-ears grinned sardonically.

"Good . . . Chiang will start his attack at 5 A.M. the day after tomorrow. The Red regiments will be encamped to the northeast of the city. Chiang will attack the encampment first, then converge in a narrowing circle into Chapei, Nantao, and the Chinese City. The Reds who escape him will come running into the foreign sectors. We'll wait four hours. We'll start our attack in the foreign sectors at 9 A.M."

So it had all been prearranged between Big-ears and Chiang!

With stiff lips, Fish translated. Fiori's eyes glittered.

"I knew I was right! Now, as to deployment of the weapons and trucks . . ."

They went on to discuss details, Fish translating mechanically, Fessenden taking no part. Agreement was quickly reached. When the two foreigners rose and took their leave, no one said good-bye.

As the door shut behind them, Fish started convulsively to rise, but Big-ears put a heavy hand on his shoulder.

"Didn't like it, did you, Little Fish?" He grinned mockingly. "Always hated Chiang Kai-shek, didn't you? I grant you, Kai-shek is basically shit-rotten. A crazy man with a crazy temper. But he's *hungry*. There's no limit to his envy and his ambition. And that suits us very well . . . Trouble with you, Little Fish, you were born rich. Born-rich people never get hungry enough."

The malice in his voice showed plainly. Fish sat still as a statue, fury bubbling in him as irrepressibly as milk on the boil. Big-ears dug him in the ribs.

"Well, back to business. I've got those five thousand men lined up. They'll have to be paid very well, in advance. It'll be a short war, but fierce. I need money. A million dollars, Fish. By eight tomorrow night. Cash, of course."

Fish gasped. Where in the deepest pits of hell was he going to get a million dollars cash by eight tomorrow night?

Big-ears slid an arm around his shoulders, forced him to turn and face his sly grin, the spiteful glint in the hooded eyes.

"You can do it, Little Fish! You're such an excellent manager!"

Fish was forced to keep silent while the armed guard escorted them back to the courtyard, but he exploded as soon as they were back in the car.

"That shit-rotten, stinking hoodlum . . ."

Zung's hand closed hard on his wrist and Zung's head jerked toward the driver's back.

"We'll talk about it when we get home," he said quietly. "We needn't get too anxious. He must have some back-up arrangement. He can't be depending entirely on our producing something close to a miracle." His lips turned down in a grim smile. "What I find more amazing is that they're pushing Chiang Kai-shek into the presidency. A super warlord, head of a super bandit government . . . But they don't care about that, as long as it suits the empire they're running . . . It's our empire too, you know."

"Not mine!" Fish spat out. "I'm quitting! I don't need those scum!"

"You do, you know," Zung murmured. "If you want to stay alive. You can't quit. You've been initiated. So have I. Remember all those vows?"

"Those idiotic vows, each one stupider than the one before!"

"Yes, but they can hook us on them anytime they want. Calm down, Fish. Take it easy. We can talk as much as we like when we get back to the compound . . . What the devil's happening?"

The car had rolled to a stop in what seemed to be a sea of milling people. Cursing, Fish wrestled open the door on his side against the press of the crowd, and stepped out onto the running board. Over the hundreds of bobbing heads, he could see as far as the corner of the road, where it turned from French Town into the Chinese City. There, at the corner, soldiers were erecting a barricade, heavy wooden trestles wreathed in rolls of barbed wire, thick and strong enough to stop a regiment.

The Northern March had arrived! The foreigners were getting ready to defend extraterritoriality against all comers, Kuomintang and Red alike!

Zung, on the opposite running board, called over the top of the car.

"No use trying another road! They'll be putting up barricades at every intersection where the foreign and Chinese sectors join. We might as well leave the driver to get through whenever he can and walk back."

Fish nodded. Zung instructed the driver, and they left the car and began to shoulder their way through the crowd, past the long line of vehicles that had already been halted by the barricade. At first the people seemed more excited and curious than afraid, but as they approached the barrier a sense of panic began to burgeon. People were pushing, calling out that their children, their spouses, their parents, were on the other side, they had to get through, they had to pass. Someone with a bullhorn was shouting patiently for calm. But calm was sadly lacking. The closer they got to the barrier, the more frantic people became, pushing and jostling in a mad crush. Fish lost Zung and struggled on alone.

The barricade was composed of five huge trestles, a pair together on each side of the road, a single one in the middle that could be moved to allow vehicles to pass through one at a time. On the French Town side of the barricade, soldiers were busy erecting machine-gun nests, piling sandbags into low walls. Beside one of these emplacements, a tiny gap had been opened between the trestles and the wall to allow one person at a time to pass. A soldier with a rifle was guarding the gap, scrutinizing the people as they struggled through.

The soldiers were Volunteers. Each foreign nation represented in Shanghai had a regiment of Volunteers who were called up in emergencies. The man who was guarding the pedestrian gap was pleading for order, telling the pushing crowd not to be afraid, not to push, to get in line, they'd get through faster . . . But it was hopeless. People were too frightened to listen.

When the Volunteer caught sight of Fish, he used his rifle to wedge open a path for him.

"Sorry for the inconvenience!" he said ruefully.

Fish forced a genial smile. "I suppose we'll be seeing a lot more of this kind of thing."

"Afraid so. Every Volunteer in the city has been called up, and the British are rushing regulars from Hong Kong. The Kuomintang army is all around the city, and the Reds are rabble-rousing to drum up a big welcome for Chiang Kai-shek. Things are getting a bit dangerous."

For whom? Fish thought viciously as he smiled his thanks and fought his way through the gap in the trestles. For a few thousand damned foreigners determined to preserve the extraterritoriality that their damned "treaty rights" gave them? What about the millions of Chinese who'd be caught between two fires when that devil-cursed Chiang Kai-shek and Big-ears' devil-cursed gangsters attacked the Reds?

Anger simmering, he began to push his way through the

crowds on the other side of the barricade. Now he was in the Chinese City. The people, all Chinese, were running, pushing, shoving, shouting, loading carts and carriages with suitcases, bedrolls, even furniture. An old man sat a small boy on top of a bedroll—an eldest son, his head shaved except for a square patch on the top where the hair had grown long and was plaited in two skinny pigtails. The child was sobbing woefully. The old man comforted him: "We'll soon be there!"

"*Where?*" Fish snapped.

"Our village," the old man said. His voice trembled. "We should never have left it! I told my son that the land would never betray us! But my son said we couldn't stay, there was too much fighting. And the fighting has followed us here! *Chee-sah! Chee-sah!*

Sorrow, sorrow . . .

Fish walked on, beginning to feel dizzy. What did he care about these stupid people, running from east to west and west to east in a hopeless search for safety? Nobody was going to be safe anymore, nobody! Not with a madman like Chiang Kai-shek in power! It was all over. Everything was over. The very thought of Big-ears and Chiang Kai-shek turned his stomach. That piece of garbage. That degenerate lunatic. He had to get away from them. Cash in. Raise as much cash as possible, and get out. He could easily raise millions with his beautiful compound as collateral, the furnishings, the carpets, the magnificent curios. And the cash in the *hong's* accounts. He could go anywhere he liked. Hong Kong, Japan, Hawaii. He would take Susu. Funny, how he swung to aging Susu and away from beautiful Noelle. Susu had always suited him perfectly. Noelle—let her go back to England. She was tied in too deeply with all that stuff he was aching to get rid of—the life-duty, his father, Great Dragon, Julie. Julie . . . Anyway, Noelle was getting too difficult. Always asking questions, refusing to be put off, listening to his answers with a judgmental frown. Too troublesome. Take Susu.

He felt enormous relief. Just this one last thing to do for Big-ears. To spite Big-ears and leave him open-mouthed with anger. Big-ears didn't really expect him to produce a million dollars by tomorrow night. Big-ears wanted him to fall on his face . . .

And suddenly he knew the answer. The morphine in the teacher's house! Years ago he and Zung had decided to accumulate morphine. Neat little waterproof paper packets, much easier to handle than opium, and many times more valuable than opium. Not so easy to get hold of when they'd started to hoard it years ago, but a fine investment. The stock in the teacher's house would easily fetch a million dollars!

He hurried on toward Mali-lu, through thinning crowds. Should he tell Zung of his decision to flee? No. He'd tell nobody but Susu. After tomorrow's attack there'd be many days of turmoil in the city. Banks would be closed, but he knew of moneylenders who owed him favors. He'd have to discount his collateral a little, but that didn't matter. He could get hold of the money. Cash. Gold bars. Diamonds. Letters of credit from a couple of damned crooks he knew to their relatives abroad. He'd hide out with Susu while he was negotiating the funds.

Ahead, he saw Zung banging at the gate of the compound. He ran to catch up with him. His heart felt light. His feet sped over the cobbles.

"The morphine!" he said as he reached Zung, and Zung said, "Of course!" They grinned at each other.

They banged again on the gate. There was the sharp click of the peephole opening. Fish showed himself to the tiny eye, calling out, "Open! We had to leave the car behind!"

The gate was hastily opened, and they walked into the compound, turning automatically toward the teacher's house, Zung producing a big bunch of keys from his pocket. The courtyard was so lovely, Fish thought. A shame to leave it. But it was nothing compared to getting away from Big-ears and Chiang Kai-shek.

Outside Susu's house, Zung paused.

"How shall we move the stuff?"

Fish seated himself on a bench beside a tubbed tree. He felt lighthearted and calm. He smiled at Zung. Zung came and sat beside him, looking puzzled.

"What's the matter, Little Fish?"

"Nothing . . . Let's decide what to do with the stuff."

"Well, I've got a list of buyers who'll be only too glad to get a chance at it. I thought I'd go and see them today. Give them a chance to get cash together. Tell them we'll deliver tomorrow at the Blue Villa."

"We can't move those little packets. We'll have to bag them."

"Yes, I thought of sacks of rice. Shove them down into the rice, and send the rice through on flatbed carts in the ordinary way."

"What about the barricades?"

"Yes. It'll take some time to get through those, so we'll have to start very early. Six o'clock. I'll go with the carts. Should be at the Blue Villa by four. I'll go from the Blue Villa direct to Big-ears'. Should be there well before eight. . . . But our real problem isn't the barricades. It's Fiori. The arrangement with him is that we won't move stuff through French Town during the day, and when we move it, it'll be in closed carriages. If we take the rice carts through one of the French Town barricades during the day, and Fiori's men get wind of it, you can bet your head they'll seize the whole lot."

"You're right . . ."

He couldn't take the slightest chance on that. He had to do this last thing for Big-ears in impeccable style.

"Well, then, we'll have to send the stuff through the Settlement."

"We don't have Fessenden's agreement."

"No, but how will Fessenden know? The French are watching for us to trip up. The British aren't. The Settlement is much safer."

"All right. How about the Markham Road intersection? It's closest to the Blue Villa."

"Yes! The Markham Road intersection."

They rose. Zung went ahead toward the teacher's house, jangling his keys. Fish followed, feeling elated, feeling in control.

Chapter XVII
April 10, 1927

NOELLE WOKE when Fish's valet came tiptoeing into the bedroom. She lay still. The valet murmured to Fish, who rose quietly and left the room. The valet gathered up his clothes and followed him.

She opened half an eye and peeped at the window. It was barely dawn. Fish would be gone at least all morning, perhaps all day—this must be one of his mysterious meetings. A day free of Fish! She stretched luxuriously. Susu would come to visit. She'd been afraid at first that one of the servants would tell Fish about Susu's visits, though Susu said they wouldn't. Susu was right, none of them had breathed a word. They loved Susu as much as they disliked and feared Fish. He was becoming more and more morose. The tension between herself and Fish heightened daily. He hated her asking him questions. But the questions buzzed around in her mind and had to be asked . . . She pushed away the troubling thoughts and snuggled down. Time for another two or three hours sleep before Susu came.

Susu came at nine o'clock, bringing Lonnie.

"I kept him home from school today because my girls are away visiting my parents and he's feeling lonely and bad-tempered. So when Fish went so early I decided to let him come and play with Donnie."

The boys rushed out into the pink marble courtyard, and Noelle and Susu happily settled on the sofa in the living room.

"D'you know where Fish has gone, Susu?"

"No. He left with Zung. They took the new German car. We'll hear the klaxon blaring when they're on their way back, and I'll have time to rush home, so we needn't be on eggshells."

They laughed together. They never lacked things to talk about. For all her wisdom, Susu could barely read and write and was completely ignorant of the world beyond China's shores—indeed, beyond the limits of the city and her parents' village, which was only sixty miles away. She never tired of listening to stories of life in London, of English mores and customs, of the single god that the English worshipped in tiny chapels and magnificent cathedrals, of that god's priests who didn't sell passports for the safe conduct of one's spirit to the King of Hell. She never tired, too, of stories about Noelle's ancestors and Fish's, of the way their lives had been intertwined for five generations.

"Six, really. Fish had four ancestor tablets. Fish himself is the fifth generation. And Lonnie and Donnie are the sixth . . ."

"I don't hear them!" Noelle cried, and ran to the window, heart bumping. She would never forget the moment the gardener stepped from the reflecting pool with Donnie's limp little body in his arms. But the reflecting pool was shining and unruffled under the clear spring sky, and the gardener was calmly clipping one of the tubbed trees. Otherwise, the courtyard was empty.

"They're not in the courtyard, Susu!"

Susu made a sound of annoyance. "They must have gone into the main compound. I should have locked the gate!"

Noelle ran with Susu to the door, but Susu stopped her.

"You can't come out with me, Noelle. The guards at the main gate will see us together, and *they*'ll tell Fish. Fish hires them himself. I have nothing to do with them."

"But I want to go with you to find Donnie!"

"Put your cloak on, then—the one that covers your hair."

Noelle ran to get it, swathed herself in it, and the two of them ran together across the pink courtyard, through the gate, and into the lane, or driveway, formed by tubbed trees and bushes, that led from the pink courtyard into the main compound. When they emerged from the lane, they would be visible to the guards at the main gate, at the far end of the main courtyard. The distance was considerable, but still their two figures would be clearly visible.

Susu said, "We'll walk side by side, slowly—don't make any quick movements—straight to my house." She pointed to her right, where the little house stood about fifty yards away. "From my front windows we can see most of the main courtyard."

They smiled at each other, not really anxious yet, just annoyed with the children, but indulgent, prepared for a little scolding and quick forgiveness. They each took a big breath and, together, walked out into the main compound.

Noelle had passed through it a thousand times in a car, but she had never before walked in it. Where her own courtyard was of pink marble, this one was milky white marble, veined in silvery gray. Beautiful. Old and mellow and somehow caressing to the feet. Loving people had walked here. She peeped out from under her hood. To her left, behind her now, was the lovely little ancestors' house. Beyond, quite distant, the big, imposing family house. Then the gate and the gatehouse. Five or six men were standing in front of it, talking. They seemed intent. One of them glanced toward the two women, but paid no further attention.

A moment later, they slipped into Susu's little private courtyard, laughing, breathing simultaneous sighs of relief. Susu led the way quickly into the house, through a kitchen, into the front room where a large window looked out on the main courtyard. A reed blind had been let down over the window to shut out the sun. Susu rolled it up a little, and they kneeled beside the window to peer out. Almost all of the main courtyard lay before them, but aside from the guards at the main gate, they could see no one. Susu exclaimed.

"Maybe Lonnie took Donnie to the ancestors' house. I have duplicate keys to all the houses, and he knows where I keep them. He's been naughty since he woke up today . . ."

Faintly, somewhere to their right, they heard the children's voices.

"They're in the teacher's house!" Susu cried. "I'd better rush and get them back immediately. Fish strictly forbade anyone, even me, from going into that house. If he found out the children have been there, he'd have a *fit!* You stay here, Noelle. I'll slip over and bring them back."

She went out quickly. Noelle knelt again in front of the window, looking to her right. In a moment, Susu appeared around the corner of the house and began walking fast toward the teacher's house, about a hundred yards distant. Were the guards watching? Noelle glanced to her left. The guards were now clustered around the gate. They seemed excited. She looked back to her right in time to see Susu enter the little courtyard of the teacher's house. A few seconds later Susu came out again, holding the boys' hands. Relieved, Noelle turned back toward the gatehouse.

And felt her heart leap into her throat. The gate was open, and Fish was walking through it, followed by Zung! Had Susu seen them? She glanced anxiously to the right: Susu had slipped behind some tubbed trees and was taking an oblique course. A few moments later, she and the boys passed around the corner of her house and were no longer visible to Fish.

Heart thudding, Noelle glanced back in Fish's direction. He and Zung were walking toward her. Instinctively, she flinched away from the window. Susu came hurrying back into the room.

"I told the boys to stay in the kitchen. Where's Fish now?"

"He's walking this way . . ."

Together, they crept back to the window, peeped out. Fish and Zung were almost level with the window. Zung seemed a little hurried, but Fish walked leisurely, smiling. Zung said something. Fish went to a stone bench beneath a tubbed tree, not ten yards from the window, and sat down. Zung followed. They began to talk. Noelle and Susu leaned forward, straining to hear, but the voices came only faintly through the glass. With the gentlest of movements, Susu eased the window open an inch . . .

Fish was saying, ". . . those little packets. We'll have to bag them."

Zung: ". . . sacks of rice. Shove them down . . . send the rice through on flatbed carts in the ordinary way."

A gust of breeze rose that blew the next words away.

Then Fish said, ". . . how will Fessenden know? . . . The Settlement is much safer."

Zung said something, and Fish nodded.

"Yes! The Markham Road intersection."

They rose and walked on toward the teacher's house, Zung leading the way, jangling his keys.

Susu sank back on her heels.

"Thank the gods, I snapped the padlock shut!"

Noelle nodded absently. What had they been talking about? Packets. Rice sacks. Fessenden. The Markham Road intersection . . . She felt strange and uncomfortable, as though somehow she should know . . . But how could she?

Susu said, "Noelle, they've gone into the teacher's house. You'd better take Donnie and rush back to your own house. Wrap yourself in the cloak . . ."

Noelle came to with a start. Of course! She snatched up the cloak and swung it round her, ran with Susu into the kitchen.

Lonnie and Donnie sat at the table, Donnie holding a small packet wrapped in brown waterproof paper while Lonnie poked at it with a chopstick. They were so absorbed that they did not look up, and their mothers involuntarily stopped, peering to see what they were doing. At that moment, Lonnie jabbed sharply, the chopstick penetrated the paper, and a little white powder dribbled out of the hole it made. With great satisfaction, Lonnie said, "I told you!"

Donnie looked up at his mother, blue eyes shining with excitement, and said with great clarity, in English—he was bilingual in English and Chinese, "Look, Mummy! It's Jesus Opium."

Something in Noelle turned to ice and froze her throat so that she could not draw breath. Susu, not understanding the English words, grabbed Lonnie by the shoulders and shook him.

"What have you done? What is that?"

He looked surly.

"I know I'm not supposed to go to the teacher's house, but one day I saw those little packets, and we had a class in school . . ."

Lonnie went to a progressive school where, one morning a week, guest speakers were invited to talk to the children on "social" subjects like traffic safety, health, tooth-brushing, drugs . . .

Noelle said mechanically to Donnie, her breath returning in a gasp, "Come—we must hurry back to our house."

He jumped up without arguing and took her hand. She said to Susu, "Come over as soon as you can."

Then she was walking back to her own courtyard, Donnie skipping along at her side, saying anxiously, "Are you angry, Mummy? I didn't know it was naughty."

Baby-amah came running, looking terrified.

"I couldn't find Donnie! I got such a fright!"

Noelle said numbly, "He went outside. You take him, baby-amah. Take him upstairs."

The woman took Donnie's hand but didn't move away. Her eyes were still wide with fright and excitement.

"Mistress, did you know that the master and Zung came back *walking*? They had to leave the car in French Town. There are barricades at all the intersections . . ."

Noelle stared at baby-amah. The Markham Road intersection . . .

"We'll all be killed!" baby-amah wailed. "There're soldiers all over, the guards say! The Kuomintang army is outside the city! We'll all be killed!"

"Hush!" Noelle tried to sound reassuring. "Nobody can get into this compound. We'll be quite safe. Take Donnie upstairs now."

Gulping, baby-amah turned away.

Noelle sat down on a bench and stared at the reflecting pool, blue sky, and puffy white clouds mirrored in it perfectly. But what she saw were the loving, tender pictures of her first years with Fish. The achingly tender pictures. Oh, it was hard! So hard, so painful! Her heart was being squeezed in a nutcracker. She rose blindly and went into the house. She would give Fish the chance to clear up all these doubts and misgivings. As soon as he returned home, she would put her arms around, look him in the eyes, make him look into hers, ask him plainly, "Fish, those packets in the teacher's house—do they contain morphine? Is it yours?"

And he would explain it. It was something to do with the Bureau. It was stuff that had been confiscated, that for some reason he had stored in the teacher's house. He would explain it . . .

The phone rang. Automatically, she lifted the receiver and said "Hello."

"Noelle?" said Fish's voice.

She couldn't answer.

"Noelle?" he said again. "I'm sorry, but I'm extremely busy. I won't be able to come home till late. Perhaps not all night."

Where was he? Susu's house? The family house?

She said, "Where are you, Fish?"

"Downtown," he said smoothly. Then, with irritation, "Do you always have to ask questions?"

With desperation, she tried again, "Where are you, Fish?"

He made an angry sound. "I can't argue with you now! Stay at home. Don't try and leave the courtyard. If you hear the sound of guns, don't be frightened. You're safe where you are. I'll be home perhaps tomorrow, perhaps the next day. If not, I'll call you."

The phone clicked in her ear.

Slowly, she put down the receiver, stood staring at it.

As Fish was the son of Jin-see, so she was the daughter of Donald . . .

She picked up the phone book and looked for the number of the Shanghai Municipal Council. Cranked the handle of the phone and put the receiver to her ear. As on the day of the strike two years ago, the line was full of static. She waited patiently. At last the operator answered, and she gave the number. At the other end, the phone began to ring. A harassed voice answered, "S.M.C." She asked for Mr. Fessenden. The voice translated itself into clicks, hums, static, then more ringing. The phone was picked up again, and astonishingly, a man's rough voice said, "*Wair?*"

It was the vulgar Chinese telephone-answering syllable. Strange that it should be used in Mr. Fessenden's office. But she answered in Chinese, "I want to speak to Mr. Fessenden."

The voice said, "Who're you?" again using the vulgar Chinese expression, and she answered in Chinese, "I am the wife of Wei Ta-yu."

There was a slight pause. Then the voice grunted, the phone clicked, and a male English voice said, "Yes?"

"May I speak to Mr. Fessenden?"

"I'm sorry, he's extremely busy."

"It's extremely important."

"I'm sorry, we have an emergency and Mr. Fessenden is unavailable. I'm his secretary. If you wish to leave a message, I'll see he gets it as soon as possible."

"I must speak to Mr. Fessenden himself. I am Mrs. Wei Ta-yu. Noelle Wei. Noelle Mathes."

"Oh!" The voice sounded startled. Then, "Hold the line, please."

A short wait, and he was on the line.

"Mrs. Wei? Fessenden here."

She said slowly and distinctly, "Mr. Fessenden, please don't ask me how I know, but I do know that, probably soon, a number of carts loaded with sacks of rice will go into the Settlement through the Markham Road intersection. Those carts should be stopped and the rice sacks examined. Shoved down inside the rice will be packages of . . . white powder."

Silence. She heard him breathing. Then, guardedly, "Mrs. Wei, do you know what you are saying?"

"Yes."

Another pause. Then, gravely, "Thank you very much, Mrs. Wei."

"You'll stop the carts?"

"I certainly will!"

He sounded cheerful. But a moment later, he was sounding anxious.

"Where are you, Mrs. Wei? You know that barricades are up at all the intersections? If you're still in the Chinese City, you mustn't try to come into the Settlement alone. I'll send an escort—"

"No, no!" she cried, horrified at the thought of a squad of British soldiers marching into Fish's compound. "I'm at home. I'm quite safe."

"*At home?*" He sounded startled. "I had assumed . . . Obviously, there's something I don't understand. I don't want to press you to tell me anything you don't want to tell me, Mrs. Wei. I'm already extremely grateful for what you *have* told me. But if at any time you need help, just telephone me at the office or at home. If I'm not there, someone will take a message. Will you promise to do that?"

"Yes," she said. "Thank you."

He gave her numbers that she wrote down on the pad beside the phone, and they hung up.

He hadn't been astonished that white powder would go through the Markham Road intersection hidden in rice sacks.

He had only been astonished that she had told him and was still in her own home.

He must know Fish.

He must know, like Didi, that she had got it wrong.

The rest of the day passed quietly. She felt languid. Her heart ached steadily. She dozed and read a little and, in the evening, played a game with Donnie. After supper, they walked in the courtyard under the new spring moon. In passing, she tried the gate. It was locked.

She slept restlessly and woke early to a gray, misty day. After breakfast she walked again in the courtyard and again tried the gate, which was still locked. She dawdled, staring through the bars. The main courtyard was very busy, crowded with people and the two-wheeled flatbedded carts used for transporting rice. She passed on, heart thumping.

Again, she dozed, and read, and played with Donnie. Fish didn't come. Once or twice she tried the telephone, but it was dead.

In the evening, baby-amah came with a message from Susu. It had been impossible for Susu to come because of all the activity in the main courtyard. Noelle was to stay calm. Everything would be all right soon. Susu had sent some of the orange-peel tea and begged Noelle to drink a big cup of it before going to bed, and to give Donnie a big cup too. It would help them sleep.

Baby-amah had already brewed two big cups of the tea: she was prepared to enforce Susu's plea. Noelle laughed a little, in spite of the heaviness of her heart. Everyone loved Susu!

Donnie, playing at her feet, asked suddenly, "Where's Lonnie? Lonnie didn't come today!"

"He can't come now," she said. "It's dark already."

She lifted Donnie onto her lap, and held one of the cups of tea for him to drink. At first he made a face, but then he mumbled appreciatively and drank the whole cup. He started to climb off her lap, changed his mind, cuddled down. Very quickly, he was asleep. She caressed his soft black hair. Holding him, she took up her own cup and sipped at it, gazing dreamily into the dark courtyard, feeling herself relax. After the third yawn, she got to her feet and carried Donnie to bed. Baby-amah came, but she dismissed her. It wouldn't matter if Donnie wasn't washed tonight. He was so beautifully asleep! When she put him down, his eyes opened slightly: half-moons of piercing blue, catching the night light. Her heart moved in her breast. How her father would have loved his grandson!

She went to her own bed, yawning, hardly conscious of undressing and slipping under the covers. In the delicious moment between wakefulness and sleep, the thought occurred to her that Susu might have added something to the tea. It was so incredibly relaxing.

Years later, sitting in an English garden, she remembered the moment and marveled that the thought had not alarmed her. Like everyone else, she had loved and trusted Susu without question. . . . She folded the letter in her hand and put it back into its much-stamped and postmarked envelope. Tears blurred her eyes. Her small son came and stood at her knee—another son, an English son. She took him onto her lap and hugged him, the tears dropping gently onto his blond head. He was called Donnie too. She had wanted to replace that other black-haired, turquoise-eyed Donnie whom she had thought was lost.

Chapter XVIII
April 12, 1927

THE FOUR MEN seated themselves around the table in the secret room behind Jade Flower's office. For a moment no one spoke and the room was very quiet, the kind of quiet that increases the heartbeat and quickens the breath. Zung, nerves twanging, thought that their positions at the table were in the pivotal sequence of the four winds in the game of Mah-Jong. Big-ears sat in the East seat, for East is always the banker. Tall-short, his oldest lieutenant, sat at his right hand in the South seat. Zung himself, his newest lieutenant, sat at his left in the North seat. Opposite, sat Fish, in the West seat.

In the game of Mah-Jong, the discard of all four West Wind tiles in succession is held to be an apocryphal action condemning one of the players at the table to death, for "west" and "death" are the same word. Tonight, in Zung's fancy, that action had been taken, and the player condemned to death was Fish.

Fish didn't know it yet. He leaned across the table, arrogant and scowling, his bold eyes on Big-ears.

"Can we get on with this? What's so important that you had to get me here at two o'clock in the morning?"

Big-ears said softly, humbly, mocking Fish; "The money, Little Fish. The million dollars. Where is it?"

Fish sat up sharply, "You should have had it before eight last night! Zung was supposed to accompany the carts, collect cash from the buyers, and take the cash directly to you!" He swung round to Zung. *"What happened, Zung?"*

Zung kept quiet. Earlier, Big-ears had said to him, *"I will talk to Fish. You say nothing."* So now Zung kept his tongue in his head and his eyes fixed on the opposite wall. Big-ears answered Fish, sarcastically imitating his tone, *"What happened, Zung? Zung was supposed to collect from the buyers. Zung was supposed to bring me the cash. We could have done without you, couldn't we, Little Fish?"*

From the corner of his eye Zung saw Fish turn crimson with rage, saw him push his chair back and rise with a reckless, triumphant smile.

"Good! You can do without me starting *this minute!* That suits me fine! I'm quitting."

There was a moment of deep silence. Zung stared at the opposite wall. Had Fish gone mad? Did he really think he could quit?

Big-ears let out a savage bark of laughter. "There's only one way you can quit, and that's in a coffin! *Sit down!"*

Fish remained standing, the reckless smile still flattening his lips.

Tall-short rose and went around the table, put a hand on Fish's shoulder, pressed him back into his chair. It might have been a friendly gesture, but for the pistol in Tall-short's other hand. Fish resisted Tall-short's pressure, then suddenly plumped down into his chair, staring at the pistol, the blood fleeing his face, leaving it white and crinkly. Zung swallowed and closed his eyes. Whatever dream Fish might have had of quitting had blown up. He knew now that his life was in the scale.

Big-ears rasped, "See how it is, Fish? *Stay down.* I'm going to tell you what happened yesterday. . . . The rice carts got through Markham Road very easily. It was almost as though the British *wanted* them to get through fast. And—what d'you think?" He grinned his shark grin. "They *did!* As soon as all the carts were through, they stopped all of them at once. Soldiers unloaded the rice sacks and emptied them right there on the street. Shook out all those neat little packets and carried them away. Left the rice where it was, a bonanza for the neighbors."

Fish glared defiance, eyes huge in his bloodless face.

"Are you accusing *me?* The only ones who knew how that stuff was going to be moved were Zung and me, and *I* told nobody!"

"And you think Zung told the British?" Big-ears licked his cracked lips. "Not Zung, Little Fish. Your blond English wife. You told her, and she told Fessenden."

The shock hit Fish like a bullet. Zung saw him gape. But an instant later, he was again fulminating.

"I told nobody! Ask Susu! I went to her as soon as Zung left me day before yesterday, and I stayed with her until Tall-short came tonight to fetch me! I was with her continuously! Ask her! She knows I couldn't have told Noelle!"

Big-ears sneered. "Ask Susu! And Susu wouldn't lie for you, of course!"

Fish screamed at him, "I didn't tell my wife! I didn't tell anyone!"

"Then how did your wife know to tell Fessenden?"

"She couldn't have!"

"She did. The man I've got at the Council offices actually spoke to her on the telephone. By chance, he intercepted the call. She asked for Fessenden and he asked her who she was. She told him 'the wife of Wei Ta-yu.' "

"Any woman could have said that!"

"But not any woman could have known that rice carts were going through Markham Road intersection and should be searched. Immediately after your wife spoke to Fessenden, he called the British Ambassador, the chief of police, the commanding officer of the British troops, and told them all very excitedly about rice carts and Markham Road intersection."

Fish stared incredulously at Big-ears, slowly turning a pasty gray. Big-ears glanced at his watch.

"Well, we can't waste any more time. Zung got to me early enough yesterday so I could get the money from other sources. The five thousand men are armed and posted. Chiang's attack will start at 5 A.M. as scheduled—two hours and forty minutes from now. We'd better get going."

He rose, signaling to Tall-short and Zung. When Fish made to rise, Big-ears waggled a finger at him. "Not you." Fish subsided, his face ghastly. Big-ears leaned toward him and spoke reflectively, with a kind of enjoyment.

"You know, Little Fish, you overdo things. You always salt the pot twice . . . Take One-eye. I knew he was past it. I knew I had to get rid of him. You already had the advantage. But you weren't satisfied. You baited him in front of me, to show him up. He was older than you, and he was your teacher, he brought you into the Red Gang, but you had no respect. That's why I gave him a chance against you in the sampan that night, and almost hoped that it would be you that the boatman killed. . . . And take Ah-fet's opium. You used the Red Gang to get hold of it, but you thought it should all belong to you. I was going to give you a good share, but you weren't satisfied. You went behind my back and gouged a ransom out of the widow. . . . And take Chiang Kai-shek. You don't like him. But when you realized that the Red Gang had chosen him, did you compromise and hide your hatred? No! You *paraded* it. *Stupid*."

Great beads of sweat were trickling down Fish's face in rivulets and waterfalls, as though giant hands were wringing out his body fluids. Zung clenched his hands and stiffened his knees to keep himself from trembling.

Big-ears laughed. "Too hot for you in here, Little Fish? Well, never mind. Soon you won't feel the heat, or the cold either." His smile became very cruel. "You forgot something, Little Fish. The initiation. All those vows you took. Most of them were nonsense—Pock-marks invented them, he has a sense of drama. But one of them wasn't nonsense—the last one, the one you swore on the heads of your sons. . . . Red-pole is dealing with them now. Then he'll be here to deal with you. Tall-short will keep you company until then."

Without another glance at Fish, he turned and went briskly to the door.

Fish threw himself across the table, arms stretched toward Big-ears' retreating back, voice rising in a thin scream, "I didn't tell her! I didn't tell her!" Tall-short stepped behind him and jabbed the pistol into the back of his neck. He froze like a badly sculpted statue, lips contorted, face twisted against the table in a pool of his own sweat. His popping eyes swiveled madly toward Zung. The scream died away into hoarse gasps. "Zung . . . Zung . . . tell him I didn't. . . ."

Dry-mouthed, Zung squinched up his eyes and rushed from the room.

The corridors of the Blue Villa were dark and quiet: there had been few revelers on this night of fear, the Kuomintang army at the gates of the city, the foreigners patrolling their barricades, the Reds roving about, unaware yet that the hammer of doom hung over them. Stomach quaking, Zung hurried through the silent house and caught up with Big-ears in the courtyard. As Big-ears' bodyguards closed around him for the short walk to the cars, Zung called over their shoulders, "Sir, I have some urgent personal business . . ."

Big-ears glanced round. "You have until eight tonight."

"Thank you!"

Zung melted into the darkness and began walking as fast as he could toward Mali-lu. He was still shaking, his mind flinching away from the final sight of Fish, from the awful sound of Fish's final plea. "Zung, tell him I didn't . . ." But if he hadn't told Noelle, who had? Fish must have told her. She'd asked one question too many, and in one of his bursts of fury Fish had blurted it out.

Well, Zung would do what he could now to help Noelle and Susu. Red-pole must by now have dealt with the two boys—he gulped down a sharp lump in his throat—and he couldn't leave them to shift for themselves. He owed Fish that much. Fish had been his stepping stone. Not that he had ever deliberately planned to replace Fish, but as Fish's moods became more and more vicious, he had felt that a time might come . . . In spite of his perturbation, his heart suddenly bumped with excitement. Fish's shoes would fit him well!

At first it had been a kind of game, exciting and lucrative. The money from Fish, in addition to the bonuses from the Bureau, had made him rich beyond the wildest dreams of his poverty-stricken childhood. And who wouldn't pick up money that was there for the lifting? Only that crazy Didi! But he had got used to the money, to lavish spending, and he'd had to have more, and Fish had given him more, and it had become more exciting, matching his wits against Fish's, secretly exulting when Fish adopted an idea of his, pretending that it was his own. And then had come his initiation. Unlike Fish, he had realized forcefully that every stupid, babbled vow held a hook that could one day yank him out of the water. He'd thought cautiously of backing off, but instead events had pushed him forward—into Fish's shoes.

He hurried on, his mind jumping. What had Red-pole done with the children's bodies? Left them there for someone else to get rid of. Over the years, Red-pole had grown arrogant. He caught a vision of the two mothers weeping over the bodies of their sons and shivered, hurrying faster. Get this over with as quickly as possible.

He passed the barricade easily—the streets were almost empty. From there it was only a few minutes to Fish's compound. The gate guard made no trouble letting him in.

"The master hasn't returned."

"I know. I've come to fetch something from the inner courtyard."

"It's locked. The Tai-tai has the key."

Susu was the Tai-tai, the mistress. Noelle was "the foreign woman."

"Thanks. I'll get it from her."

He strode across the main courtyard. The tubbed trees were shadows that loomed as he approached them, darker than the night. He knocked at the gate of Susu's courtyard. Knocked again. Surely she was there! Suddenly he heard her voice behind him.

"Zung! I knew you would come!"

She emerged from the lane that led to the inner courtyard and touched his arm, indicating that he should follow her. She went before him, a quick, slight shadow, back into the pink courtyard, and into Noelle's house. One of the lamps in the living room was lit. It glowed softly on her face as she led him to a sofa. For the first time since he had known her, she showed her age. Black rings deepened her eyes and thinned her cheeks. She was keyed up so tightly that he thought her skin might quiver if he flicked it. She said very softly, "What has happened to Fish?"

Not "Where is he?" or "When is he coming back?" but "What has happened to him?" She knew. He had thought of various ways of telling her, but now he said simply, "He will not return."

She sighed on a long breath. Then, very low, "I will think of it tomorrow . . ." He thought how strange it was. He had seen Fish every day for years, worked with him side by side, obeyed his every whim, quaked at the awful sight of him waiting for death in that little room. And then had quickly passed on. Now Susu was passing on. Fish would leave no hole, no vacancy, no regret, no sorrow.

She echoed and magnified his thought, "All those years . . . Seventeen years I spent with him. All that evil. I *felt* it sometimes—often, lately—but I couldn't believe it. I couldn't believe in such absolute evil. Until he himself told me yesterday. . . . Yes. I will think of Fish in the time to come, and be glad that he is dead."

She fell silent and he kept silent too, respecting her withdrawal, though he tingled with urgency. Where were the boys' bodies? Where was Noelle? Why were they sitting here in her house, and she not present? Was it possible that the women didn't yet know what had happened to their sons?

Susu said, "Zung, I have many things to tell you."

He stirred restlessly, but something in her face kept him quiet. She began to tell him how she and Noelle had become friends, what they had done together. He listened in growing wonder. When she told how she and Noelle crouched behind the screened window, listening to Fish and himself discuss the transportation of the morphine, he had a mad desire to burst out laughing. It was the irony of ironies! For once in his life Fish had told the unvarnished truth, and been condemned for it! He burst out, interrupting Susu, "Did you know that Noelle telephoned the British and told them that the rice carts were going through the Markham Road intersection?"

Her eyes gleamed. "Good for her! I didn't know. I haven't spoken to her since she rushed back to her own house with Donnie while you and Fish were in the teacher's house. As soon as you left the compound, Fish came here. He made me lock Noelle in. He phoned her that he wouldn't be going home, and then he made me cut off her telephone. He stayed with me until the messenger came to fetch him tonight. Zung, he told me everything . . . all the evil. . . ."

Her eyes were wide and shiny. He had an eerie sense that she could see into the future. She was in that rare state of sensitivity when one knows what is going to happen.

"He told me how he murdered his brother and sister and took control of the *hong* in order to black-market opium. How he murdered the one-eyed man, on the way to his initiation. About the initiation. About Big-ears. All the evil. He was boasting of it. It was clever. Brilliant. He was far above the trashy garbage criminals. He was going to break with Big-ears. He was going to cash in and go to Hawaii. I was to go with him . . . I knew it was the end. No one can run away from the Big-ears of this world."

His heart was thumping like the engine of a train, but she was calm, a woman delicately treading a thin line, with confidence, knowing exactly what she was doing. He felt awe of her.

"He talked for hours. And then he dozed off. I hurried. First, I sent Lonnie away . . ."

He sighed softly with relief.

". . . Lonnie had been with me often to my parents' village by train, and he remembered how to go, and I explained it all again. He's smart. He'll get there safely. And then I sent some orange-peel tea to Noelle and Donnie. I put into it some of the white powder from the packet Lonnie brought from the teacher's house. I wanted them to sleep *very* soundly. Then Fish woke up again, and I went back to him and questioned him, pretended I would go with him to Hawaii . . . He told me more and more. He seemed to be in some kind of trance. And then the messenger came to fetch him away."

He licked his dry lips. Red-pole must have come very soon after that. Lonnie was safe, but where was Donnie?

As though reading his mind, she said, "I hid him. As soon as Fish left, I rushed over here. Both of them were sound asleep. Noelle is still upstairs, sleeping. I took Donnie and hid him. I barely got out of the pink courtyard before the other man came— the executioner. I hid behind the bushes in the lane. First, he went to my house, and of course he didn't find Lonnie. The house is empty—my girls were already with my parents. And then he came to this house, and of course he didn't find Donnie."

"Of course?" he croaked.

She smiled. "I hid him very well. . . . Zung, the boys can't reappear. We have to send Noelle back to her people without Donnie. There will be headlines in all the English papers—

Noelle is saved, but her poor little boy Donnie has disappeared. Those headlines will make Donnie safe. But if the English papers write that Donnie is with his mother, that will be Donnie's death certificate, and maybe Noelle's too. People like Big-ears who rule by ruthlessness can't afford to let anyone get away with anything. He'll have to see that Donnie dies, and he might order Noelle killed too as a warning to anybody who's thinking of defying him. Besides, there's the executioner—he has to retrieve his honor."

He stared at her. She had it summed up exactly right. She might have known Big-ears and Red-pole intimately for years.

"But how can we persuade Noelle to go without Donnie?"

"Easily. She'll be fast asleep."

"And what about Donnie?"

She hesitated for the fraction of a second. Then, "You'll take him and give him to Didi."

"Wh—Wh—What?" He was so startled that he stammered. "You're crazy, Susu! What if I can't find Didi? What if he's dead? He's a Red, you know, and in a couple of hours they'll be hunting Reds all over the city! And what if he doesn't want the child?"

"If you can't give him to Didi, you'll bring him back to me, and I'll take him, and he'll be as my own son. But we must try to give him to Didi. He and Didi have the same ancestors, and Didi has their soul tablets."

He considered, mind and heart ticking fast. What was to prevent him trying? Where Didi lived was the safest part of the city, where there would be no fighting. He couldn't take Donnie through a barricade—if he woke and opened his eyes, their color would arouse instant suspicion. But he could take him to the Nantao docks, get a sampan, and be rowed downriver to one of the landing places along the Bund, in the center of the Settlement. No fighting in that holy of holies. A rush of refugees, no doubt, but no actual firing. From the Bund he could make his way to Didi's house with ease. Didi might be glad to have Donnie. In any case, he would see Didi again. The man for whom he still felt a strange, pure love.

"All right," he said. "I'll try. But I must go at once. The attack is due to start at five, and it's already after four."

Her eyes were bright with satisfaction.

"First you must telephone the British to come and fetch Noelle. I can't do that."

"All right."

He went to the telephone. Who to call at this early hour? He saw the letters "Fess. . . ." scrawled on the pad beside the telephone, and under it two numbers. More proof, if needed, that Noelle had phoned Fessenden. He chose the number that indicated a residential area. Fessenden's sharp, clipped English voice answered on the first ring. It took less than a minute to arrange to have Noelle fetched.

Fessenden said, "She didn't want soldiers. I'll send plainclothes men."

"Better an ambulance."

"Is she hurt?"

"No, not at all. But she's heavily sedated."

"Oh. Her son will be with her, I suppose?"

Zung put down the receiver softly.

Susu said, "Now I'll show you where I hid Donnie."

She led him out of the house and into the pink marble courtyard. The predawn light was the same color as the marble. The whole world was a pure, pearly pink. She went quickly across the courtyard, around the reflecting pool, to the little doll's house that marked the grave of the baby Olan had lovingly killed. She stood with her hand on the little tip-tilted roof.

"Fish had Julie buried here, in the same grave with her baby sister. They had to move the little house to open the grave, and the roof fell off and broke. They couldn't find marble of the same color, so they made a new roof of tin and painted it. Nobody can tell the difference by looking at it. But I knew. Look!"

Like a magician, she folded the roof back and lifted it off in one piece. The roofless house was like a large lidless box. At the bottom, lying on a white pillow, a blanket wrapped around him, was Donnie, fast asleep.

His heart leaped with joy, astonishment, admiration.

Watching his face, she laughed with pleasure, then bent and lifted the child out of his hiding place, cradled him in her arms, the laughter leaving her, her spirit growing solemn and sad.

"It's to save his life . . . If you throw a stone into that reflecting pool over there, the ripples go on and on as though they'll never stop. I wonder if the evil that Fish did will ever stop . . . Well, Noelle is very young. She will marry again and have other children. English children, in England, where she belongs. And one day I will manage to write to her and tell her that Donnie lives."

She handed the child to Zung. "Go quickly."

He took the child. "If I can't give him to Didi, I'll be back by seven this evening."

"Yes. Take care . . ." Then, as though she could see into his spirit, "Zung, don't follow too closely in Fish's footsteps."

He glanced at her as he turned away. Her face was palely lighted by the dawn. A plain, middle-aged face, its expression tentative now, half afraid, unsure whether the plans she had made and put in motion so effectively were really good. Nothing at all in her look and stance to indicate the wit and courage of her spirit.

At the gate, he told the guard, "I am taking the child to his father. Soon, some foreigners will come to fetch the mother. Open the gate to them without question."

The guard grunted. He was glad, Zung knew. All the servants, except perhaps Donnie's amah, would be glad to see the foreign woman and the half-foreign child with the strange-colored eyes leave the compound. They were bad luck.

He stepped out into the alley, the child heavy in his arms, and began to walk toward the river. The streets were eerily deserted. Ordinarily, at this dawn hour, the life of these streets was already well begun, but today all the shops were tightly boarded, the shutters of the houses closed. Only a few people hurried along, whose concerns were so desperate that they outweighed fear.

As he neared the docks, the attack started. The sky exploded with reddish light. A splintering roar shattered the infant day. It was distant—the Red encampment was miles away on the other side of the city—but it seemed very close at hand, a terrifying new kind of thunder and lightning. He began to run, keeping tight against the walls of buildings, his ears ringing and his teeth aching from the crackling, tearing sound of spreading shrapnel. The few people in the street were running, scattering, hiding, but nearby a voice shouted—a rickshaw coolie, a ragged scarecrow, waving his arms.

"Hop in! Hop in!"

Zung scrambled into the rickshaw, glad for relief from the child's weight, and the coolie spurted forward, shouting wildly, "Here! Fall here, you bombs! Fall on this starving body!"

Zung had to pound his heels on the rickshaw's floorboards to get the coolie's attention.

"The docks! Take me to the docks!"

"To hell if you like!" the man yelled, and careened onward, the rickshaw bumping madly.

As they neared the river, the tenements fell behind and the view opened. Thick, gray smoke was fulminating over the horizon, shot with jagged flashes of flame. The roar of the exploding shells, the teeth-jangling whine of shrapnel, filled the air. The coolie staggered to a stop. Zung thrust a handful of notes at him. He grabbed them and flung them into the air, laughing madly as they fluttered away.

Clutching the child, Zung sprinted across the road onto the nearest dock. At first glance the riverfront seemed deserted and his heart sank, but a head appeared over the edge of the wharf, then an arm and hand holding an oar. A sampan was tied close alongside, its rope caught on a capstan. Zung swooped, freed the rope, and flung himself and the child into the tiny boat. It rocked violently and he fell across a thwart, dropping Donnie into the bilge. The boatman, holding his oar rigid in the water to still the boat's wild swinging, shouted, "The rope! The rope!" Zung saw that the rope was snaking about in the water, weighing the boat down heavily on one side. He began to draw it inboard, the boatman yelling encouragement. When the rope was coiled, he shipped his oar and began to shift the boat under the dock, pushing and pulling at the pilings, calling to Zung to help. When they were as far under the dock as they could get, the boatman quickly tethered the boat to a piling and picked Donnie up out of the bilge. Donnie opened his eyes a little and whimpered, and the boatman sat down on one of the narrow thwarts, propped a sinewy bare foot on the other, and cradled Donnie, crooning to him in a sing-song barely audible to Zung under the continuous sound of the shelling.

"Poor little boy! How ugly your eyes are! But be good, be wise, and one day you'll find a woman to love you!"

Zung sat down on the thwart beside the boatmen's foot,

hysterical laughter bubbling in his throat while his ears rang and his teeth ached and his stomach spasmed. But Donnie quieted and edged closer to the boatman and was soon fast asleep again.

The boatman looked up proudly.

"I am good with children. In the sampan shelter downriver, they always call me when a child is sick."

Zung was to remember that day as the strangest of his life. They sat in the little boat in a forest of splintery, barnacled pilings weirdly streaked with sunlight leaking between the boards of the dock overhead, in an isolated world that smelled dankly of age and rot, assaulted by restless masses of debris that tried stealthily to wash over the gunwales. The savage noises of the shelling crackled all around, muted by the wet wood and the oily water, a kind of fierce lullaby for the child asleep on the boatman's lap. The boatman was old, his face the color and texture of worn and cracked leather, his hands and feet gnarled, his breath heavy with garlic.

He said, "The child is half foreign. He is not your child?"

"No. I am taking him to his relatives."

"Ah. He was lost? Never mind, don't tell me. It doesn't matter. Perhaps nothing matters anymore. Have you thought of that?"

There was a new burst of firing. Zung listened, but the echoes bounced about the boards over their heads and he couldn't tell how near or far it was. The boatman said, "It's frightening at first, isn't it? You think of the people's flesh bursting and their blood gushing out. But then you think of death and you remember that everything is fate, and perhaps nothing matters, and if so you needn't be frightened . . . I've heard this before, you know. When I was young, when the foreigners brought their great fire ships to the Taku Forts."

Zung looked up, startled. That was—1860! When the British and French armadas destroyed the Taku Forts on the way to Peking to force the emperor to ratify the Unequal Treaties. 1860!

The boatman smiled, showing two yellow teeth.

"You're surprised, eh? I was eight or ten years old then. I was in the Great North Fort, one of those 'monkeys,' they called us, who ran about carrying gunpowder to the gunners and arrows to the archers who shot the great crossbows. But the foreigners' shells sprayed bits of red-hot metal all over, and before we knew it, we had two thousand dead men, and the rest had run away."

He shifted his position to make Donnie more comfortable. "You know," he went on reflectively in his cracked old voice, "what I said about perhaps nothing matters anymore. In the last few days I have rowed many people across and across the river, some going east, some going west, some running away from the city, some running into it . . . does it matter? The people were factory workers and bank workers and all kinds of workers, and some were soldiers and some were Reds. Reds have no money, not like the owners and managers of the factories who have their own launches to cross the river in. Most of those rich ones are Kuomintang. But the Reds have to hire us sampan boatmen to take them across the river, and they talk to us while we're rowing. What they say makes sense if you own nothing. But if you own your own launch to go across the river, what they say is terrible. How can that be, I've been wondering. They say the Kuomintang and Reds are together, liberating the people. If so, what is happening now? This killing can't be the liberation of the people. It's very hard to know what is happening. So I wonder—does anything matter anymore?"

Zung thought of the initiation vows: I swear I will never reveal any secret of the Red Gang. But in this dim, eerie, watery world, did anything matter anymore? Recklessly, he said, "The Kuomintang and the Reds are not the same. They are joined together for the Great Northern March to conquer the warlords. But beyond that, the Reds are for the people, and the Kuomintang is for . . . itself. So the Kuomintang must split away from the Reds, and today the Kuomintang is hunting Reds."

The boatman bowed his head sadly and said nothing.

They heard the sputtering roar of powerful launches. Peering between the pilings, they could see the launches approaching, their bow waves peeling away in great swathes. The launches roared straight up to the dock under which they were crouching, coming alongside two or three at a time, then storming off while others took their place. Soldiers leaped out of them in a human tide and went thundering off across the dock.

The boatman said, "Kuomintang. They have boots on."

The converging operation was beginning: Kuomintang troops approaching the city in a concentric circle, flushing Reds before them into the foreign sectors—the factory districts, the peripheral slums, not the immaculate purlieus like the one where Didi was living.

The boatman said, "When I was a boy at Taku, foreigners came to kill Chinese. But now Chinese are killing Chinese. Not, mind you, in a drunken fight where men might kill each other, not meaning to. Nor in passion—a man finding a lover in his wife's bed, or a burglar in his house. Not even like slaughtering pigs for meat. Just killing. What is happening?"

What *is* happening? Zung thought. What am I doing in this tiny boat, crouching under a dock? Fish dead, Noelle gone, Susu soon to go. And Didi? Gone too? Dead? And even if he lives, can I find him? Will he want the child? I must go! I have only a few more hours!

He stood abruptly, rocking the boat.

"Sit down," the boatman said. "It's not yet time."

Zung sank down again. The boatman was right. It was only a little after nine. The slaughter in the city must only just have started. For hours yet they would be hunting Reds, bashing down doors and windows, dragging out those who hid behind them. Who could tell from the blank face of a door whether it sheltered a Kuomintang or a Red or even a plain Chinese, a poor fool who thought it was all right just to try and earn a living, bed a wife, raise a family?

The sounds of fighting slowly changed, from the roar and crackle of shrapnel to the rat-tat of small arms fire. The boatman fumbled in a pocket and produced a crumpled pack of cigarettes. Zung held his match for him. He inhaled pleasurably and blew out the smoke, carefully turning his head away from the sleeping child.

"You said the Kuomintang and the Reds are not the same," he mused. "I suppose you are right, otherwise the difference in their wealth and poverty couldn't be so great. The Kuomintang must hate what the Reds say."

"What *do* the Reds say?" Zung asked.

"Oh, many things. That the rich are too rich and the poor too poor. That the rich are careless of the poor as fire of the wood it burns. That the rich grow rich by evil, like selling opium. That the government of China is like the quilts the women make, sewing together bits of rags. Now, everything is ragged. China is a quilt of holes held together by bits of thread. There is nothing more that can be patched. There must be a great fire that will burn all the rubbish, and from the ashes China will rise again like the phoenix. In that new China all men will be brothers and none will be careless of another."

"Do you believe that?"

"I don't know. But I do know that the rich are careless of the poor as fire of the wood it burns. That opium is a very evil thing that the rich sell and the poor buy with their life's blood."

"The rich are careless of the poor as fire of the wood it burns." That sounded like *New Culture*, like the pen of Didi's wife. That plain, frail woman with the brilliant mind. Fish had envied Didi his possession of her. Fish, with beautiful Noelle in one house and wonderful Susu in another, had fiercely envied Didi for his wife. Not only for his wife. For everything. Sitting there in the dim, dank forest of pilings under the dock boards, Zung suddenly realized that Didi was enviable. He had liked Didi—loved him—but had always felt for him a kindly patronage. More fool he! Didi was no well-intentioned blunderer. It wasn't stupid not to pick up money that was there for the picking—it was honest. And clever. You didn't land up, like Fish, in a little, airless back room, waiting for death, Tall-short your last companion. Zung shivered. He was wearing Fish's shoes now, but he wouldn't follow too closely in his footsteps. That's what Susu had said—don't follow too closely in his footsteps. Or was he already too close?

He stirred restlessly. The boatman said, "Was this child given something to make him sleep?"

When Zung nodded, the old man said nothing, as though that were ordinary.

They sat for a time in silence. The old man dozed, woke, smoked another cigarette, dozed again. The firing died down, burst out, died down. The sun slowly shifted. The streaks of light that came through the boards narrowed, like knife slits in a dark fabric. Under the dock, the day dimmed.

Zung thought of Didi. The things that Didi had done for the

Reds were as smart and sharp as any of the smart, sharp things Zung had done for Fish, and would do again for Big-ears. And Didi was far braver. Zung would deliver Donnie if he could, or take Donnie back to Susu, and then would rush to Big-ears and the armored cars and the submachine-gun-toting bodyguards. But Didi—if he were not already dead—where would he go? Certainly not to armor-plated shelter.

Suddenly, weirdly, excitement filled him. Didi was alive! He would find Didi in that house on Bubbling Well Road! Didi would take the child—of course he would!

The old man said, "You are happy."

"Yes! Is it time to go?"

They listened. The firing was sporadic. Zung's watch said it was almost four in the afternoon. Seven hours since the attack in the city had started. The worst must be over.

The boatman said, "Let's try."

He laid Donnie down and they began to shift the boat out, pulling and pushing on the pilings. When the boat slipped into the open, Zung raised himself over the edge of the dock. Traffic was moving on the waterfront—a great crush of traffic. The threat of death by bullets must be over. People had left the shelter of their houses and were rushing about, as the boatman said, from east to west, from west to east, into the city, out of the city. Did it matter? He almost laughed.

"Will you take me downriver?" he asked the boatman. "Any of the landing places along the Bund will do."

The old man looked crafty. "A *dollar?*"

Zung grinned. The ordinary fare would be a few cents. Under the dock it had been a different world. Out here, there was a rare chance to make a dollar.

"Whatever you say," he told the boatman.

The old man fitted his oar into the oarlock and began to row.

"You must be rich," he said reflectively. "But not *rich,* in the way the Reds say."

"I am not a Red."

"No!" The old man chuckled. "The Reds pay in coppers."

They came to one of the flights of stone steps that led down from the Bund into the water. The boatman brought his little craft expertly alongside. Zung gave him a dollar and he tucked it carefully away. Zung hopped out of the boat onto the lowest step, and the boatman handed Donnie to him, smiling, saying the age-old farewell: "Take care!"

By the time Zung, fighting his way through densely crowded streets, reached the house on Bubbling Well Road it was almost six o'clock, and dusk was falling. The house was dark and silent, the gate in the high wall blank and repelling. Zung pulled the chain that dangled from a hole in the gate, but the bell inside had been muffled. He knocked on the gate with his knuckles, then with a bunch of keys. He heard nothing, but suddenly knew that there was someone on the other side of the gate. He knocked again and said, low-voiced, "Let me in. It's Zung." There was no response.

He thought of the letter he had stolen from Didi the day Didi's ancestor tablets arrived from Shansi. It had fallen out of the box and he'd picked it up on impulse and thrust it into his sleeve, meaning to return it after he had read it—"Is this what you were looking for? Found it under the desk." But once he had read it, he had kept it, of course. It was valuable ammunition against Fish that one day he might need. He had carried it always on his person, afraid to leave it where one of Fish's spies might find it. Now, he shifted Donnie's sleeping weight and fumbled the much-worn letter out of his wallet, slipped it through the crack between the gate and the wall, heard a tiny rustle as it was picked up on the other side.

Then at last, Didi's voice: "Zung?"

"Yes! Let me in, please! I'm alone, except for a child. I have to talk to you. *Personal.*"

Bolts clicked and the gate was slitted open. He pushed in quickly and the gate was shut and bolted behind him. Didi was no more than a tall shape in the dusk. He said quietly, "Walk in front of me to the house. I have a pistol pointed at your back."

Didi, with a pistol! Hardly breathing, Zung walked carefully along a sandy path, up a few steps, across a porch, through a door that opened as he approached. The door was shut behind him before a dim light was turned on. Didi's voice said, "All right. Turn around."

He turned with a strange eagerness. He hadn't seen Didi for five years! He was much the same. His face a little thinner, the lines more finely drawn. But the eyes! No longer mild and accommodating. Sharp, assessing, prepared to pass judgment. Zung looked into Didi's eyes and drew a quick breath, almost of fear.

Didi said tonelessly, "What do you want?"

A thin, pale woman with eyes too big for her face came out of the kitchen and stood beside Didi, looking gravely at Zung. Belle. He spoke to her.

"I brought you the child. Donnie, son of Fish and Noelle Mathes."

The woman made a little sound. She was staring at Donnie, her eyes very bright. Didi said roughly, "Why did you bring him to us?"

"It's a long story."

The woman said, "Let him explain. Come into the kitchen."

She opened the door and let them into the pleasant kitchen, pushed forward a basket chair in which Zung deposited Donnie, waved them to chairs around the table.

Didi said, "All right. Explain."

Zung licked dry lips and told the story as briefly as he could. At the end: "You and the child share the same ancestors. We thought you should have him. He should be with his family. But if you don't want him—"

"Oh, we want him!" Belle cried. She was looking at her husband, her face radiant. Watching her, Zung understood why Fish had envied him.

Didi said, "Yes, of course we want him."

She ran around the table to the basket chair, fell on her knees beside it. In that moment, Donnie opened his eyes.

"His eyes are blue!" she cried.

The child regarded her gravely. She held out a hand to him. After a moment, he put his hand in hers. But then he looked up and saw Didi, who had risen and was standing behind Belle. He withdrew his hand from hers and held both arms out to Didi, a beam of relief and recognition flashing over his face.

"Papa!" he cried.

When Belle had taken the child upstairs, Didi smiled at Zung—his old smile.

"Thank you! The child is a gift from heaven. My wife cannot

have children. You've made us very happy. And our ancestors too!"

Zung felt ridiculously glad. He tried to be casual.

"So—you forgive me for stealing that letter out of the box of your ancestors' tablets?"

"Of course! You'd never have got in otherwise."

"I'm glad I found you. I was afraid—"

He stopped, and Didi said gravely, "That I might have been killed in today's slaughter? Many died today. Many . . ."

He paused. To pay respect, Zung thought. Not in fury, like Fish, but to pay respect, to give the benediction of a moment's sorrow, and then to go on.

". . . but we had some warning. When they attacked the Red regiments outside the city, we knew what was going to happen inside. Belle and I are going to be badly needed for the rebuilding of the Party, so our superior instructed us to stay indoors. This house is practically impregnable—and it's in the elitest part of the Settlement." He smiled a little. "Did you ever think you'd be grateful for British protection? We were, today!"

"Yes—but after today? You're well known, Didi! Organizing that strike two years ago gave you a tremendous reputation. You're a target, Didi!"

Didi regarded him reflectively.

"Thank you . . . I know. But you've broken some sort of vow by telling me. I'll tell you something in return. In an hour, Belle and I and Belle's mother, and Donnie, of course, will leave this house and everything in it. We'll each just take a small bundle of clothes and walk out of the city with all the thousands of refugees running to and fro. We'll cross the river at Lung-hwa, and make our way, mostly on foot I suppose, to Kiangsi province. There's a mountain there—Chingkanshan—that's been a bandit stronghold for centuries. That's the designated gathering place for what's left of our forces. There the *tung-chih* will rebuild."

Tung-chih. Comrades. "In that new China none will be careless of another." Zung shook himself. It was a dream.

Didi said, "Come with us. We'd like to have you. You'd like it too, I think."

Zung laughed. "Walk across half of China on foot! What makes you think I'd like that?"

He heard the jauntiness in his voice, and his heart ached, and he went recklessly on: "Besides, I'll also be taking a trip. By train. To Yunnan province. We're exporting opium from Yunnan to compete with the British for the French and Dutch monopolies. Soon, we'll be smuggling as far as Indochina, Burma, Malaya, the Dutch East Indies."

Didi said nothing and the silence grew. Zung sought anxiously to break it.

"What are you going to do with your soul tablets? Take them with you on your walk across China?"

"Yes. You saw them—they're small. They'll fit into our little bundles."

"Mmmmm." Zung sipped from the tea cup Didi had poured for him. It clattered as he set it down. Why was he so nervous?

He rose abruptly. "I must go."

"All right."

They walked silently to the gate. Didi unbolted it and held it half open. It was dark beyond, dark and cavernous. For one crazy moment, Zung almost turned back to Didi. Then, with an absurd sense of loss, he stepped through the gate.

Epilogue

1950

BLUE-EYES PEERED cautiously between the branches. The man was a hundred yards away, slumped on the ground, back against a tree. Blue-eyes had spotted him a half-hour earlier when the last oblique rays of the sun had glinted on his heavy leather shoes. A White. A Kuomintang. Funny! They shed their uniforms and disguised themselves in farmer's blue cotton or coolie's rags, but they clung to those shoes! Didn't they realize what a giveaway they were? Shoes must be addictive. He had had shoes once, when he was four years old—not that he remembered what shoes felt like. . . .

He moved forward a few stealthy steps. The White didn't stir. He was sleeping, gathering his forces for the final push. Sometime during the night he would make for the border, for that wild triangle where Yunnan province meets Burma and Laos. It was a year since Mao Tse-tung proclaimed the People's Republic from the high rostrum of the Gate of Heavenly Peace, two years since Chiang Kai-shek fled to Taiwan. Most of the White soldiers left behind, poor, bewildered draftees, some as young as eight or nine, had been gratefully absorbed into the People's Republic. But there were still White commanders holding out, trying to make it over the borders.

Blue-eyes crept forward. If he could get close enough to the man, he could hold his pistol on him before waking him. The man might then give up immediately, and there need be no bloodletting. He moved closer, his straw sandals noiseless in the dust. Twenty feet. Ten feet. Very gently, he knelt, cocking his pistol.

And then the man spoke, a single word that rocked Blue-eyes back on his heels. If he had been given a million guesses he would never have guessed what that word would be.

The man said, "Donnie . . ."

Blue-eyes froze, the breath escaping his lungs in a gasp. Nobody had called him Donnie since Grandmother Mei-mei died on the Great Snow Mountain! He was Blue-eyes now to everybody, even Willi!

The man's eyes slitted open. He was pale, gaunt, dirty, unshaven, exhausted. But his eyes smiled.

"Saw you before you saw me . . . Saw your eyes . . . Can't be another blue-eyed Red in the whole of China . . ."

Blue-eyes began to tremble a little. A secret was creeping out of his subconscious, a marvelous secret. But still, he was cautious.

"If you were so near that you could see my eyes, why didn't you kill me?"

"Kill my brother?" the man murmured.

The secret burst forth in all its glory! The man was Lonnie! Lonnie!

Blue-eyes laid his pistol on the ground between himself and Lonnie. Lonnie moved his left hand, which had been concealed by his body, and laid his own pistol beside the other. Then joy flooded out and they embraced each other, laughing, saying each other's names over and over, withdrawing to look into each other's faces, hugging again, tight and warm and full of love. At last Lonnie's arms fell away weakly, and Donnie cried, "You're exhausted! Can you manage a little walk? About a mile? My wife will have dinner ready."

He gave Lonnie his water flask, and Lonnie drained it, then gathered his legs under him. Donnie helped him up, stuck the two pistols in his own belt, put an arm around his brother to support him. They walked slowly, side by side, Donnie's heart soaring. Lonnie was still taller than he! Lonnie still had that little swagger, his shoulders that carefree look as though they were about to shrug nonchalantly. Donnie laughed aloud, a small boy again, walking beside his all-knowing big brother in a pink marble courtyard.

Lonnie glanced at him sideways, smiling.

"You said, your wife?"

"Yes!" A new wave of joy surged through Donnie, as it always did when he thought of Willi. "We've been married four months. We met when we were children, way over on the other side of the country, in Shansi. We never saw each other again until I was posted to border duty here, and here she was, the village schoolteacher!"

Lonnie was smiling his big-brother smile.

"And marriage is good?"

"Wonderful! I wouldn't have believed how wonderful! But of course you know—you must be married too."

"No . . . I've had wives, but not the kind you marry."

"Willi's my first!" Donnie cried, and then blushed as Lonnie glanced at him with amusement.

"And you're—let's see—twenty-seven?"

Donnie felt a little embarrassed—but it was natural and good to speak of such things with one's brother! He said frankly, "I was four years old when I climbed the Blue Mountain, and the very next morning I was a Little Red Devil. From then on, for many years, I recited the Rules of the Red Fighter every morning. Obey orders promptly. Be strictly honest. Be courteous to everyone. Be sanitary. Respect every man's wife and daughter. I guess it's pretty hard for any of us who grew up on the Blue Mountain not to respect wives and daughters, and I never met a woman yet who wasn't someone's wife or daughter!"

He shot a glance at Lonnie. Was he being naive? Lonnie had always been so sophisticated . . . But Lonnie had stopped walking and was grinning with love and laughter, and they embraced again, thumping each other's backs.

From close by, Willi called, "Blue-eyes! You were so late I came to find you."

He turned and waved to her. "Come here, Willi! You won't believe what's happened!"

They watched her approach, a slight, erect figure in the dusk, her lithe movements having both dignity and authority. When she reached them, Donnie put an arm around her.

"Lonnie, this is my wife Willi. Willi, this is *my brother* . . ."

She searched Lonnie's face with grave eyes. Then: "You are welcome, brother of my husband."

"Are you sure?" he asked, as gravely. "I am—was—a Kuomintang commander."

She said, "Our house is away from the village. No one is likely to see you. For tonight, you two are brothers, and I am the wife of one and the sister of the other. Come . . ."

She led them down a forested path to a little clearing in which stood a mud-walled, straw-thatched house, its chimney smoking invitingly. The smell of wood smoke, cooking, evening moisture gathering on the dry thatch, went marvelously with Donnie's happiness. He showed Lonnie the outhouse where there were soap and a towel, then hurried in to Willi to thank her. It was true that it might be dangerous to have a Kuomintang commander in their house. Before he could say a word she stopped him with a kiss.

"For tonight, he's not white or green or any color. He's your brother."

He hugged her. At ten he had commanded a squad of Little Red Devils. At sixteen a squad of Red Fighters. At twenty, a regiment. Yet this tiny little thing now commanded him, and he obeyed without question!

Lonnie came into the room, his shoes clumping on the rough wood floor. Donnie's joy erupted again into laughter.

"Don't you Whites realize that those shoes are a dead give-away?"

Lonnie shrugged ruefully. "I can't walk without them! My feet hurt!"

Donnie looked down at his hard, brown, callused feet.

"I don't remember wearing shoes, but I do remember running along, trying to keep up with you, in a lovely, smooth, pink marble courtyard."

"Your mother's courtyard!"

Again, Donnie began to tremble a little. Belle was, of course, the woman he had loved almost all his life as Mother. But there was that other mother, whose fleeting memory came to him now and then—smiling eyes as blue as his own, misty blond hair, an aura of love.

"Lonnie, do you know what happened to my English mother?"

"She went back to England . . ."

Willi was laying dishes on the table, but she stopped and came to stand behind Donnie, putting a hand on his shoulder. Lonnie did not look at her, but went on talking to Donnie in a quiet, big-brother voice.

"As soon as the city began to calm down after the attack on the Reds, the British police launched a big search for our father, and for you. Our father's body was found in an alley. You, of course, were never found. So your mother went back to England. . . . But—perhaps she knows now what happened to you. Some years later, Zung came to see my mother in our village, and she got him to write a letter to your mother telling her all about it. They sent the letter care of the British ambassador in Shanghai. Perhaps she received it."

Donnie felt unreal, as though something in his breast was melting. Willi put her arms around him from behind and held him tight.

"She got the letter! The mails are very efficient, especially the English mail!"

He glanced up at her, smiling, feeling real again. She didn't know any more about the mails than he did, even the Chinese mail, which was only now being restored after the years of war. He touched her hands, clasped across his chest, and thanked whatever gods were above for the fate that had brought them, by their widely separated ways, from that lovely valley in the Shansi mountains to this miniscule village on the Yunnan border.

She finished laying the dishes on the table and they began the simple dinner. After a few mouthfuls, she and Donnie stopped eating and, smiling, watched Lonnie clean up the food. At last he put down his chopsticks with a sigh.

"I think I'm going to live, after all!"

She began to clear the table. "Talk, you two. I can hear."

But they were silent for a while. The little one-roomed cottage was warm and glowing in the light of the kerosene lamp. The bed stood in a corner behind a curtain. There was a scarred old wooden cupboard, the table, three stools, the clay cooking stove, shelves for pots and dishes, hooks for clothes: the furnishings the village had proudly assembled for their schoolteacher. It was the first roofed and floored home Donnie had ever known, apart from the marble-paved courtyard home that he barely remembered. He looked around, mind buzzing with contentment.

Lonnie said, "What's it like, being a Red? I know, of course, that you eat babies and murder grandmothers when it becomes too expensive to feed them. But apart from that, what's it like?"

Donnie burst out laughing. How he loved Lonnie!

"It's just—living. Like you . . ."

"*Not* like me. I can't walk without shoes on. Come on, Donnie. Tell me from the beginning, after Zung took you to Didi and Belle."

"Well—I suppose the beginning was climbing the mountain. That's the first thing I really remember . . ."

It wasn't just a mountain. It was a huge, great series of peaks and valleys and plateaus. They had started climbing early in the morning, he and Didi and Belle and Grandmother Mei-mei. He climbed until his legs ached so much that he couldn't help crying, and Didi had picked him up and carried him. They rested every now and then and drank water from streams. When the sun set and dusk fell, the mountain turned blue. A varied color, in the valleys almost purple, over the peaks as blue as the sky. When he cried out in amazement that the mountain was blue, Didi said it was only a trick of the light, but for him it had always been the Blue Mountain. He had loved it. It had been home. They had stopped wandering about, walking, begging rides in oxcarts, hiding in the freight cars of trains, and settled down in a leaky old tent on the Blue Mountain, and it was home.

A proper home, with playmates. The Little Red Devils— orphans created in battle, whom the Red Fighters carried along with them, to whom the Red Army was mother and father. They fetched and carried for the Fighters, whom they proudly called *tung-chih*, comrades, and loved dearly. It was a Little Red Devil who had first called him Blue-eyes, declaring that a boy with blue eyes couldn't be a Little Red Devil. But he had fought him a few times, and soon everyone was calling him Blue-eyes, and he remained a Little Red Devil.

Every day, men came up the mountain to join the Red Army. Not for money or material benefit—there was never enough to eat, and nobody from the smallest Little Red Devil to Mao Tse-tung himself got a salary. They came because they hated the Whites. It was the same old thing all over again—injustice, abuse, oppression, degradation, only worse because the Whites had claimed to be saviors and the people had hailed them with wild joy, and they turned out to be no better than any oppressors who had come before. They were worse. The Reds called themselves "fighters" because the word "soldier" held the most odious connotations on account of what White soldiers did, aping their commanders, and the commanders aping their generals, all the way up to the Generalissimo, and he the worst of all, being the most powerful. So men who longed and yearned and ached for justice climbed the Blue Mountain.

"I thought it was very natural," Donnie said, laughing. "I thought everybody would like to come to that wonderful place. Everybody was friendly and full of enthusiasm and—a kind of purity. I didn't recognize it then, of course, but now I know what it was. The Rules of the Red Fighter were the declaration of a . . . religion. A kind of religion that everybody believed in. And everybody was the same. You couldn't tell a fighter from a commander by looking at him. Everybody lived the same and ate the same and wore the same, mostly the clothes they'd climbed the mountain in. Nobody wore stripes or golden epaulets or decorations like, I saw later, you Whites wore. The only thing everybody had was a small red star. I wore mine pinned on my sweater, but I had to move it about a lot because of the holes. Belle tried to tie the loose ends of wool together when the first hole started, but she soon had to give up. Who cared? The only thing was it got cold at night, but I'd just snuggle up to a *tung-chih*."

Willi finished washing up the dishes and came to sit at the table beside Donnie. Donnie took her hand, and smiled at his brother.

"I'm doing all the talking. Tell what you did after we were separated."

Lonnie shrugged lightly. "Nothing as exciting as you. I stayed in our village with my mother and sisters and went to school. My sisters got married and moved away. I left school at sixteen and immediately got drafted. At sixteen one is bright-eyed and hopeful and full of ideas about honor and justice, especially if one is Susu's son. They thought I was officer material and sent me to the Whampoa Military Academy."

He stopped and seemed reluctant to continue, so after a minute Donnie went on.

"In 1934 we were forced to leave the Blue Mountain . . ."

"The Fifth Communist Extermination Campaign," Lonnie said, and Donnie nodded.

"Yes—the Fifth. The first four were a joke. I remember the fighters coming back from chasing Whites all over the landscape—the squads coming back up the mountain, laughing, to report what they had captured. Weaponry from rifles to field mortars. All kinds of ammunition and supplies. Trucks, even! The Red Army armed itself well on what it captured from the Whites in those first four campaigns. . . . It was a marvelous time! Didi was organizing communes among the farmers all around the mountain. Belle—you know, she was a well-known writer. There weren't many educated people on the Blue Mountain, but those who were educated recognized her name at once. She was put in charge of organizing a dramatic troupe to perform in the villages. She wrote all the skits and trained the actors. It was a great way of educating people to the Red Army's aims, and of passing on news of what was happening. Her troupe was so popular that the list of scheduled performances was six months long!"

But at last, in 1934, seven years after they arrived at the Blue Mountain, the Fifth Extermination Campaign, for which Chiang Kai-shek had got German advisers, began to squeeze the Reds out of their mountain stronghold. In October they started out on the Long March, six thousand miles, from Kiangsi to Shensi in the far northwest, to escape the Whites.

"And to fight the Japanese! All the skits Belle wrote at that time were concentrated on that theme: Chinese were fighting Chinese while the Japanese gobbled up our country! If Chiang Kai-shek wouldn't fight the Japanese, *we* were going to do it! I was eleven years old, commanding a squad of Little Red Devils. How proud we were! We were going to fight the Japanese! So we started out . . . Well, the Long March is famous by now . . ."

He stopped because Lonnie seemed to be sleeping, slumped at the table, head down. But he wasn't sleeping for he said almost harshly, "Go on."

Donnie went on.

"Didi died at the crossing of the Tatu River. The Whites had withdrawn all the boats to the opposite bank and were strongly guarding all possible crossing places. The Red commanders decided to make for a bridge two hundred miles upriver. The gorges are very high there, and the river very narrow, very far below. At night, our torches were reflected in the river. It seemed like a river of light. It was so beautiful. And so desperate. If we didn't get across the bridge before the Whites stopped us, we were all dead. . . . We marched day and night, double quick time, stopping for ten minutes rest now and then, eating raw rice for there was no time for cooking . . ."

The bridge was a suspension bridge, planks lashed to two thick chains that spanned the chasm. The White garrison had removed the planks from the Red side of the bridge, leaving only the chains. The Red commanders called for volunteers. Of the many who stepped out, they chose thirty. With guns, ammunition, bayonets, and hand grenades strapped to their backs, the thirty swung out on the chains, hand over hand. The White garrison opened up from their machine gun nest. They got ten of the men swinging from the chains before the rest reached the shelter of the planks that the Whites had not removed. The first Red to climb up onto the planks had perfect aim. He threw a hand grenade straight into the White machine gun nest. That was it . . . Two days later the entire Red Army had crossed the river on the restored suspension bridge.

But not Didi. He was one of the ten killed by White machine gun fire. His body spun slowly, gracefully, as it fell the long, long way down into the river.

Donnie's voice echoed in his own ears with the pain and horror of the moment. He went quickly on to finish with the telling. Belle had died soon after that. It was a wonder to everyone that she had pushed her frail body so far. When her husband died, it seemed that she let herself die as quickly as she could. She was buried by the roadside in a little forest.

There were still two thousand miles to go and seven mountain ranges to cross, sweltering in the lowlands, freezing on the mountaintops. Donnie's squad of Little Red Devils adopted Grandmother Mei-mei. She joked and made them laugh and kept their spirits up, and they boosted her over the hard places and hauled her up the cliffs. She died on the Great Snow

223

Mountain, almost at the sixteen-thousand foot summit—sat down to rest with them, laughing, and simply failed to get up when they got up to go on. They buried her there, in the snow.

Lonnie stirred and stretched himself, flung his head back, stared up at the roof thatch.

"So you were the only one of the family to make it to Shensi. And you didn't eat any babies."

Donnie laughed and stretched himself too, glad that Lonnie was returning from the secret place into which he had retired.

"Not a one! Didn't eat much of anything, in fact. Though the peasants all along the way helped us as much as they could. Gave us all the food they could spare, took in our wounded, warned us of White movements . . ."

Lonnie barked a short laugh. "That's not what we heard in Chungking! The peasants hated the Reds, we heard. Turned them in at every opportunity, or murdered them if they could. But then, what we heard in Chungking was mostly what the Generalissimo wanted to hear."

"You were in Chungking!"

"Yes. I didn't quite realize when I entered the Academy that I was committing myself to a career in the Kuomintang Army. I don't know that I'd have chosen otherwise, but as it turned out I had no choice. I was attached to the Generalissimo's personal bodyguard, and spent most of my war in Chungking."

Donnie waited, but Lonnie said no more. Once again, his expression became remote and withdrawn. Rather anxiously, Donnie started talking again, hoping to entice him back.

"Willi and I met in a beautiful valley high up in the Chungtiao Mountains in Shansi. As soon as we Reds had settled down in Shensi, we started again to build communes. One of the main things was to get rid of poppies . . ."

"Poppies?" Lonnie said sardonically, eyes fixed on the roof. "How did you get rid of poppies?"

"We're not entirely rid of them yet—but soon . . . It's not hard. It just becomes uneconomic, you see. Reds have no money to buy opium—only Whites bought it. Farmers didn't grow opium for themselves—they grew it to sell so they could pay their taxes. In Shensi the farmers told us that the White government charged them forty-four different kinds of taxes, plus

224

a 'happy tax' to promote happiness on the day that they had to pay their taxes!"

He laughed, hoping that Lonnie would laugh too, but Lonnie only raised an eyebrow and continued staring at the roof. Hesitantly, he continued:

"In our communes, the farmers were forgiven all taxes for the first three years, so they didn't have to grow poppies, and even if they did they couldn't sell the opium, so naturally it was more profitable for them to grow food. Some of the older Little Red Devils were sent around to find out which farmers were still growing poppies and persuade them not to. I was on the squad that went to Willi's valley, where Willi's father was the headman. Willi was there—she was six years old— standing by her father and staring at me. And suddenly she piped up, 'He has blue eyes! Is he a foreigner? Do they let foreigners into the Chinese army?' When everybody laughed, she ran away . . ."

He smiled at her, oblivious for the moment of Lonnie's silent presence, carried back over the years to that beautiful valley. His love for her, sweet and tumultuous, flooded his spirit. She smiled back at him and touched his hand and for an instant they were one, indissoluble.

Lonnie stirred, sat forward, reached for the teapot, poured himself a cup of tea.

"You probably wouldn't believe how often I thought of you all those years in Chungking, Donnie."

Donnie turned to him gladly. "Why didn't you come to us? Many Kuomintang came, and every one was welcomed!"

Lonnie shrugged. "It was . . . too late."

"What d'you mean? Every year, as we expanded, it became *easier* to come to us!"

Lonnie shrugged again. Then, absently, "I think my mother would have gone over . . . She's dead, you know . . . I told you, Zung came to see her in our village. He wanted to marry her but she refused him because of his connection with that criminal who killed our father—Big-ears Doo. I heard a few days ago that he's dead too. In Hong Kong. He ran away there in 1947. Zung went with him . . ."

He sipped tea, and then sat, head down, staring into his cup.

"My mother made our father give her a lot of money over the

years. She was very practical"—he smiled sadly—"and she wanted to be sure that her children would be taken care of. It was in gold bars. She believed in gold bars, that had weight and solidity. Not like paper. A lot of people believed in gold bars. . . . But they found a way to make all those people give up their gold bars for paper. Big-ears Doo and his partner-in-fraud of many years, Soong Ai-ling, and her husband Kung, and the Generalissimo. The experts. They found a way to get their hands on every gold bar in China."

Donnie sat silent, hardly drawing breath, longing for his brother to speak out loud the bitter secrets of his heart, to speak them and thus be rid of them.

Lonnie said, "When an egg came to cost a quarter of a million dollars in our old paper currency, those experts replaced it with a new one—Gold Yuan, which they said was worth four to an American dollar. They decreed that everyone who owned gold bars must turn them in to the Central Bank in exchange for paper Gold Yuan. It took just five months for the Gold Yuan to fall from four to an American dollar, to one million."

He stopped to laugh at Donnie's amazement.

"Yes, one million Gold Yuan for one American dollar! My mother had to use a rickshaw to cart enough money to the market to buy food. Nobody could count a rickshaw-full of paper, of course, so the money passed in packets of ten thousand that the Central Bank was supposed to have counted and sealed. Later, the Gold Yuan was passed by weight. On the trains you weren't allowed to carry more than twenty kilograms of paper money. . . . In those few months, my mother became a pauper. Not only she, of course—millions of others. It was the last and greatest fraud of all. I couldn't get the Generalissimo's permission to leave Chungking to go to my mother. By the time I got to her, she was dying."

"Why didn't you come to us *then*?" Donnie cried.

Lonnie didn't answer for a time. Then, very low:

"I told you—it was too late. I had stayed too long."

"You should have come to us!" Donnie cried again, agonized. "Why did you stay?"

Lonnie said nothing.

Donnie jumped up and went to the bed, fumbled under it, brought back a package wrapped in a torn and dusty towel.

"Lonnie, these are the tablets of our ancestors . . . Didi carried them with him wherever he went. Just before he swung out on the chains over the Tatu River, he gave them to me, and I have carried them with me ever since."

He loosened the towel and set the tablets up on the table: a pair in white marble carved in gold so pure that it shone as though carved yesterday, for Wei and the Englishman Charlie, nicknamed the Red Barbarian. A pair in dark green jade for Jin-see and Great Dragon. And a fifth tablet—a plain, squarish piece of river stone, scratchily carved by an amateur's hand.

He picked it up. "This one I carved myself. I took the stone from the bank of the Tatu River and carved on it every minute I could spare until I had carved out Didi's name—for he is the man I loved and honor as my father. For our real father, yours and mine, there is no tablet."

Lonnie rose slowly. They stood, shoulder to shoulder, gazing at the tablets. Then, by tacit consent, they knelt together and kowtowed to their ancestors.

When they rose, Lonnie was once more his big-brother self.

"Don't the Reds hold ancestor worship to be reactionary, counterrevolutionary, thoroughly reprehensible?" He slapped Donnie's shoulder, grinning. "Haven't you just broken some Red law? Well, I won't tell on you . . . It'll be dawn in an hour. I've got to go."

With anguish, Donnie cried out, "Stay with me!"

"Sorry, I can't."

"Why not? *Why not?*"

"Told you—it's too late. I stayed over there too long. I did some wicked things myself—it's easy, when everybody's doing them. Besides, I have a friend waiting across the border in what Zung used to call the 'golden triangle.' It's got good soil for poppies. The trade's already rich."

Donnie stood speechless before his brother, unable to find words to make the plea that he knew would ache in his spirit everlastingly if he didn't make it. At last, hoarsely, "I'm supposed to stop you . . . I have your pistol . . ."

"But you'll give it back to me. You'll let me go."

It was Willi who answered:

"Yes, he will let you go. He is a happy man, innocent and good, and you would change that. So he will let you go."

She went to the stool on which Donnie had left the two pistols, picked up one, handed it to Lonnie.

He gave her a little bow. "You are wise. My brother is fortunate."

Then, to Donnie, a quick, painful grin. "Good-bye, little brother."

When he had gone, Donnie could not move or speak. He heard Willi moving behind him, but he did not look around, he did not care, for some essential part of his being was going with his brother toward the border.

She came and turned him round to face the table. Dazedly, he saw that she had laid a white cloth on it, and two lighted candles, and placed between them the five soul tablets, in a row. They caught the light from the candles and glowed softly, even the common one of river stone.

She said, "Blue-eyes, it's true that ancestor worship is forbidden now, but forbidding is not what makes good and bad . . . Shall we now, you and I, in this dawn, kowtow to your ancestors and report to them that we love each other, that we have married—and that soon we will present to them a new descendant?"

She took his hand and placed it on her body below her ribs. He looked into her luminous eyes and forgot his brother. The essence of his being returned to him, and joy filled him. He took her in his arms and kissed her with a kind of magical tenderness. Then, together, they kneeled and kowtowed to the ancestors.